HARD RULES

HARD RULES
A DIRTY MONEY NOVEL

LISA RENEE JONES

ST. MARTIN'S GRIFFIN
NEW YORK

HARD RULES. Copyright © 2016 by Lisa Renee Jones. All rights reserved. Printed in the United States of America. For information, address St. Martin's Press, 175 Fifth Avenue, New York, N.Y. 10010.

www.stmartins.com

Designed by Omar Chapa

Library of Congress Cataloging-in-Publication Data

Names: Jones, Lisa Renee, author.
Title: Hard rules / Lisa Renee Jones.
Description: First edition. | New York : St. Martin's Griffin, 2016. |
    Series: Dirty money ; 1
Identifiers: LCCN 2016002083 | ISBN 978-1-250-08382-1 (trade paperback) |
    ISBN 978-1-250-08386-9 (e-book)
Subjects: LCSH: Corporations—Corrupt practices—Fiction. |
    Man-woman relationships—Fiction. | BISAC: FICTION / Romance /
    Contemporary. | GSAFD: Romantic suspense fiction. | Erotic fiction.
Classification: LCC PS3610.O627 H37 2016 | DDC 813/.6—dc23
LC record available at http://lccn.loc.gov/2016002083

Our books may be purchased in bulk for promotional, educational, or business use. Please contact your local bookseller or the Macmillan Corporate and Premium Sales Department at 1-800-221-7945, extension 5442, or by e-mail at MacmillanSpecialMarkets@macmillan.com.

First Edition: August 2016

10 9 8 7 6 5 4 3 2 1

HARD RULES

That was the beginning of the end of our thing.

—*Anthony Casso*

PROLOGUE

SIX MONTHS AGO

"Tequila and tonic number two," I say, setting the drink on top of a MARTINA'S CASA napkin for the dark, good-looking stranger who'd come in asking for my brother.

He ignores the drink, his dark brown eyes on me. "Thank you, Teresa."

"You know my name."

"I make it a point of knowing a pretty woman's name."

"You know my name because you know my brother."

He straightens and I am momentarily distracted by the way his lean, athletic body flexes beneath the material of his white button-down shirt. That is, until he murmurs, "Holy shit. You're Adrian's sweetheart sister?"

"Ah . . . yes. I guess you didn't know."

"No. You're fucking waiting tables." He holds up a hand. "Sorry. They say he beats the crap out of people that flirt with you."

Sorry for flirting, not cursing obviously. Sorry for daring to cross my brother. Sorry for ever talking to me, I suspect. Anger rolls through me, lighting up every nerve ending this stranger has hit. I lean on the table and look him in the eye. "If that were the case I'd be a virgin, now wouldn't I? Or maybe I just found a man braver than you." I start to move away and he grabs my hand.

"I'm sorry. I offended you."

"Apology number two," I say. He might be a stranger, but he's managed to get under my skin in all kinds of wrong ways. "Are you apologizing because you mean it? Or because you're afraid I'll tell my brother?" His lips tighten but he doesn't reply, and I suppose I should be sympathetic. My brother scares a lot of people, and with good reason. "Now you're afraid of me."

Seeming to read my thoughts, he defends himself. "He's the leader of a drug cartel. What do you expect?"

"My father's the boss."

"Your brother practically owns every official in Denver."

He's right. He does and he's about to own this man as well. "Let me give you some advice. You're obviously doing business with him, so what I expect is what he'll expect. That you grow some balls. Take that advice, or you'll be nothing but prey to him. His prey never survives."

"Teresa."

I suck in a breath at the sound of my brother's voice and whirl around, shoving my hands in my apron pockets. He stands there, tall, broad, and tattooed, in jeans and a T-shirt with his long, dark hair tied at his nape, his brown eyes sharp, hard. He'd kill for me, and that kind of terrifies me at times. Like now. "Adrian," I manage.

"Leave us. Ed and I have business to attend."

I nod and step around him, walking to the bar and rounding the counter to watch as Ed stands and joins my brother. They head to the corner offices and I have a really bad feeling about this. I watch them disappear and several of my brother's men follow them. I inhale for courage and realize I might have just gotten that man hurt. I can't let that happen.

I round the bar again and rush across the restaurant, down a long hallway toward my brother's office where the door is shut. I lean against the door, pressing my ear to the surface and for once, I'm happy they are hollow and thin. "Man, I'm sorry," I hear the stranger say. "I didn't know she was your sister. I'm working for you. I got you into college-level sports."

"And I got you a win on the football field, Coach. Thanks to my drug, your athletes perform better and test clean."

"I know."

"You don't know or you wouldn't be hitting on my sister. There are rules and 'not knowing' is not acceptable."

"How would I know?"

"What if you offer the drug to the wrong person? You have to know who you are approaching. One mistake can land us all in jail. You have to pay."

"Pay? How?"

"Strip him naked," my brother orders and I cover my mouth to stifle my gasp. Oh God. What is he going to do?

"No," Ed says, and even through the door, I hear his fear, which is exactly what my brother wants. "No," he pleads. "No. I won't. You aren't—" A thud hits the door and I jump back, my heart thundering in my chest and I decide it must be Ed trying to get away. A harder thud rattles the door, followed by my brother's voice at close range.

"I'm going to beat you," he says. "And if you shout, I will beat you more."

I look down and my hands are trembling. How can Adrian be so loving to me and so brutal to others? Why is this my life? Why? Ed grunts and I know he's being beaten. I can't help him, though. I can barely help myself. I rush down the hallway and duck into a small office. Grabbing my purse, I pull the strap over my head and across my chest when my gaze catches on the image in the mirror, my long dark hair falling in waves at my shoulders, my brown eyes filled with torment. I hate how much I look like every other Martina. How so much of their blood is my blood.

I rush out of the office and down the hall, not stopping until I'm at the exit, pushing the door open. Once I'm outside, a cool evening wind gusts over me, the mountains offering sweet relief from an abnormally warm October in Colorado. I start walking, no destination in mind, thankful the hustle and bustle of the downtown area during the midday is absent at ten o'clock on Monday night.

I need air. Space. Time to think.

I've just turned a corner, headed toward a little twenty-four-hour coffee shop I know, when a black sedan stops next to me and the window rolls down. The minute I see *him*, adrenaline races through me. He's been gone for weeks, since I told him who my brother was. I thought he too was scared away. He motions me to the car and I don't even try to play coy. I race forward and the door opens, the window sliding up. In an instant, he's pulling me to his lap and I'm straddling him, shoving open his suit jacket.

His fingers tangle in my hair and he drags his mouth to mine.

"Miss me, sweetheart?"

"I thought you wanted out," I whisper.

"I had to leave town, but I'm here now."

His mouth slants over mine and the rest of the world disappears, as does the driver, leaving me alone with the only man who's ever possessed me and made me like it.

There's no such thing as good money or bad money. There's just money.

—*Lucky Luciano*

CHAPTER ONE

SHANE

I park the silver Bentley convertible, which my father gifted me last year for saving his ass, into my reserved spot in the garage of the downtown Denver high-rise building owned by our family conglomerate, Brandon Enterprises. It's a car he and I both know was far more about his attempt to drag me to the dark side, and aligning me with his way of doing business, than the thank-you for keeping his ass out of jail. I'd have refused the damn thing if my mother hadn't begged me to take it, insisting I'd bruise him when he's already fragile and cancer-ridden. Like my father ever fucking bruises and he damn sure isn't fragile. And if he knew I'd coddled him, he'd most likely spit in my face, and tell me I'm a disappointment.

Killing the engine, I exit the vehicle and stare at my older brother's white Porsche 911, also a gift from my father, ironically and most likely for getting us into the very mess I'd returned to Denver to clean up. Jaw clenched, I shove my keys into the pocket of the gray two-thousand-dollar suit I'd bought back in New York, a reward to myself for winning a high-profile case for one of the most prestigious law firms in the country. I wore it today to remind myself that I'm a few well-played cards from conquering the challenge I took when I returned home: becoming the head of the family empire when my father retires and replacing all the dirty money running through six of the seven asset companies with good, clean cash. Namely, the revenue produced by Brandon Pharmaceuticals, or BP, the newest asset I'd forced into acquisition only three months ago.

I head toward the elevators, when my cell phone buzzes with a text. Fishing it from my jacket pocket, I glance down to read a message from my secretary, Jessica: *Seth just called. Needs to speak to you urgently. I told him you had a meeting at the BP division this morning and he hung up on me. Knowing Seth, he'll show up at your meeting.* Seth Cage was the one person I brought to the company with me, and the only person other than Jessica who I trust now that I'm here.

I punch the call button for the elevator, and dial Seth. "I'm pulling into the BP parking lot now to see you," he says by way of greeting.

"I just pulled into the garage downtown."

"Son of a bitch. I'm pulling a U-turn at the security gates. I have something you need to see now, not later, and I can't talk about it on the phone. Is your brother in the building?"

I glance at the Porsche. "His car's here so I assume he is as well. What the hell has Derek done now?"

"Let's just say I'm not sure it's a good idea that he's in close range when you find out. Let's meet outside the office."

"Fuck me," I growl.

"No," he amends. "More like fuck us all."

"I don't even want to know what that means," I say, catching the elevator door that's opened and already trying to close. "Meet me at the coffee shop."

"That still puts you in the same building as him. I don't think that's a good idea."

"Just hurry the hell up and get here," I order testily, ending the call and stepping into the otherwise empty car where I punch the L button on the panel to my left. In the short trip to the lobby level, I manage to come up with at least five ways my brother could fuck over the plays I have in action, and I'm still counting.

Exiting into the gray marble corridor, I walk toward the huge oval foyer of the building and then to the right, where a coffee shop is nestled between a restaurant and a postal facility, both of which rent from Brandon Enterprises. I head to the counter when Karen, the owner of the coffee shop—a robust forty-something woman with red hair and a big attitude—appears, leaving me no escape from her habitual chitchat.

"Well, well, well," she says, leaning on the counter. "Now I know what I'm missing on the morning shift and I do declare that seeing Shane Brandon himself, instead of his secretary, is a better 'wake-me-up' than any java shot I sell. But then, you Brandon boys came by those looks honestly. That father of yours is a looker."

And therein lies the reason she irritates the shit out of my mother and I happily treat Jessica to afternoon coffee to have her bring me mine. Karen's not only a chatterbox and a flirt, she has it bad for my father.

"All right now," Karen says, grabbing a cup and pen, and preparing to write. "Large latte with a triple shot?"

"Just what the doctor ordered," I confirm, though I have a feeling once Seth arrives I'll be wishing for a bottle of whiskey.

"Will do, honey," she says, giving me a wink before moving toward the espresso machine. "I'll add it to your tab."

I retreat to the end of the counter where the orders are delivered, resting my elbow on the ledge, retreating into my mind and chasing problems made worse by the division between Derek and me. He's thirty-seven, five years my senior, and the rightful successor to our father. I'd happily stepped aside and started my own life, but damn it to hell, I know things now and I can't walk away.

My order appears and I straighten, intending to claim my coffee and find a seat, when a pretty twenty-something brunette races forward in a puff of sweet, floral-scented perfume, and grabs it.

"Miss," I begin, "that's—"

She takes a sip and grimaces. "What is this?" She turns to the counter. "Excuse me," she calls out. "My drink is wrong."

"Because it's not your drink," Karen reprimands her, setting a new cup on the counter. "*This* is your drink." She reaches for my cup and turns it around, pointing to the name scribbled on the side. "This one's for Shane." She glances at me. "I'll be right back to fix this. I have another customer."

I wave my acknowledgment and she hurries away, while my floral-scented coffee thief faces me, her porcelain cheeks flushed, her full, really damn distracting mouth painted pink. "I'm so sorry," she offers quickly. "I thought I was the only one without my coffee and I was in a hurry." She starts to hand me my coffee and then quickly sets it on the counter. "You can't have that. I drank out of it."

"I saw that," I say, picking it up. "You grimaced with disgust after trying it."

Her eyes, a pale blue that matches the short-sleeved silk blouse, go wide. "Oh. I mean no. Or I did, but not because it's a bad cup of coffee. It's just very strong."

"It's a triple-shot latte."

"A triple," she says, looking quite serious. "Did you know that in some third-world countries they bottle that stuff and sell it as a way to grow hair on your chest?" She lowers her voice and whispers, "That's not a good look for me."

"Fortunately," I say in the midst of a chuckle I would have claimed wasn't possible five minutes ago, "I don't share that dilemma." I lift my cup and add, "Cheers," before taking a drink, the heavy, rich flavor sliding over my tongue.

She pales, looking exceedingly uncomfortable, before repeating, "I *drank* from that cup."

"I know," I say, offering it back to her. "Try another drink."

She takes the cup and sets it on the counter. "I can't drink that. And you can't either." She points to the hole on top, now smudged pink. "My lipstick is all over it and I really hate to tell you this but it's all over you too and . . ." She laughs, a soft, sexy sound, her hands settling on her slender but curvy hips, accented by a fitted black skirt. "Sorry. I don't mean to laugh, but it's not a good shade for you."

I laugh now too, officially and impossibly charmed by this woman in spite of being in the middle of what feels like World War III. "Seems you know how to make a lasting impression."

"Thankfully it's not lasting," she says. "It'll wipe right off. And thank you for being such a good sport. I really am sorry again for all of this."

"Apologize by getting it off me."

Confusion puckers her brow. "What?"

"You put it on me." I grab a napkin from the counter and offer it to her. "You get it off."

"I put it on the cup," she says, clearly recovering. "*You* put it on you."

"I assure you, that had I put it on me, we both would have enjoyed it much more than we are now." I glance at the napkin. "Are you going to help me?"

Her cheeks flush and she hugs herself, her sudden shyness an intriguing contrast to her confident banter. "I'll let you know if you don't get it all."

My apparently lipstick-stained lips curve at her quick wit but I take the napkin and wipe my mouth, arching a questioning brow when I'm done. She points to the corner of my mouth. "A little more on the left."

I hand her the napkin. "*You* do it."

She inhales, as if for courage, but takes it. "Fine," she says, stepping closer, that wicked sweet scent of hers teasing my nostrils. Wasting no time, she reaches for my mouth, her body swaying in my direction while my hand itches to settle at her waist. I want this woman and I'm not letting her get away.

"There," she says, her arm lowering, and not about to let her escape, I capture her hand, holding it and the napkin between us.

Those gorgeous pale blue eyes of hers dart to mine, wide with surprise, the connection sparking an unmistakable charge between us, which I feel with an unexpected, but not unwelcome, jolt. "Thank you," I say, softening the hard demand in my tone that long ago became natural.

"I owed you," she says, her voice steady, but there's a hint of panic in her eyes that isn't what I expect from this clearly confident, smart woman.

"What's your name?" I ask.

"Emily," she replies, sounding just a hint breathless. I decide right then that I like her breathless but I'd like her a whole lot more if she were *naked* and breathless. "And you're Shane."

"That's right," I say, already thinking of all the ways I could make her say my name again. "I've never seen you here before."

"I've never been here before," she counters and I have this sense that we are sparring, when we're not. Or are we?

My cell phone rings and I silently curse the timing, some sixth sense telling me that the minute I let go of this woman, she's gone, but I also have to think about whatever explosion Seth is trying to contain. "Don't move," I order, before releasing her to dig my phone from my pocket. I glance down at the caller

ID to find my mother's number, and just that fast, Emily darts around me.

I curse and turn, fully intending to pursue her, only to have Seth step in front of me. Considering the man equals my six feet two inches, and is broader than I am wide, he stops me in my tracks. I grimace and he arches a blond brow that matches the thick waves of hair on his head. "Looking for me?"

"You'll do," I say, reaching for my coffee and bypassing it to pick up Emily's instead, or rather holding it captive for the return I doubt she'll make.

"Good to see you too," he says, the words dripping with his trademark sarcasm, which five years of knowing him has taught me to expect.

"Bring me good news for once," I say, motioning us forward, leading the way through several display racks of chocolates and coffees, as well as a trio of empty tables, to claim a seat at a corner table facing the entryway.

Seth sits next to me rather than across from me, keeping an eye on the door, the ex-CIA agent in him ever present, his skills and loyalty paired with his no-nonsense attitude only a few of the reasons I recruited him from my firm in New York. He opens a large white envelope and pulls out a picture, setting it in front of me. "The private security company we contracted to do surveillance on your brother delivered this to me about an hour ago."

I stare down at the image of my brother handing a large envelope to a man I've never seen before. I eye Seth. "Who is he?"

"He works for the FDA."

Any remnant of pleasure I'd taken from the exchange with Emily disappears. "Obviously it's related to the pharmaceutical division and I don't even want to think about how many laws we broke in that exchange."

"That's why I wanted you to see it right away."

"Do we know what was in the envelope? Do we know any-thing?"

"The FDA employee's name and tenure. That's about it, but I authorized the security team to follow him as of today."

I glance at the picture, wrestling with anger that will get me nowhere but the hell to which my brother is trying to drag me. "This is the aftermath of last week's stockholder meeting. I walked in there singing the praises of BP profit margins, with the promise that once the FDA approves our new asthma drug, it would allow us to let go of all the dirty money."

"And all they heard was the chance to double their money," Seth supplies. "Enter Derek, who promises to make it happen in a ploy to claim the table. You knew this could happen. We talked about it. Dishonest people don't suddenly become honest."

"No," I say tightly. "They don't. And I haven't been operat-ing with the same killer instincts as I did in the firm or this wouldn't have happened."

"Because you still haven't let go of the firm."

"It's not the firm I haven't let go of. It's my brother. Because despite my denial, I knew staying meant my brother became my enemy."

Seth leans closer. "Listen to me, Shane. I'm thirty-five years old. I did seven years in the CIA and five years of contract work all over the world before I happened to take a job that threw us together. I've seen monsters. I've seen criminals. I've seen your family and I say this not just as the person you hired to have your back, but the friend who would have it anyway." He taps the image of my brother in the photo. "*This* man is your enemy. And I'm not going to let you forget it."

"He's also my brother, and this is my family, who I want to save."

"You may not be able to."

"I'm aware of that and if I don't take this company as my

life, the way I did my law career, I won't succeed. And believe me, I've navigated enough family-driven litigation to know that blood divides as easily as it unites, especially when money and power are involved. I have to get ahead of this before we all end up bloody or in jail."

"So we agree. This is war."

"It's always been war. I didn't want to name it, but I am now. It's time we go to battle."

"Meaning what?"

"I played nice for my brother's sake. Today he put me—us—into the line of fire with the law, and I'm done pulling punches. The number-one obstacle is my need for the board's vote to gain control."

"And when exactly is that vote? Because the last I heard, your father wasn't exactly retiring to hit a bucket list. If he hadn't dropped twenty pounds in six months, I could forget the man is dying of cancer."

If only forgetting made it not true. "Whatever the case, a vote now would not be in my favor and since we've agreed there isn't a cure for corruption, our board needs to go away. That's the only way I can freely dissolve the root of all of our problems, which is Brandon Financial, where my father's spent decades hiding people's money and doing dirty deals for them. The rest of the companies—trucking, restaurants, real estate, and steel—they're nothing but shells to hide money for us and those clients."

"You won't get rid of them without playing hardball."

"I didn't win the case I won, or save my father's ass from the Feds, by playing softball. This is a chess game, and you can ask my father and brother. I'm damn good at chess, both on the board, and off. Hire the staff you need and get me the kind of leverage I can use to push them out."

"Dirt or leverage?"

"Isn't it one and the same with these kinds of people?"

"There can be a fine line."

"And I'll evaluate when I have data to analyze but if I don't do this in one fatal blow, my family will push me out before I can."

"I've already pulled enough substantial 'dirt' on everyone to force an exit, with the exception of Mike Rogers. He's reading clean to me. The man owns a professional basketball team and twenty percent of our stock and I can't figure out why he's even risking the liability he knows exists here. He has to have hidden money with your father, but we can't use that without the threat of the company being exposed."

"His money is exactly why he's involved. He has a boatload to hide and invest. He has more to lose when we shut down the investment division than anyone. Interestingly enough, Mike is the only one, aside from me, Derek, and my father, who has the complete list of transactions for the financial division. He could rally people together. He's dangerous."

"Why would your father put him on the board and give him that kind of power?"

"Good question, because my father isn't one to give anyone else power. I'll ask my mother what she knows. In the meantime, get me what you have on the others."

"You're sure your mother's still on your side?"

"Believe me. My mother doesn't think orange jumpsuits work for her. Last year's brush with the law scared the shit out of her. Fortunately for her, I plan to make Brandon Enterprises something far bigger, and more prosperous, than ever before." I grab the picture and stuff it in the envelope.

"What are you going to do about that?" he asks.

"Use my father to rein in Derek to buy us some time while I prepare to leash him myself. And speaking of Derek, are we sure he doesn't have anyone inside BP on his payroll?"

"I'm working on that answer." Seth glances at his watch. "I'm meeting with the head of security at BP in an hour to pick up the logs and camera feed. I'll review it all tonight and let you know what I find." He stands, pausing to say, *"Cave canem"*—Latin for "Beware of the dog"—before he heads for the exit.

I stare after him, chewing on the words, *my words*, I'd said almost daily at the firm right before I went toe-to-toe with opposing counsel, and I understand why Seth repeated them now. It's a reminder that it isn't about family anymore. It's about winning and the "dog" isn't opposing counsel. It's my brother, who I fully intend to put on a fucking chain before he ruins us all.

Grabbing the cup off the table, I stand and tip it back, drinking a long, deep swallow, the sweet rich taste of chocolate awakening my taste buds and reminding me of the woman who'd ordered it. Crossing to the trashcan, I decide I know exactly what drew me to Emily. She was strong, but also sweet and soft in all the ways this life, and my family, has made me hard. She's the kind of woman who would be eaten alive in my world. I toss the cup, and decide it's a good thing she ran.

Five minutes later, I step off the elevator onto the twenty-fifth floor and pause to stare at the words BRANDON ENTERPRISES painted on the wall, my gaze focusing on the lion emblem beneath them. It's meant to represent my father—the king of our jungle, in his own words—and I'd seen him that way until I was about fourteen. From that point forward, he'd become the man he is now, the monster who'll eat any sheep who dare cross his path and a few who don't. And I have that killer instinct in me, but I will never be him. It's a thought that sets me into action again, walking toward the double glass doors of our corporate offices.

I enter the reception area, dominated by a horseshoe desk in the center of a fork of hallways; the bulk of our offices are on the other side of the building. Kelly, the new, twenty-something brassy blonde who handles the desk, straightens on my approach. "Good afternoon, Mr. Brandon."

"Is my father in?" I ask, stopping directly in front of her.

"Yes, but I believe your brother's with him."

"Perfect," I say. "Don't warn him I'm headed his direction."

"But he said—"

Waving a hand at her, I dismiss her objection, cutting left down a short hallway. In a few steps, I'm entering the enclave that is the exterior of my father's office. And considering my father just burned through his third secretary this year, there's no one to stop me as I pass the mahogany secretarial desk framed by a giant painting of the Denver skyline to reach the double, floor-to-ceiling wooden doors of his office. Without a knock, I open them and enter the room to find my father sitting behind his ridiculously large half-moon oak desk.

Derek springs from one of the two high-backed leather visitor's chairs to face me, his tailored blue suit an expensive product of everything wrong with this company and family, and he doesn't give a shit. In fact, he's proud of it.

"What the fuck are you doing here, Shane?" he demands. "Don't you know how to knock?"

I ignore him, closing the distance between me and my father, who just watches my approach, choosing not to speak until I stop in front of his desk, opposite Derek.

"Yes, son," he demands then, his voice low and controlled, like everything he does. "What the *fuck* are you doing?"

I'm not fooled by the obvious reprimand, all too aware of the gleam in his eyes that has nothing to do with irritation and everything to do with amusement. He thrives off the war for control he's stirred between his sons. He's not repenting for his sins with the grim reaper on his doorstep. He's daring him to come take him, and as much as I'd like to blame his brain tumor, I can't. I love my father because he's my father, but he's a bastard, which is exactly why I swore I'd never work here.

I reach inside the envelope and remove a photo, tossing both down in front of him. "Do you know who that is?"

Derek replies before my father has the chance. "You said the FDA was keeping us from doubling our money. They aren't anymore."

There is pride and victory in his voice that has me checking my anger, and slowly rotating to face him. "Did you read the reports that said the drug isn't ready for market? We can't endanger lives." And because my brother doesn't seem to have a conscience I add, "It opens us up to lawsuits."

"That we'll be able to afford," Derek argues, "because we're rolling in cash. And we have you to fight them."

"People will die," I bite out.

"Every drug company takes calculated risks," he counters.

"The drug *isn't* ready."

He rests his hands on the back of one of the two leather chairs separating us. "No one says we don't keep working on the quality of the product, but I've paid to ensure we can take it to market whenever we so choose."

I mimic his position, my hands settling on the second chair. "Poorly hidden lump-sum payments to various organizations got this company in trouble last year, in case you don't remember."

"And you cleaned it up as I'm sure you'll do again if need be."

"If this goes sour, I won't defend you."

"The pharmaceutical property was your acquisition. You're linked, baby brother. No one will believe otherwise."

There's no missing the threat beneath those words. If he goes down, he'll do whatever is necessary to take me with him. "You want to play God, do it with one of the other six companies under our umbrella."

"That's the difference between you and me," he says. "You want to be God. I, on the other hand, prefer the fires of hell."

"Until they burn you alive."

His jaw clenches, his eyes glinting with anger, and while we might look alike, today I face the fact that we share nothing else anymore, most especially this company.

"Come now, brother," he says, a hint of amusement shading his voice. "You know you wanted that drug approved. And now we have an inspector in our pocket. We should be celebrating."

I turn to face my father. "You asked me to stay and protect this company after I cleaned up your mess. Rein him in, or the only *legacy* you'll end up with will be jail, because I'll leave. I will walk the fuck away and your little game will be over. And when this explodes in your face, like the last mess did, I won't fix it this time."

My father's lips tighten, eyes sharpen, darken, and while mine might be the same shade of light gray, I refuse to ever let them be as hard and cold. "You do know I'm dying," he says.

"Which means you have nothing to lose but that legacy," I say with brutal honesty, because brutal is all he understands. "I have everything to lose and that's too much. I won't go to jail for you."

His lips twist wryly. "This company survived twenty years without your sense of morality."

"And then you got on the Feds' watch list with that trade deal that went south. I covered that shit up despite everything I believe in." Anger and guilt burns through me. "Because you said I had a chance to make things right here once and for all." I glance at Derek. "You're still my brother and I am trying to keep you out of jail."

"Whatever you have to tell yourself to look in the mirror, Shane."

I don't justify the snide remark with an answer that will only ignite another attack, instead refocusing on my father. "You know what it takes to keep me here. It's nonnegotiable." I turn on my heel, striding toward the door, and the moment my hand closes on the knob, I hear my father speak. "Brandon Pharmaceuticals is yours. Derek will stand down."

I don't turn, pausing only long enough to hear Derek's low curse, nor do I stay for the argument certain to follow. I exit to the exterior office, shutting the door behind me and traveling the secretarial enclave with long, purposeful strides meant to lead me to a stiff drink I normally don't entertain at this time of the day. An agenda that is derailed as I reach the hallway and my mother steps into my path.

"Shane, sweetie," she greets me, looking forty when she's actually in her fifties and sporting a sleek black dress that hugs her curves in a way no son would approve. "Is your father in?" Her brows dip, her hand closing on my arm. "You're upset. What happened?"

It never ceases to amaze me how quickly she reads what I know is not on my face. "Nothing I can't handle." And knowing this isn't the time or place to talk to her about Mike Rogers, I say, "I have work I need to attend to."

"You mean you don't want to talk about it." Narrowing her pale blue eyes on me, she delicately swipes a lock of her long, dark hair behind one ear. "I don't even need to know details because we both know you still aren't listening to me. Take control and then make changes. That's the only way this works." She releases me. "I'll talk to him. Call me later." She moves around me and I step forward, only to have her stop me. "Oh and honey. If you plan to do more than fuck the woman who put that lipstick on your collar, I expect to meet her."

I have no idea how lipstick traveled to my collar, and really don't care, but damn if a taste of the woman who put it there doesn't sound really damn good right about now. And if I had her, my mother, and my entire damn family for that matter, wouldn't be allowed anywhere near her.

Behind every great fortune, there's a crime.

—Lucky Luciano

CHAPTER TWO

SHANE

Within fifteen minutes of my mother's "lipstick" announcement, I'm already behind my cherrywood desk in the corner office opposite my brother's, trying to focus on work, when Jessica, a tall blonde with spiky hair and an attitude, steps into the office.

"Your fresh shirt has arrived," she says, indicating the garment in her hand. "And let me just say, if the woman responsible for your change of clothes put that scowl on your face, I'm personally requesting there's no do-over."

"The lipstick on my collar isn't what it looks like," I say, dropping my Montblanc pen on the desk. "If it was, I'd definitely be in a better mood."

She hangs the shirt on the back of the door. "Sounds like an interesting story we both know you won't tell me, so I won't ask." She crosses to stand in front of my desk and sets two folders in front of me. "The top one contains the top ten most profitable drugs in the world, along with risk assessments, lawsuits, and drug studies. The bottom contains the profiles of the key players who brought them to market."

"Ever efficient," I say. "Good work. Is——"

"Yes. Derek returned to his office just after you did."

In other words, my father shut him down, which is, at least, a small piece of good news.

"Anna, his new secretary, followed him into his office and shut the door, a recent habit they've developed. I'm really quite thankful the walls in this place are thick because, I assume, he too will be in need of a fresh shirt. I guess it's good to have a full-service assistant. She can do it all. I don't. I won't. But I promise you, I'm better than her."

"Ah, Jessica. Leave it to you to keep things in perspective. I keep waiting for the day my brother tries to hit on you to get to my secrets. I want popcorn and front-row seats."

"Please give me a reason to go Rocky on that man. I'll leave you to your work." She crosses the room, disappearing into the hallway and pulling my door shut without me asking. The woman is a jewel in a sea of stones.

I grab the folders and go to work, looking for our next play in the market, the one where the rest of Brandon Enterprises no longer exists. I start reading and I don't stop, analyzing alliances I might form, products we might produce. My interests lead me to Internet research and an e-mailed list of prospective hires that I shoot to Seth. I'm deep into the second half of folder number one when I blink and look up to find Jessica setting a coffee on my desk, along with a bag I know has the croissants I favor inside. "It's seven o'clock."

I blink and look up at her. "How long have I been sitting here?"

"I believe you stretched your legs and walked to what I assume was the bathroom—I certainly hope so—at about four o'clock. So, three hours, not including the three before that break. What can I do to help?"

"Go home."

"You've been here late every night for a month, Shane. You haven't even changed your shirt. You need rest."

"Thank you, *Mother.* I'm fine. Go home."

"I'm twenty-nine years old, about to be thirty. For your safety, do not call me 'mother.'"

"Go home," I repeat.

"Fine," she says, turning on her heel and marching toward the exit, disappearing into the hallway and shutting the door behind her. I rotate my chair to face the floor-to-ceiling windows wrapping the room. The city is soon to be aglow in light, but it will never compare to the view from my Manhattan office. Frustrated at myself for going there, I face forward again.

It's time to go home, order a pizza, and just work, but I don't get up. Instead, for at least the tenth time, my mother's words replay in my head. *Take control and then make changes*, followed by my thought of, *Not a chance in hell.* I need a play, a game changer that forces everyone to follow me if Seth fails on the leverage side. I stand and grab my briefcase, shoving the files inside, and damn it, my gaze catches on the view behind the glass. For almost a year now, I've craved my return to New York, but it's time I face facts. I have to be here and be present to win this war, or give up. I dig my phone from my pants pocket and text the realtor I've been dodging for months: *I'm ready. Find me a house. I'll call you tomorrow.*

Shoving my briefcase strap over my shoulder, I cross the room, exiting into the dimly lit outer office, and I'll be damned if Derek doesn't do the same. We both stop outside our doors, the tension between us damn near making the floor quake. In unison it seems, we start walking, neither of us stopping until we are toe-to-toe at the hallway, inviting both our departures.

"The company doesn't need to be saved," Derek bites out, as if we're mid-conversation. "Father might be playing a game with us, but we both know he won't watch his pride and joy be gutted."

"Wake up, Derek. He'll be dead and you'll be in jail if we don't make changes. We can make those changes together."

"We can't do shit together, Shane."

"We're *brothers*. We used to be inseparable."

"I was your babysitter, then left for college before you even hit high school. We barely know each other and anything we were damn sure ended when you returned home and became everyone's moral compass." His jaw sets. "Go back to your world. This is mine."

His. This is all about the company and money. Power. And still, the brother in me who used to idolize Derek wants to cave and give him what he demands, but he's made that impossible. "Together," I say again.

"Fuck off, Shane. How do you not see how much I hate you? Right isn't right because it's your way, and you'll find that out soon. You have my word." He steps back and walks down the hallway. I step to the center of the hall, staring after him, willing him to turn back, and wondering how we've gotten to this place where we are now enemies. He rounds the corner, disappearing.

Gone. But he's not completely lost yet. I refuse to let that happen.

The sound of the lobby door opening and closing signals his departure, and ready to get the hell out of the building, I waste no time following in his path. By the time I'm in the corridor outside Brandon Enterprises, he's already departed in one of the eight elevators. Another opens for me quickly.

Once inside the car, my mind doesn't go to Derek, but rather to my father. He's always been brutal, the ways he terrorized me in my youth too many to count. Derek had been older, but there had been a window of time we'd shared a hatred of him, and yet both of us had craved his attention and the love I'm not sure he's capable of giving. I don't crave that anymore, and yet he's dying and I think maybe I should. My mind travels to the past, to me at sixteen, and him forcing me to run laps until I threw up after I got a ninety on a test, a failure in his eyes. I guess I should thank him, though. I did get into Harvard.

Holy fuck, I want out of this elevator. I step to the doors, waiting impatiently for them to open, and the second they part, I cut through the deserted building toward the parking garage. Once I reach the steel door, I hesitate, the idea of my empty apartment hitting all the wrong nerves. I head back toward the lobby, which leads directly to the Sixteenth Street strip mall lined with restaurants and bars. I'll prepare for my brother the way I did my cases in New York. In a corner booth of a restaurant, only this time it won't be with a never-ending pot of coffee, but an expensive bottle of whiskey. I'm halfway to the front door when my gaze catches on the security booth in the corner and I stop dead in my tracks.

Unless I'm dreaming, my sweet-smelling coffee thief is indeed here again and seems to be arguing with the guard. Suddenly, a little conversation doesn't sound so bad after all. I remind myself that she is completely wrong for how fucked up my life is right now, but the truth is that's exactly what makes her appealing. Besides, I don't want to own the woman. Well. Not when she has her clothes on, and if I have my way, she won't for long. I start walking in her direction.

EMILY

"I understand the Lost and Found is locked up for the night," I say to the stoic, gray-haired guard behind the security desk. "But surely you can make an exception for a cell phone. I'm expecting a very important call. I can't be without my phone."

"I understand, miss, but there are rules."

Rules. There's a concept that hits a raw nerve. "Fine," I

concede, reaching for my wrist, missing the bracelet that should be there but is not. "I'll come back. How early can I be here?"

"Seven in the morning."

"Six forty-five it is," I say, rotating to depart, yelping as I smack into a hard body, and a pair of large, manly hands settles on my waist, steadying me. "I'm sorry," I say, glancing up in shock to realize the hot man from the coffee shop is standing in front of me and my palms have landed on his incredibly hard, broad chest.

"We meet again," he says, his voice a soft purr of seduction, and his eyes are still a perfect steel gray just like the tie that matches his suit.

"Yes, I . . ." I swallow hard. "I'm sorry. I didn't see you."

"I'm not sorry and I did see you."

"You . . . what?" I step back, his hands falling from my waist. Mine slide away from his chest, where I wouldn't have minded them lingering a little longer, but that would be bad. And inappropriate, which is exactly what I'm trying never to be again.

He glances at the guard. "Is there a problem, Randy?" he asks, and good gosh, no wonder I ended up in that exchange with him this morning. The man is the definition of "tall, dark, and handsome."

"The lady is looking for her cell phone," Randy explains, "and Lost and Found is closed for the night."

Shane arches a brow at the man. "Closed? How does Lost and Found close?"

My thoughts exactly, but I bite my tongue, considering "Randy" had actually displayed quite a lot of patience with me, when I'd asked the same question in a far more pushy way. And Randy is actually looking quite uncomfortable, his reaction indicating that Shane is more than a random hot guy in this building who likes his coffee ridiculously strong. "I'm the only guard on duty," Randy explains. "I can't leave the desk."

"I'll watch it for you," Shane states, and it's not an offer. It's an expectation. Everything about this man is a smooth command that manages to be sexy, not obnoxious. A rare skill few men, or women, successfully harness, though I've known many who tried and failed.

"Yes sir," Randy says. "I'll be back in five minutes."

The guard rushes away, leaving me stunned at his quick departure while Shane rests an arm on the counter and faces me. "You ran away today."

My eyes go wide. "That's the way to get right to the point. And for your information, I had someplace to be."

"You didn't even take your coffee with you."

"I didn't have time to drink it," I say quickly, no stranger to thinking on my feet.

"You ran," he repeats.

"You're kind of intimidating," I counter.

Amusement lights his gray eyes. "*You* aren't intimidated by me."

"Are you saying you *are* intimidating to others?" I challenge.

"To some I am, but not to you."

"You base this assessment on what, exactly?"

"Anyone intimidated wouldn't be brave enough to say they are." He closes the distance between us, the scent of him, autumn leaves and spice, teasing my nostrils. "Are you intimidated now?" he asks, the heat in his eyes blisteringly hot.

"No," I say, suddenly warm all over, when lately, everything has made me cold. "I'm *not* intimidated."

"Good news," the guard announces, jolting me back to a reality that does not include hot strangers who could find out more than I want them to know. I quickly take a broad step backward, distancing myself from Shane, to face Randy.

"You found my phone?" I ask, hopeful.

"I found *a* phone," he confirms. "I need you to verify the first number in the contacts."

I hesitate, but having no other option, admit, "There are no numbers in my phone at all."

"You are correct," the guard says, sliding the phone onto the counter. "I've never known anyone to have no contacts in their phone."

"It's new," I explain, picking it up and slipping it inside my purse, and realizing it's a lame excuse, I add, "I need to sync my numbers. Thank you." I rotate to face Shane to find him staring at me with the kind of interest and curiosity I'm not in a position to invite. "And thank you," I add, motioning toward the door. "I should go."

"I was about to go grab dinner and a drink at one of the restaurants nearby. Join me."

"I really should get home," I say, trying not to sound as regretful as I am. I'm flattered, but then, what woman wouldn't be with this man?

"I won't keep you long."

"I have plans in the morning," I counter, and it's true. I'll be waiting for the phone to ring and thinking about how much I wish I'd said yes to his invitation.

He glances at the guard, who quickly takes a hint and murmurs, "Good evening," before stepping back behind his post and busying himself.

The instant he's gone, Shane once again closes the space between us, this time bringing us intimately close, and I think he might touch me. I *want* him to touch me. "Here's how I see us meeting again: the odds are next to zero. That means you have to have dinner with me."

"Have to? Is that some rule or something?"

"Not just a rule. A hard rule I just made up."

"Does making up rules work often?"

"Yes. Is it working now?"

Yes, I think, but instead, I say, "I wish I could."

"*You can.* Just say yes, Emily."

Emily. I hate that name, but he has somehow not only re-membered it, but made it silk and seduction. *He* is silk and se-duction, a magnificent man who no doubt has so many woman lining up that I am a mere flicker on the screen. And actually, that isn't a bad thing. In fact, it's freedom. This is about tonight. *Just* tonight. He won't want to know my past or my future. He's looking for a diversion, and the truth is, if I spend one more night alone, trapped in guilt, worry, and my fast-looping replay of how I got to this point, I might go insane.

"Emily," he prods, using that name again, *my* name, and I swallow hard. "Say—"

"Yes," I supply. "Yes, I'll have dinner and drinks with you."

Satisfaction fills his eyes and he waves the guard forward, handing the man his bag. "I'll pick it up on my way out," he tells him. The other man nods, and a moment later, Shane's full at-tention shifts back to me, and I'm jolted by the way I *feel* the im-pact, or rather, I feel *him,* a warm spot forming in my chest and spreading low into my belly. He offers me his arm. "Shall we?"

I hesitate a few beats, reminding myself that "alone" prom-ises safety, but I can't live that way forever. This dinner with this man is a no-harm, no-foul way to practice being the new me. I accept his arm.

You just know how to hide, how to lie.

—*Tony Montana*

CHAPTER THREE

EMILY

Arm in arm, Shane and I cross the lobby, and as crazy as it is, for the first time in a very long time, I don't feel alone. It's a façade, of course, but one I'm happily wallowing in. A fantasy and an indulgence: this night that can never become another night.

"How's Jeffrey's Restaurant two blocks down?" he asks.

"I've never heard of it," I say, "but I'm sure it's fine." Because I'm not going with him for the food. It's for him. No. It's for *me*, for once.

"It has a mixed menu, a full bar, and it's relatively quiet," he replies, releasing my arm to open the building's exterior door, and wave me forward.

"Sounds perfect," I say, and somehow our eyes collide, and I don't know how or why, but that tiny connection has my stomach fluttering. I dart forward and outside, a cold breeze lifting my hair and sliding along the bare skin of my neck. Shivering, I hug myself, chilled on the outside but pretty darn warm in all those intimate places he continues to awaken. I start to turn to face Shane, but suddenly he is beside me, his arm draping over my shoulder, dragging me closer, his big body sheltering mine from the cold, and my chest hurts with the silly idea he's protecting me. No one protects me and suddenly, this dinner seems like a bad idea. I deal with being alone by *being alone.*

"Don't you just love Colorado in May?" he asks, angling us left and into the heart of downtown Denver and a cluster of restaurants and shops. "Random snow showers, cold at night, and warm in the day."

I open my mouth to tell him this is new to me, and snap it shut, frustrated at how easily I almost invited questions about where I came from, and why I'm here. "I should have brought a jacket," I say simply instead.

"I'm glad you didn't. Gives me an excuse to keep you close."

"Somehow, I doubt you're a man who needs an excuse for much of anything."

"And you make that assessment based on what?"

"Pretty much every one of the limited, but colorful moments I've known you."

"Colorful," he says. "There's an interesting description."

"I'm just glad it was you whose coffee I stole and not some really cranky person who would have yelled at me."

"I have my moments, but never over something as trivial as a cup of coffee."

"The world would be a better place if everyone thought like you."

"There's a cynical statement."

"You've obviously not worked retail or you wouldn't call that cynical."

"And you have?"

"As a college student," I say, quickly wishing I could pull back the words that invite questions into my past.

But I am saved as he announces, "And we're here." He leads me under a covered overhang toward a wooden door, where he surprises me by stopping, facing me, his hands coming down on my arms. "I'm glad it was me who found you in that coffee shop," he says, the dim glow of overhead lights catching like fire in his gray eyes, but what steals my breath are the shadows banked behind that fire. He doesn't want to be alone tonight either, and I find myself wanting to know why.

I dare to reach up and press my hand to his chest. "I found *you*," I say, giving him a smile, wanting *him* to smile. "And you should know that I'm on a roll of mishaps today. The chance that I will spill, dump, or break something during our dinner is high."

His eyes and mouth soften, any residual effect of those shadows I'd spied disappearing. "Then we'll laugh and clean it up," he says, motioning toward the door. "Let's go inside."

"I'd like that."

He opens the door, allowing me to enter the dimly lit restaurant, where I pause to wait on him, glancing around at my surroundings. To my left is a padded leather wall, and directly in front of me are rows of uncomfortable looking wooden tables and chairs with flickering candles in the center of each table. Shane steps to my side, his hand intimately settling at my back as we advance toward the fifty-something dark-haired woman dressed in all black who is manning the hostess stand in the right corner.

She offers me a friendly smile and then glances at Shane. "Good evening, Susie," he greets.

"Good to have you in tonight. Jeffrey will be sorry he missed you."

"He's still giving me a hard time about the Broncos losing this year anyway. Tell him he lives in Denver. He can't root for Texas."

Just hearing the name of my home state, which I can't claim, twists me in knots. I have to get over this reaction.

"We've been in Denver for twenty years," she replies, giving me the impression she might be Jeffrey's wife. "He's never giving up the Cowboys. You want the bar or restaurant?"

"Is there a booth in the bar available?"

"You're in luck considering it's been a busy Wednesday night," she says, grabbing two menus. "We just had one open."

"Excellent," Shane says, and with his approval given, Susie motions for us to follow her.

Shane urges me forward, his fingers flexing where they've settled on my lower back, and we round the leather wall to a rectangular room with fully occupied high tables in the center, a bar to the right, and cozy booths set on high pedestals to the left. Susie directs us to the fourth booth of eight lining the far wall. "Can I get anything started for you?" she asks before we sit, her gaze falling on me. "Wine or a cocktail, perhaps?"

"Wine would be great," I say. "Can you suggest something sweet?"

"I have an excellent German white I recommend often," Susie replies.

"Perfect," I say, and she immediately eyes Shane.

"Cognac?"

"You know me well," he confirms, shrugging out of his jacket and proving his crisp white shirt is indeed hugging the spectacular chest my hand had promised was beneath. "And let's break out the good stuff tonight," he adds. "I'll take the Louis XIII."

She holds out her hands for his jacket and he removes his cell phone, sticking it in his pants pocket before allowing her to take the jacket. "I'll hang this up by the door as usual," she informs him, "and I won't ask if the expensive cognac is to celebrate a good day or drive away a bad one."

"That answer changed when Emily joined me."

"Oh," Susie says, giving me a curious, pleased look. "Thanks indeed, Emily, because I have been witness to this man after a truly bad day and it's not pretty."

Shane directs a playful scowl in her direction. "Begone before you scare her off and you're stuck with me alone."

She laughs, rushing away, and Shane refocuses on me. "Apparently you saved Susie from my foul mood," he jokes.

"But who'll save me?" I tease, trying to be as ladylike as possible as I attempt to climb into the high, half-moon-shaped booth.

"Me," he promises, gently gripping my waist to help me into the seat.

"Thank you," I murmur, and when I expect him to move to the opposite side of the booth, he instead slides in beside me, forcing me to scoot around. I make it to the center before he says, "Oh no you don't," and the next thing I know, his fingers have closed down over my knee, my sheer pantyhose the only thing between his palm and my skin.

He scoots closer, aligning our legs, tilting his head in my direction. "You're still running."

Not from you, I think, but I say, "Not anymore, but I admit, I did judge you at first."

He inches back to look at me. "Did you now?"

"I did. I mean, that cup of coffee said a lot about you," I say, calling on the skills I'd once thought would serve me well in a career that now seems lost. "I'm very good at reading people."

His eyes light, the shadows nowhere to be found, and it pleases me to think I've made them disappear. "What did my coffee tell you about me?" he asks, resting an elbow on the table, his body still angled toward mine.

"It was strong and no-nonsense, meant to get a job done, without any fluff about it."

"That still doesn't tell me what you think it says about me."

"Of course it does. You're a workaholic."

"A workaholic."

"That's right. It was a large triple shot. That says you are running on fumes and trying to stay focused. Oh. And you don't take no for an answer."

"The coffee told you I don't take no for an answer?"

"No. That part I gathered from you not taking no for an answer."

We break into mutual laughter that fades into a hint of a smile on his lips, the air shifting around us, thickening. There is a pureness to our shared desire that I decide is created by us having no past to color the way we feel about each other.

"Let's talk about your coffee," he says, putting me in the assessment hot seat.

"You didn't drink my coffee," I point out.

"Actually, I did."

"What?" I ask in disbelief. "Wait. You drank my coffee after I left?"

"That's right."

"On purpose?"

"On purpose," he confirms.

"Why?"

"Because I was left curious about the woman who ordered it and your drink, like mine, says things about you."

I can't believe he drank my drink after I left or that I'm about to invite him to look deeper into who I am. "And what exactly did it say about me?"

"It said—"

"I have a cognac and a wine," a waitress announces, leaving me hanging on his words.

"Wine for the lady," Shane instructs and we both lean back to allow her to deposit our drinks in front of us, giving me the opportunity to discover our waitress is a gorgeous redhead, with deep cleavage exposing DD breasts, which make my D cups feel like As.

"Are you ready to order?" she asks.

"I haven't looked at the menu," I say, reaching for it, and glancing at Shane. "You probably know what you want."

"Indeed," he says, the look in his eyes sizzling, as he adds, "Very decisively."

I flush, quite certain that yes, he has noted my brief walk down insecurity lane, and while I'm embarrassed, I am quite charmed at the way he's made sure I know my concern was without merit. I shut the menu again. "What do you recommend?"

"They're well known for their brown butter ravioli," he replies, "which I have every time I visit."

"It's amazing," the waitress interjects. "Melt-in-your-mouth good."

"You had me at brown butter," I say. "And anything with pasta and cheese makes my favorite foods list."

"Three check marks on the list," Shane says, gathering our menus and offering them to the waitress. "Two of the house raviolis it is then."

"Got it," the waitress confirms. "Any drinks, aside from what you have, with your meal?"

I shake my head but Shane motions to my wine. "Try it and make sure you like it."

It's an order, which seems to come naturally to him, but it's also him actually caring that I'm satisfied. I take a quick sip, and the fruity sweet liquid is pure perfection. "It's great," I tell him, and eye the waitress. "I love it."

"Well then," she says. "I'll put the order in to the kitchen."

She departs and Shane reaches for the glass I'm still holding, covering my hand with his. "May I?"

Heat rushes through me, the idea of his mouth where mine had been more than a little sexy. "Of course," I say, sounding and feeling breathless. And when I would offer it to him, he covers my hand over the glass, his eyes capturing mine as he tilts it to drink, then savors it a moment.

"Sweet, like your coffee."

"And you think that means what?" I ask.

He considers me a moment, before releasing my hand and reaching for his glass. "I drink my coffee the way I see the world. Harsh and brutal. And I drink my booze with a smooth kick, the way I try and face my adversaries."

This is a silly game that has suddenly made my world feel upside down and I laugh without humor. "I don't see the world as sweet, if that's where you're going with this."

"No. No, you don't. But you do compartmentalize the bad stuff, while I force myself to stay in the thick of things no matter how bad they are. I'm not sure which is worse."

I'm not sure if I'm more stunned that he's nailed me so well, or that he's actually shared something I find quite personal about himself. "And I make this assessment not from your drink, but the way you handle yourself and the look in your eyes."

The look in his eyes, I think. I was right. We're drawn together because we're both dealing with a demon or two that won't let us go.

"Am I wrong?" he asks.

"No. You pretty much nailed it. If I don't compartmentalize, I worry and obsess. It's just who I am. It started young. My mom said I could fret over my Barbie losing a shoe for hours."

"That fits the profile of someone who compartmentalizes to survive."

"And you stand in the fire and let it burn you."

A muscle ticks in his jaw. "I stand in the fire," he says, lifting his glass and taking a drink. "I don't let it burn me."

"Because you're good at whatever you do." It's not even a question.

"Yes," he says. "I'm good at whatever I do." It's confident, maybe arrogant as well, but it works for him. "What about you?" he asks. "Are you good at what you do?"

We just entered dangerous territory and I reach for my wine. "Let's hope so, since I'm on an unplanned job search."

"Unplanned?"

"Right," I say, glad to share one piece of truth. "Unplanned." I take a drink, steeling myself for his questions and my lies.

"You don't have to tell me," he says, obviously reading my discomfort.

"It's fine," I say, setting my wine aside. "I relocated here from Los Angeles to work for this very rich man, a stockholder of a big holding company."

"For him or the holding company?"

"Him. I was to be his assistant, but the job was bigger than the title. I saw it as a chance to learn at the highest level of the corporate world. He said he'd mentor me. It was exciting and the pay was spectacular. Unfortunately, two weeks after I arrived, one of his companies folded and he filed for bankruptcy."

"Now that's a fucking bad break."

"He paid me a month severance—"

"A whole month. That's generous of him."

"Hey. It's better than nothing, and like I said, my pay was spectacular."

"What did you do back in Los Angeles?"

"I was a paralegal chasing a bigger dream," I confess, and there is at least some truth to the statement, but here comes the lie. "Every time I thought I'd make it to law school, I hit a bump in the road."

"And yet you took a job that wasn't leading you to law school at all."

"I did," I say, not having it in me to say more.

His eyes search mine, probing and far too aware. "How old are you?"

"Twenty-seven. And you?"

"Thirty-two. Do you have family or friends in Denver?"

I twirl the base of my glass. "No family or friends."

"You moved here with nothing but a job?"

Not by choice, I think, but I say, "Just ambition."

"I'm impressed."

"I don't have a job," I remind him, wishing I deserved the admiration I see in his eyes.

"Anyone who dares to do what you have will come out on top. That takes balls very few men or women possess."

I grab an opening to turn the conversation back to him. "And you do?"

"Yes. I do." His reply is quick, but he is quick to turn the conversation back to me. "Aren't you just a little tempted to go back home?"

Home. I almost laugh at that word. "This is where I live now."

"Surely leaving has crossed your mind," he presses.

"No, actually. It didn't and it won't." I cut my gaze reaching for my wine, stunned when he catches my wrist before I succeed. I try not to look at him, but somehow I find myself captured in his far too astute stare.

"You're alone," he states.

"I'm with you," I say, cringing inwardly at the obvious, nervously spoken statement so ridiculous that I've invited further probing.

His hand curls around mine and he drags it to his knee, and the way he's looking at me, like the rest of the room, no, the rest of the *world,* doesn't exist, steals my breath. I haven't allowed anyone to really look at me in a very long time.

"Emily," he says, doing whatever he does to turn my name into a sin that seduces rather than destroys me.

"Shane," I manage, but just barely.

"Did you say yes to dinner because you didn't want to be alone?"

I am not sure where he is going with this, if it's about reading me or if he needs validation that I am here for him, so I give him both. "I like being alone," I say, and on some level, it really is true. "I said yes to dinner because *you* are the one who asked." My lips curve. "Actually you barely asked. You mostly ordered."

"I couldn't let you say no."

"I'm actually really glad you didn't."

"And yet you say you *like* being alone?"

"It's simple and without complication."

"Spoken like someone who's lived the opposite side of the coin."

"Haven't we all?"

"Who burned you, Emily?"

I blanch but recover with a quick, "Who says anyone burned me?"

"I see it in your eyes."

"Back to my eyes," I say.

"Yes. Back to your eyes."

"Stop looking."

"I can't."

Those two words sizzle, matching the heat in his eyes, and my throat goes dry. "Then stop asking so many questions."

He reaches up, brushing hair behind my ear, his fingers grazing my cheek, and suddenly he is closer, his breath a tease on my cheek, his fingers settling on my jaw. "What if I want to know more about you?"

"What if I don't want to talk?"

"Are you suggesting I shut up and kiss you?"

Yes, I think. *Please.* But instead I say, "I don't know. I haven't interviewed you as you have me. I know nothing about you. I want to know if you—"

He leans in, and then his lips are on mine, a caress, a tease, that is there and gone, and yet I am rocked to the core, a wave of warmth sliding down my neck and over my breasts. He lingers, his breath fanning over my lips, promising another touch I both need and want, as he asks, "You want to know if I what?"

Everything. "Nothing."

"The food has arrived," our waitress announces, and I jolt, tugging my hand from Shane's and feeling like a busted school-girl and bringing attention to myself I don't need or want.

"Here you go," she says, setting a plate in front of me, the scent of butter and spices teasing my nose, but I am suddenly no longer hungry. In fact, I feel a little queasy.

Noting the way the waitress has set her stand in front of Shane's side of the table, I grab my purse and round the seat opposite him and murmur, "I'm going to the ladies' room." I don't look at him but I feel him watching me, willing me back to my seat, while he remains somewhat, thankfully, trapped.

"In the back of the main dining room," the waitress calls after me.

"Thank you," I mumble, pretty sure it's not loud enough to be heard, already almost to the bar exit. I pass the leather wall and I stop, my gaze landing on the front door and an easy escape.

"Bathroom?" Susie asks.

"Yes," I say. "Please."

"Behind me and all the way to the back and left."

"Great. Thanks." Following her directions, I cut left, away from the exit, relieved Shane hasn't shown up, and actually thankful I haven't made it out the door. If I'm to start a new life, I can't hide in my apartment out of fear. I have to pay the bills, which means navigating Shane and every other person, and situation, I might face. This is my life now and I have to learn to cope with questions I don't, and won't, answer.

I pass through the dimly lit dining room that is far too long, giving me way too much time to think and yet I can't think. I reach a long hallway that cuts left. I'm almost at the bathroom door when suddenly my wrist is shackled, and another second later, I'm against the wall, with Shane's big body crowding mine.

My hands land on the hard wall of his chest, his legs framing mine. "What are you doing?" I demand.

"You're upset."

"You just shoved me against a wall in a hallway," I say. "Yes. I'm upset."

"That's not why you're upset."

"I'm a very private person."

"Good. So am I."

"You have me shoved against a wall," I repeat. "In a public place. And you kissed me. *In a public place.*"

He cups my face. The act is possessive, a claiming driven home by the way that autumn scent of his teases my nostrils. "That wasn't a kiss," he declares, his mouth closing down on mine, his tongue pressing past my lips. The instant it finds mine, the taste of spiced cognac fills my senses. Another lick and I moan, my fears, the public place, and my secrets fading away, for the first time in an eternal month. This, him, is what I craved this night. Not brown butter ravioli and fancy wine. I don't fight to remember the privacy I've declared I value. My fingers curl around his shirt, and suddenly I am kissing him back, my body swaying into his, the warmth of his seeping into mine, but it doesn't last.

As if he was waiting for my total submission, he tears his mouth from mine, denying me his kiss, and I'm left panting. "That was an appetizer," he declares, his voice a low, sultry rasp. "And you were right. Alone is better, which is exactly how I planned to spend this night. Until I saw you and alone wasn't better anymore. And now I know why. You want what I want."

"Which is what?"

"No complications."

Relief and the promise of the escape I now know I'd hoped for rushes over me. "Yes. Yes, but you keep—"

"Thinking about kissing you. That's all I could do sitting at that table. And I should warn you. When dinner is done, I'm going to do my damn best to convince you to go somewhere else with me where we can be alone." He covers my hand with his. "Come. I'm going to feed you, because if I have my way, you're going to need your energy."

He starts walking, taking me with him, and I grab his arm. "Wait." He pauses and turns to look at me, those intense gray eyes of his stirring a giant dose of nerves in my belly that I shove aside. "I don't want to go back out there."

He narrows his gaze on me, his big hands settling on my shoulders. "What are you saying?"

"I prefer somewhere else," I say, and my voice is remarkably steady considering I'm so out of my comfort zone with this man and my actions tonight that I don't know what I'm doing. But what I do know is that I don't want to spend the one night I have with this incredible man at a dinner table.

He stares down at me, his expression unreadable, seconds ticking like hours before he asks, "You're sure?"

"Yes," I confirm, and it's a relief that I mean it, that nothing dictates this choice but my own wants and needs. "I'm sure."

Again, his reply is slow, and he seems to weigh my words before one of his cheeks presses to mine, his breath a warm tease on my ear and neck as he whispers, "I want you to leave with me, but be clear. That means I will fuck you every possible way, with the full intent of ensuring that I'm the man you compare all others to."

Every nerve ending I own is suddenly on fire with the bold words that I know are meant to test my resolve. I do not intend to fail. Not this night. "You can try," I whisper.

He eases back to look at me, the gray of his eyes now flecked with pale blue fire. "You, Emily, are a contradiction I cannot *wait* to explore." I don't have to ask what he means. I am a contradiction, and in ways he can't begin to understand. He takes my hands again. "Let's pay the bill and get the hell out of here."

"Yes," I agree, barely speaking the word before he's walking again and this time I let me lead me forward.

Together, we enter the dining room, side by side, walking through the rows of tables toward the hostess stand, and I am more affected by my hand in his than anything else before this. It's the unity, I think, the sense of being with someone, a façade of course, and that alone cuts deep. I am not with him. I am not with anyone at all and yet tonight I am pretending I am. Maybe that's the appeal of one-night stands. You get to live the fantasy, experience human touch. Pretend you matter to someone, and them to you, until it's over.

We're almost to the hostess stand when abruptly, Shane stops walking. A moment later, he's in front of me, his back to the entryway, blocking it from my view, his hands on my arms. "My father is here and he's the last person I want to see right now. I'm going to grab a waitress and pay the bill. Wait for me at the back door."

Stunned, confused, I stammer, "I . . . yes . . . okay." Embarrassment follows, and I turn on my heel, intending to dart away, only to have him snag my hand, and angle me back toward him.

"I'll be right there," he says, his voice thick with promise.

Unable to process the wave of emotions overwhelming me, I manage a choppy nod and he releases me. I pretty much lunge forward, and still, the short walk feels more eternal than his long, gray-eyed stares. He doesn't want to be seen with me. He doesn't want to introduce me to his father, and that is fine, I tell myself, but it feels bad. Really bad. Why would he bring me to one of his regular places, if this is how he was going to react if we ran into someone he knows? Why do I care? It doesn't matter. I do. Illogical as it might be, I do care. What was I thinking coming here in the first place? Low profile went right out the window and it's time to get myself back under control.

Rounding the wall to the hallway again, I continue onward and cut the corner where I spy a BATHROOM sign right next to one that reads EXIT. Exit wins. Double-stepping, I close the distance between me and it, hoping to escape before Shane follows, *if* he follows. That he might not is a humiliation I really can't stomach right now. I reach the door and forcefully shove the heavy steel open, finding myself on a street with mostly retail stores that are now closed. I scan for someplace to disappear to, not about to be some sort of obligation to a man I barely know. I cut left when I spot an open coffee shop.

I all but run toward it, a gust of chilly wind lifting my hair from my neck, and I swear this Texas girl pretending to be a Cali girl will never get used to chilly summer nights. Reaching the entrance, I glance right without meaning to, at the same moment the back door of the restaurant opens. My heart leaps and I quickly enter the coffee shop, traveling the narrow path between the vacant round wooden tables.

Passing the register, I wave at the person I barely look at behind the counter. "Bathroom before I order," I murmur, entering yet another hallway and immediately finding the bathroom. I turn the knob, entering the tiny box intended for one, and lock myself inside. Falling against the door, I shut my eyes and touch my lips, remembering that kiss Shane had surprised me with, and I swear I can still taste remnants of cognac on my tongue, remnants of *him*. I bury my face in my hands, dreading my empty apartment and bed that might have been filled with Shane. Yet another part of me is relieved. I push off the door, dragging my fingers through my hair, staring at my pale face and now messy chestnut hair, and I swear, I look like my mother and I'm making the same mistakes she did. Only she could have turned back time, and made them right, and I can't. And I was about to add tonight to the list. If anything had happened to me, no one would even miss me. But that's the point I guess. For one night, I wanted someone to know I exist again. Actually, I wanted him to know. Just him, and I don't know why.

It hits me then that I haven't even checked my phone. I dig it from my purse and look for the call I'm expecting, and find the screen blank. Blank, damn it. What the hell is going on? Nothing I can control, that's for sure, or I wouldn't be in Denver. I wouldn't be doing a lot of things. I drop the phone back in my purse. I need to go home. Okay, not home. That apartment is not home. I just . . . I need to go. I grab the door, yanking it open, only to gasp at the sight of Shane standing there. "What are you doing?"

He holds up his hands. "Just hear me out and if you want me to leave, I will."

"I do. I want you to leave."

"He wasn't with my mother."

I gape. "What?"

"The woman my father was with wasn't my mother." There is a rasp to his voice, and steel in those gray eyes. "I couldn't have you be a part of that potential confrontation."

The wall I've placed between us falls away, my chest pinching with the familiar emotion of betrayal he must be feeling. A feeling I know all too well but wish I did not. "I'm so sorry."

"*I'm* sorry. I know what I made you feel. Like I was embarrassed to be with you and that simply isn't the case." He offers me his hand. "Come with me."

I could say no, but I don't want to. And I should ask where we're going, but very out of character for me, I simply don't care, nor do I think about any of the reprimands I gave myself in that bathroom. This isn't about an agenda I must follow. This is about one night with this incredibly sexy man. I slide my hand into his.

I never lie to any man because I don't fear anyone. The only time you lie is when you are afraid.

—*John Gotti*

CHAPTER FOUR

SHANE

The instant Emily's delicate little hand settles against mine, I close my fingers around hers, holding on tight, wanting her to the point of almost need. This night, somehow, she's become the light in the darkness that is my fucked-up family.

I drag her to me, my hand molded to her lower back, hers settling over my thundering heart, her eyes on my chest. "Look at me," I order.

She tilts her chin up, those pretty blue eyes filled with desire, but also trepidation that I will take great pleasure in tearing away. "This isn't," she begins. "I don't normally . . ."

"I know."

"You know?"

"Yes. I know and I don't make a habit of taking women I just met to bed."

"Then why me? Why tonight?"

"Because it would be unfair to someone else for me to fuck them while thinking about you. I want you. Just you."

"Yes, but—"

"Because you're you. That's the only answer I have for either of us."

"I don't know what that means."

"Neither do I, but we won't figure it out standing here in yet another hallway."

She studies me for several long moments, and I fight the urge to pressure her, but I wait, and when she finally nods her approval, the relief I feel defies all reason and my understanding of who I am as a man. But I don't question it or give her time to change her mind. I take her hand, leading her through the tables, me in front, simply because it's the only way I can hold on to her. Now that I have her, I'm not letting her go. I want this woman. I'm not letting her get spooked and run again.

Once we are at the door, I pull her in front of me, holding it open for her, but staying close, my hand on her back. We exit, a gust of especially cold wind greeting us and she faces me, hugging herself. "I really need that jacket right about now."

"Take mine," I say, shrugging out of it, feeling protective of this woman when I barely know her.

"No," she says, holding up her hands. "I can't do that. It's very—"

I settle it around her, holding on to the lapels as she murmurs, "Expensive," and I am looking at her lips, thinking about my mouth on hers.

"Put your arms in," I order softly, the wind lifting that sweet scent of hers in the air, and I swear my groin tightens as if she'd touched me. Holy hell, I'm in trouble with this woman. "Arms," I say again when she hasn't moved.

She hesitates a moment longer but does as I say, laughing as her hands are swallowed by my sleeves. "You're big or I'm small."

"Considering I'm six two and I'd guess you to be a foot shorter, I'd say both."

"Hey now," she reprimands me. "I'm five four. Don't take my two inches."

"Five four," I amend, reaching for one of her arms to roll up the sleeve.

"Don't do that," she objects, grabbing my hand. "This is at least a two-thousand-dollar suit. You can't roll up the material."

For a woman who tries not to talk about herself, she's just told me there's a good chance she's been around money, even if she doesn't have it now. "The jacket will be fine. The dry cleaners can handle it. I promise."

For a moment, she looks like she might argue, but instead says, "Thank you," and there's an odd hint of something in her voice that reaches beyond simple politeness and stirs further interest in me. She interests me and remarkably, the edge of minutes before has eased slightly, and I haven't even gotten her naked yet.

I grab the lapels again and inch her closer. "My place is a mile from here. I want to take you there. This is where you say yes again."

"You know my answer."

"Say it," I demand, needing her to be clear about what she wants, and what I want.

"Yes," she whispers, then seeming to understand I'll ask for more, she firms her voice to add, "Your place is fine."

"Good answer." I don't give her time to get nervous on me, draping my arm around her shoulders to sweep her into the shelter of my body, and set us in motion down a fairly deserted section of the sidewalk. "The walk is longer from the direction we exited the restaurant," I say, noting her hands grasping her purse, not me, where they belong. "But I need to drop by the building and pick up my car. Is yours in the garage?"

"I walked," she says as we enter the dark patch just before

the bustle of Sixteenth Street. "Good grief, this back street is spooky. I'd never walk it without you."

"Just another half a block and we'll be back on the main road," I say, when someone jumps out of the darkness, and starts cursing at us. I quickly pull Emily to the opposite side of me, away from the action, and hustle us forward. The minute we're on Sixteenth, I place her in front of me and turn to find a homeless man hanging back and laughing.

"Little bastard," I murmur, joining Emily, who's now facing me. "He's not following us," I say, my hands settling on her arms. "Are you okay?"

"Now that my heart is out of my throat. That was scary."

"I'm pretty sure that was a guy known as Joe who has some notoriety around him. He's a street person who enjoys scaring people."

"Enjoys it? What a horrible way to amuse himself. And how can I be mad at him and still feel sorry for him?"

"Don't," I say, draping my arm around her neck and turning her to step us into action again. "My understanding is that he has family who've tried to help but he always ends up back here."

"Drugs?"

"Yes. Drugs. He won't stay clean. Addiction is an evil monster that comes in many forms."

"Yes," she whispers, delicately clearing her throat. "Yes. It is."

She cuts her gaze, hiding what I might find in her eyes, her response suggesting the topic is personal to her and I wonder if that has anything to do with her coming to Denver alone. "Have you ever lived downtown in a major city?"

"No. Why?"

"I've traveled enough to know that every downtown located

in a major metropolis is packed with convenience, but also comes with a rough side. I was with you tonight, but you never know when you'll run into another Joe, or someone with worse intentions."

"I'm always careful." She cuts me a look. "As you can tell, considering I'm going home with a stranger tonight."

"I'm not a stranger. You know where I work. You know a restaurant I frequent and plenty of people saw us together. And by the way, Jeffrey's really does make a damn good plate of ravioli. You would have liked it."

"It smelled and looked amazing but . . ." She hesitates. "I guess it's good we didn't decide to stay. I'm sorry about your father."

"Yes well, it really shouldn't have surprised me the way it did. I mean this is a man I caught fucking our neighbor, my buddy's mother, on our kitchen counter when I was sixteen."

"Oh God. That must have been a nightmare for you."

"It wasn't one of my brighter moments."

"I'd say it's more like it wasn't one of your *father's* brighter moments. But your mother stayed?"

"Yes. She stayed."

"So, they worked it out. Are you sure this dinner was inappropriate?"

"Inappropriate is about as 'appropriate' as it gets," I say, remembering the way the woman was hanging on my father and wishing like hell I hadn't opened the door for more questions I won't answer.

But she doesn't ask another question, instead summing things up perfectly with, "Then he's an asshole."

"Yes," I agree. "He's an asshole." Silently adding, *An asshole dying of cancer.* And yet he seems to revel in pissing people off and watching them catapult their anger to guilt.

"I love horses," she says, as a carriage pulled by a black geld-ing passes by us. "And this one is quite beautiful."

"Have you been around horses?"

"My father loved to ride. I love to ride." I'm curious about this side of her, but she's already moving on. "I'm glad the car-riages only work the section of Sixteenth closed to traffic. The animals seem well cared for too."

"Unlike the ones in New York City," I say, reluctantly allow-ing her to divert the topic from herself. "My apartment was right next to Central Park. Those poor animals are in the middle of traffic getting their hoofs beat to hell."

"You lived in Manhattan?"

"Yeah. I moved there right out of law school and stayed there until I moved back to Denver last year."

She stops dead in her tracks and turns to look at me. "You're an attorney?"

"Didn't I mention that?"

"No. You *did not* mention that. You sat there and listened to me talk about law school and you didn't say a word."

I step to her, my hands settling at her waist, under the jacket. "I'm telling you now."

"What kind of law?"

"Corporate."

"Where'd you go to school?"

"Harvard."

She gapes. "Harvard? You went to Harvard?"

"Yes. I went to Harvard."

"And then you were recruited out of college to work in New York?"

"That's right."

"Money or passion?" she asks.

My brows dip. "What?"

"Are you in it for the money or the passion?"

"Why can't I have both?"

"Is that possible?"

"Not always. But sometimes." I study her a moment, and that sexy trepidation I've noticed several times before has returned with a vengeance. "Emily," I say softly, lifting my chin toward our destination. "We're ten feet from the building, and my car, which means us leaving together, and we aren't moving any closer to achieving that goal. Is this nerves or second thoughts?"

"I really want to know about you and Harvard and—"

"Understood. And I'll tell you, but we're still standing here."

She glances at the building and then back to me. "I wasn't, but now that you just pointed all of that out, I am. It's been a while and you're . . ."

"I'm what?"

"You. You're just you, and don't ask me to explain that because like you, I can't."

There is something so damn sweet about this woman that hits all the right spots and I reach over and caress hair from her face. "We're going to be good together. We already are. I feel it. You have to feel it, too. *Do you* feel it?"

"Yes," she says. "I do."

Pleased with her answer, I link our arms again and we cross a walkway toward the building. "I don't have to ask to know you're a good attorney," she comments a few steps later. "You're very persuasive."

I laugh. "Some would say I'm an asshole."

"Are you?"

"If I'm dealing with an asshole, then yes, I'm an asshole. Have you taken the LSAT?"

"Even if I had, I wouldn't tell you. I have no desire to compare scores."

"Now you've really made me curious."

"Why?" she asks as we reach the glass doors to the building. "It's nothing you haven't already done and done very well."

I key a code into the security panel and open the door. "What was your score?" I press again.

Her answer is to purse her lips and stride into the building, making a beeline for the elevators. I laugh and pursue, snagging her hand. "I need to get my bag," I say, leading her in the opposite direction. "And then I'm going to get your scores out of you."

"I didn't even say I took the test."

"We both know you did."

Her cell phone rings, she stops walking to reach into her purse, and I release her and motion to the desk. "I'll grab my bag."

She nods, and I head for the security desk, giving Randy a wave. By the time I reach the counter, he's set my bag on top, and leans close. "Your father was with a woman tonight."

"I know," I say. "I had the misfortune of running into them. Do you know her?"

"No, but I saw her with your brother a couple of weeks back at a restaurant around the corner."

My fucking brother is manipulating and spying on my father. Why does this surprise me? "Thanks, Randy. Do me a favor. Make me a copy of tonight's security feed and send it to my apartment. Be sure to wipe the original clean before replacing it."

"Consider it done."

I give him a nod and grab my cell phone from my pocket, turning to find Emily standing in profile near the elevator corridor, her head tilted low. I text Seth: *My father's at Jeffrey's with a woman. Randy says he saw her with Derek off location. I know nothing else.*

I wait for a reply, watching Emily as she turns just enough for me to see the anger on her face, a perfect match for what I'm feeling right now. Well, not a perfect match per se. She's sweet at her core, while I'm not sure what the hell I am, but it's not even close to sweet. I'm everything she is not, and that makes her damn appealing.

Deciding to hell with Seth's reply, I stick my phone in my pocket, and start walking toward Emily, a man on a mission to get us both naked as soon as possible. No more delays and I really have no clue how I went from furious in that restaurant to laughing on the walk over here, but I'm damn sure not laughing now. Neither is she. Her spine is stiff, her long brown hair hiding her face, but I can hear her muffled, terse whispers. I'm almost on top of her when she ends the call and faces me, all but jumping out of my jacket in the process.

"You scared me," she says, stuffing her phone back in her purse. "Sorry about that." She cuts her gaze. "It was my landlord and he's—"

"You don't need to make up stories for me."

Her gaze jerks to mine. "What?"

"You don't lie well and that's a compliment."

"I'm not—"

"Don't," I order softly, shackling her hips under my jacket, her hand settling on my chest, where it balls rather than flattens. She pales. "What?"

"Say nothing or tell me everything, but don't lie to me."

Her fingers grip a section of my shirt. "Nothing then."

"Understood," I agree, but the fact that I want to convince her to tell me everything is a problem I'll either deal with later, or holy hell, maybe not. I cup her face. "Here's how this is going to play out: whatever, or whomever, is tormenting you can't have you tonight. That's what you need to know. Not tonight. Understood?"

"Yes," she breathes out. "Please."

"Yes and please. Remember those words and my name because I'm going to make you say them over and over again."

She sucks in a breath, a mix of shock and interest in her expression that burns hot in my blood. She has never been properly fucked and I damn sure like the idea of being the one to remedy the situation. I take her hand and lead her to the elevator, punching our floor. The doors open instantly and I lead her inside, punching the ground level. I don't turn to her or I'll shove her against the elevator, fuck some of this anger out of my system, and Randy will have a show before he deletes the footage.

The doors open in less than sixty seconds, and I take her with me as I exit the elevator and enter the garage, where my car sits alone, a centerpiece of nothing. Interesting, considering my father is only two blocks away, but I'm sure it has to do with hiding his evening activities. Fishing my keys from my pocket, I click the locks, and the lights flicker at the same moment my cell phone beeps. I release Emily to grab my phone, and look down at the text that reads: *Sending a man now*. Simple and to the point, that's how Seth operates, and I like it that way. I stick my phone back in the pocket of my pants, my attention riveted on Emily who is standing at the trunk of the car, her finger tracing the Bentley emblem, with what I assume is nervous energy.

She glances in my direction, her eyes meeting mine from a distance. This time I'm not sure what I read in her face, but holy hell, I feel this woman in ways that make no sense. I start toward her and she rounds the car, making her way to the passenger door. I'm there in time to open it for her but she doesn't get in the car. She faces me.

"A Bentley was my dream car," she announces, apparently throwing her vow to say nothing to the wind. "No," she amends, gripping the rim at the top of the window. "*Is* my dream car. And Harvard's my dream school. And you have them both and somehow I'm with you. I'm not sure if you're a kiss good-bye to my dreams or a promise they aren't over."

"Don't let the universe decide what it means. Don't let it have that power. And don't let what you want get away from you." I step closer to her, my hand settling on the window next to hers but I do not touch her. "What *I want* is what I told you in the restaurant. To fuck you so right and well you never forget me." Her lips part, her eyes widening in surprise, chest rising and falling. "Now. Your turn. Don't censor your answer and don't think about yesterday or tomorrow. Right here, right now. What do you want, Emily?"

"You know what I want."

"Say it," I command, pushing her limits, a precursor to the rest of the night intended as a test to find out if she can really handle where I plan to take her.

She knows it too. I see it in the lift of her chin, and the hint of rebellion in her eyes. "You. Nothing but you."

And with that simple, perfect answer, she turns and slides into the Bentley. I immediately close the distance between us, kneeling beside her, and yanking the belt from the panel. She grabs my hand midway across her body.

"What are you doing?"

"Taking care of you."

"I don't need you to take care of me," she says, and she isn't talking about a seatbelt any more than I am, but for different reasons. I know what I see in her eyes because I've lived it. She's alone, trying to convince herself that's just fine by her.

Reaching over her, I connect the belt, my arm brushing her breast, her reaction a soft gasp that I feel in the tightening of my body. I inhale and settle back on my heels, my hand finding the bare expanse of her knee just beneath her skirt. "Tonight," I say. "You're mine and I take care of what's mine." I don't give her a chance to object as I stand and shut the door.

Rounding the trunk of the Bentley, I stop dead in my tracks as my brother's 911 pulls in and parks three spaces from my car.

Without question, he is up to something, and I can't help but think it has something to do with the woman who's with my father. Damn glad Emily is in the car, and out of his line of sight, I step forward to greet my brother.

He exits the 911, his gaze landing hard on me, a smirk appearing on his chiseled features. "Ah, sweet brother," he calls out, moving to the trunk of his car, his jacket now removed. "Working late I see."

I take three steps, bringing us close enough to ensure Emily won't overhear our conversation. "What are you doing here at this hour, Derek?"

"Rolling up my sleeves and getting the dirty work done, of course. A necessary evil considering I'm at war with my own brother, but at least I know who's in my corner. I wonder if you do."

It's not a question and he doesn't wait for an answer. He turns and walks toward the elevator, leaving me standing there, his words left behind as a taunt. His intent is to make me question myself and everyone around me. Of course, I know my father is ultimately on his side. Perhaps he even has more of the stockholders in his pocket than I suspect. Or not. In my experience, those who talk the loudest use language as a smoke screen. Why, if he had everything locked down, as he'd like me to believe, did he feel the need to plant a woman in our father's life to spy on him? And I'd bet money that's what's happening. Whatever the case, all is fair in love and war, and I'm starting to believe all there is left for Derek is war. I inhale, feeling the darkening of my mood, like a monster taking over. I need an outlet and I need it now.

I start walking toward the Bentley, and I'm pretty damn sure the woman inside, and the pleasure I'm going to give her, are about the only honest things in my life right now.

In Sicily, women are more dangerous than shotguns.

—*Mario Puzo*

CHAPTER FIVE

EMILY

Shane is a man of absolute control, readable in his every action and reaction, including his long, calculated strides toward the Bentley to rejoin me. Too calculated, I decide, and I have the distinct impression he's overcompensating for whatever emotional whirlwind he's just had stirred to life. He makes his final approach, and I steel myself for the end of a night I'd finally decided to embrace, or whatever else his mood brings to the table.

He opens the door, claiming the driver's seat, and sealing us inside, inky shadows consuming the small space. I inhale the scent of him, autumn and spice, wholly male, and it assaults my senses right along with a wave of cutting dark energy. He doesn't look at me or speak, wasting no time pressing the ignition to start the car, his hand going to the gear shift as if he can't wait to get the hell out of here. But he doesn't put us in drive. Instead, his wrist settles on the steering wheel, his spine stiff, and I'm pretty sure he's suddenly back in the battle he'd had with that man outside the car.

I don't know this man well, but I know that "no regrets" means not holding back. With another inhaled breath, I press my hand to his arm and try to turn the tables on him. "I could offer to get out of the car—"

He turns to me and my hand falls away, his expression a hard mask no amount of shadows can disguise. "No more back and forth. I need you in or out."

"I was going to say, but I won't offer. I won't get out of the car. Whoever that was—"

"My brother. *That* was my brother."

I hear betrayal in his voice and I understand in ways I can never share. And I don't think that's what he needs from me anyway. He needs something without complications and that's me. "Well then," I dare to say. "Your brother, your father, and the rest of the world, can't have you tonight. Because just as you said I am yours, you're *mine*."

Those gray eyes of his sharpen, slicing through the darkness like hot ice and the impact of this man's full attention is hard to describe. I have this uncanny sense of him seeing hidden pieces of me that I shelter with care and that he shouldn't see. And then suddenly, his fingers tunnel into my hair and he drags me closer. "I don't think I've ever met anyone quite like you."

"Is that good or bad?"

"I haven't decided yet," he says, and a moment later his mouth slants over mine, his tongue pressing into my mouth, stroking deeply, and I swear I feel it in the most intimate part of me. But more than anything I taste that harshness of turmoil in him that has nothing to do with me, and everything to do with why he's here with me tonight. And now I know why it has to be me and no one else. Because we are the same in ways that need no words to be understood.

He deepens the kiss, kissing me like I have never been kissed. Like I am his next breath and I have never been anyone's next breath. I moan and he responds by tearing his mouth from mine, his breath a warm whisper against my cheek as he lingers and promises, "You will do that many more times tonight." He releases me and settles back in his seat, and this time he places the car in gear, and us in motion. Only we've been in motion since the moment I reached for a cup of coffee that wasn't mine, but I think it was always meant for me. It's a silly, fantastical idea for a woman who, at any other time, wants to believe stealing the power of the universe is as simple as Shane directed. Simply not giving it the power.

He stops us at the edge of the garage, waiting for traffic to pass before we exit, and my gaze lands on the Bentley emblem, a "B" framed by wings. I reach out, touching it, a multitude of emotions rushing over me. I want this car. I want the life I was supposed to have, and it hits me that in the last few months I've become a victim, not because of what has happened to me, but rather, how I'm dealing with it.

"Have you ever driven one?" Shane asks, his voice snapping me out of my reverie.

"Not the Continental GT Speed Convertible." I run my hand over the tan leather on the door, glancing up at him. "With a custom color package inside and out."

"So the dream car isn't just a Bentley," he says, turning us onto the main road where we're immediately delayed by a red light. "It's *this* Bentley."

"Yes. This Bentley, which I know has an obscene price tag, but a girl has to set big goals." I sigh. "Preferably while employed."

"I have no doubt you'll get a job quickly." The light turns green and he reaches for my hand, placing it over the silver stick between us, placing us in gear, and accelerating. "Now you've driven your dream car."

I laugh, squeezing the stick as he shifts yet again. "This is not driving it but I still like it."

He cuts me a look, a bit of his dark energy at bay now. "We can change that, you know? I can pull over—"

"No," I object quickly, shocked at the offer. "I'm not driving it."

"Why?"

"I could wreck it."

"I have insurance," he says, cutting us into the driveway of the Four Seasons hotel.

"No," I say, as two doormen hurry to our sides who he waves away.

"I have insurance," he repeats.

"I don't want to drive, but thank you. You drive. Please. Let's get out of here."

He does the opposite, placing the car in park. "I live here."

"You . . . live in a hotel?"

He turns to face me. "The top floors are residential, which means we have the added benefit of room service if we so choose." He reaches up and brushes hair from my eyes, his fingers grazing my skin and sending a shiver down my spine. "You can drive the car."

"No. But thank you. Besides. I thought you wanted us to . . ."

"Should I use my highly creative imagination and fill in the blank?"

"No," I say quickly. "Or yes. But don't voice where that leads us or I might chicken out and never get out of this car."

"Too late to escape." He lifts his hand toward my window and the door opens instantly. "See you on the other side." He turns away and exits the car.

Nerves rush over me, and I am jittery inside and out. For the first time in my life, I'm going to have sex with a stranger, only he doesn't feel like a stranger anymore, and somehow that is both better and worse. It's a thought I can't begin to make sense of at this moment. Inhaling, I step out of the car and murmur my appreciation to the Asian bellman I guess to be around fifty. "Welcome, miss," he greets me, his eyes lighting with a mix of surprise and interest, and I suddenly wonder if I'm outside Shane's normal box. And how many women are in that box. "I'm Tai," he adds, as I try to shake off my concern. This is one night. "And," he continues, "I'm a regular around here, and at your service. If you need anything, don't hesitate to ask."

"Thank you," I say, darting to the awning-covered sidewalk. I turn to find Shane still on the driver's side of the Bentley, palming a tip to another man in uniform before rounding the hood of the car, and my God, the man is gorgeous and I'm about to be naked with him. And everyone knows. Oh God. That's embarrassing.

I shove my hands in the pockets of the jacket, *his* jacket, and decide, yep. They all know. How can they not? I tell myself it doesn't matter, but I have this need to control the perceptions of those around me that comes from a place that really isn't a good one. I blink and Shane's attention locks on me, his eyes warm, and his pace determined, as if he can't wait to get to me, and my worries about appearance slide into the breeze that lifts my hair.

Tai intercepts Shane by my side, and Shane palms him a bill I'm pretty sure is a generous fifty. "Keys in the car, Tai," he instructs of the Bentley. "We're in for the night."

We're in for the night. Does he mean me and him or him and the car? It doesn't matter really. My belly flip-flops anyway, and not just because of his use of the word "we," but the inference that I'm staying the night. *Am I* staying the night? I think I want to, but isn't the morning after weird?

"Always a pleasure to park the Bentley," Tai replies, sounding rather excited by the prospect.

He turns away, as if eager to get to it, when Shane stops him. "By the way, I meant to tell you. Culinary school for your daughter was a good investment. I took some clients to her restaurant last

week and we all agreed. Best meal we've had in years. I'll be
sending people her way."

Pride and appreciation flash across Tai's face. "The restaurant's gotten a slow start, so you have no idea how much that
means to all of us."

"My absolute pleasure," Shane says, grasping his shoulder.
"One day she'll make a husband fat and happy."

Chuckling, Tai pats his belly. "Just like her mother." He hurries away and Shane's attention lands on me, and I swear the connection I once again feel to this man, who is so obviously more
than his money and good looks, punches me in the chest. I've
never had a man affect me like this.

He steps in front of me, reaching into the jacket pockets to
pull my hands onto his shoulders before his settle possessively at
my waist. "I like you in my jacket," he says, his voice a low, rough
caress I feel in every part of me. "It says you're with me."

It's the exact thing I'd found concerning minutes before, but
coming from him, it's pure seduction. "I like me in your jacket
because it smells like you."

"You can keep it as long as I'm in it."

"You aren't in it now," I point out.

"You won't be either in a few minutes," he promises, turning us toward the entryway and wrapping his arm around my
waist, under the jacket. "Finally, I'm going to have you to myself."

"Which wouldn't be happening had I driven the Bentley
and wrecked it," I say as the double glass doors part for us and
we enter a fancy lobby with a long oak registration desk to our
right, and chairs and tables speckled here and there to our left.

"You weren't going to wreck it," he assures me. "And you
had other reasons for declining and we both know it."

"I don't know what you're talking about," I say quickly, and it's the worst lie I've told. I know and I'm now certain he knows that I didn't want my lost dreams punishing me any more than they already have tonight.

"Besides," he says, giving me an escape, and directing us toward the elevators, "I wouldn't have let you wreck it."

"All that confidence and command won't stop me if I want to crash, fall, or spill something, I promise you." We turn a corner and stop at what appears to be a private bank of elevators. "There's a law of nature element to it."

He punches the call button. "I don't believe in the law of nature any more than I do the power of the universe."

"Never. Not at all?"

"No. To do so would infer I have no control over the outcome of a situation and if that's the case, why keep fighting? I want control. That means I have to believe I can take it."

"What about how you just happened to come downstairs tonight when I was at the desk? That's fate. Or the stars aligning, or whatever you want to call it."

He steps to me and shackles my hips, something he does often, and I could easily get used to it, but of course, I will never get the chance. "I chose to come after you," he states.

"But you wouldn't have had the opportunity if the timing hadn't been perfect."

"Semantics."

"That's not even close to the definition of 'semantics.'"

"It is if I say it is. That's how I win over juries. I believe what I'm saying and I make them believe it too."

"So you're not just good at your job, you're good in the courtroom."

"Being good means rarely going to court."

"And you do that how?"

"Know what makes everyone tick, which means knowing

more than your client and the people influencing their situation and life. Know the same about your opposing counsel."

The elevator doors open and he leads me into the empty car, keying in a code and punching the button for what I think is the top level. The next thing I know I'm in the corner, and he's crowding me, his hands back on my waist, and the air around us thick with sexual tension.

"Right now, I want to know you." *Right now.* Those are the two words that make his attention to details sexy, not dangerous. He leans in closer and inhales. "You're the one who smells good. Like vanilla and flowers."

"It's vanilla and lilac. A special scent I have made at—" I stop myself before I place myself back in Texas, not Los Angeles. "It's the only scent I wear."

"It's addictive," he declares, his cheek brushing mine, the newly forming shadow on his jaw rasping against my delicate skin and I have no idea how but my nipples pucker in response. "You're addictive," he amends. "I couldn't stop thinking about it all day."

Oh how easily he can make a girl feel special. "You know just what to say. No wonder you never make it to court."

He inches backward, his gaze pinning mine. "Don't do that, sweetheart."

The endearment does funny things to my stomach. "Do what?"

"Don't make what I say to you about something else or even about me." His hand slides under my hair, around my neck. "I have nothing on my mind *but you*, and you have no idea how nearly impossible that is tonight. Obviously I need to work harder to make that clear."

"No I—"

He drags my mouth to his, his lips gently brushing mine,

his tongue a tease against mine that promises so much more. "*You are all that matters tonight. Understand?*" The question plays on his tongue as an erotic command, as does his hand on my neck.

"Yes," I reply, quaking inside with the way he manages to possess me and arouse me when everything about my history says those things shouldn't make me respond. But it is him I respond to, the way he somehow makes right what was always wrong for me.

The elevator dings behind us and he links our fingers, an act that, more and more, feels intimate, leading me out of the car, and it hits me then that he holds on to me like he is afraid of losing me, like I matter. And he looks at me like he really wants to see and know me, when earlier today, I was certain that I was invisible in every way.

"This way," Shane instructs, leading me left down the hallway, and the butterflies that erupt in my belly are almost too much to handle. Each step I take is laden; adrenaline pours through me like buckets of his triple-shot lattes. Too soon, we are at his door and he's turning a lock. He opens the door and he motions me forward, when he's all but led me everywhere else.

I stare at the entryway and I see it as the question mark intended, but more so, I instinctively understand he's offered me a choice. A moment of fairly profound introspection follows in which I think of all the controlling, powerful men who have come into my life by my choice, or otherwise, all with fairly devastating results, not one of whom gave me a choice. But Shane has, and not only that, he speaks of my pleasure, not his, which actually makes me want his pleasure, not mine. *He* is the contradiction and I like it. Suddenly the nerves I've been battling shift and change, still existing, still alive, but not fed by fear or self-doubt. I'm not here because I'm repeating the past. I'm here because Shane might have money, power, and good looks, but he is a rare person who is not defined by those things.

I let the walls fall away between us, letting him see the

decision in my eyes, answering his silent question, even before I say, "Yes. The answer to me wanting to be here, is an absolute 'yes.'" And with that declaration, I know that at least for now, I am choosing to let tonight exist without my secret, without the fears and danger it creates, and I enter a magnificent apartment with a towering flat ceiling, and striking dark wood floors streaked with a paler bamboo color.

I stop several feet inside, my gaze reaching beyond the open living room with tan leather furnishings to the floor-to-ceiling windows wrapping the entire apartment, a dark city spotted with lights beyond. The door shuts behind me and I feel Shane's approach, his energy a potent force wafting over me, but I can't seem to make myself turn and face him. His hands come down on my shoulders.

"I'll take this," he says, dragging the jacket from my shoulders, leaving me feeling oddly naked; my hand grips my purse I'd all but forgotten was trapped beneath. Once again, adrenaline rushes through me, fuel for my nerves that I can't escape, and I whirl around to find Shane hanging the jacket on a coatrack. My gaze falls on his hands, which will soon be touching my naked body, and it hits me that this man makes me feel naked in ways beyond the idea of taking my clothes off.

It's a disarming thought, and needing to catch my breath, I face forward, and start walking. I pass a kitchen that is stainless steel and more bamboo, continuing on through the living area, and I drop my purse on a leather chair, on my way to stand at the window. I grip the railing splitting the glass, staring out at a strange city I barely know as my own, the sky's inky canvas waiting to be painted with what I make of this new life, starting with this night. Shane appears to my right. I turn to find him standing at a bamboo minibar, the air thick with our awareness of one another.

"Drink?" he asks, lifting the topper to a crystal decanter.

"Most definitely, yes," I say, walking to stand beside the minibar, close to him. "Please."

At my eagerness, he gives me an assessing look, too damn smart not to know that I'm a ball of anxiety and not because of my secret. Because he's amazing and I want this and him in a way I am not sure I've ever wanted anyone before him. He pours a golden brown liquid into one glass only and replaces the stopper, clearly having no intention of filling another. "It's cognac," he says, picking up the glass and closing the two steps between us. "Expensive, strong, and smooth."

I take the glass and start drinking, warm spices exploding in my mouth. Three swallows in, he grabs it and stops me. "Easy, sweetheart. I said I want you to remember me."

"I want to remember you, Shane."

"But it's not me you're trying to forget."

"Something like that."

He downs the rest of the cognac, setting the glass on the table, and before I know his intentions, his hand is under my hair again, cupping the back of my neck, and he's aligned our bodies, his powerful legs pressed to mine. "What are you running from, Emily?"

I'm taken less off guard by the question that forces me back to my secret, than I am by my desire to tell him what I *can't*. "Everything or nothing," I say. "And I chose to tell you nothing."

"So you don't deny you're running?"

"Aren't we all?"

"I'm not or I wouldn't be in Denver."

"Ironically," I say, daring to tell a piece of the truth because *it is* only one night, "the opposite is true of me."

"I already knew that."

"Of course you did. You see too much."

His fingers flex at my neck, and he lowers his head, his lips a breath from mine. "I haven't even begun to see enough of you," he declares, and then his mouth is on mine, his tongue a soft caress, a tease that promises that even if I will give him nothing, he will give me everything.

I am breathless when his mouth leaves mine, my tongue flicking over my lips. "You taste like cognac."

"I'm going to taste like you," he says, and after hours of wanting this man, my sex clenches with this certainty that very soon he will make good on that promise. "Come," he orders, once again leading where he wants me to follow. This time it's the door opposite the minibar that I hadn't noticed before now. He opens it and motions me forward into a dark outdoor abyss that's a bit spooky. I step outside, and not only is Shane quickly by my side, motion detectors trigger lights, and we are instantly cast in a warm, intimate glow.

I glance around a balcony hugged by tall concrete privacy walls that successfully block the wind and cold, finding a couch and chair, and dangling teardrop lanterns that might actually be heaters. "This is spectacular," I murmur.

"The view is the best part of the apartment," he says, twining my fingers with his, and damn it, there is a hot spot in my chest that isn't about sex, but about how he makes me feel *with him*. Together, we walk toward the steel railing that sits atop a glass half wall, allowing it to feel as if we are almost standing in the middle of the sky.

I grab hold of the railing, staring out at the city, while he does the same beside me. "How high are we?"

"Fifteen floors."

"Low enough that we can see every street and building."

"But high enough to be on top of our new home," he murmurs. "It even looks worth staying from here."

I glance over at him to find he is already looking at me. "You've been back here a year," I remind him. "And you're from here."

"I didn't decide to stay until today."

"Why today?"

"It should have been sooner."

It's not a real answer, and he doesn't give me time to decide if I want to press for more. He steps behind me, his hips framing my backside, his hands at my sides. "And thanks to you," he murmurs, his lips near my ear, "I'm not thinking about what I left behind. I'm thinking about what I have right here."

The words infer more than a night, or maybe they don't, but it doesn't matter right now. He is caressing up and down my sides, his fingers grazing my breasts, and I can no longer think. My nipples are tight, aching nubs, and my sex is clenched tight. I bite my lip and tighten my grip on the railing, sucking in air as his exploration moves to my hips and then my backside. And suddenly, or not so suddenly, I want to touch him and see him. I try to turn, but he is quick to step to my side, holding me steady. "Stay facing forward," he orders, his fingers splaying on my belly where they've settled, that other hand, still branding my backside, gliding upward until his fingers find the zipper to my skirt, deftly dragging it down.

"Shane," I say, not sure why, and when I turn my head to look at him, he kisses me, a sultry, sexy slide of tongue against tongue that leaves me breathless, and wanting more.

"I like it when you say my name like it's a pleasure."

He steps behind me again, a light breeze lifting my hair and reminding me we're outside. I think I should care, but he caresses my skirt over my hips, and I can't find a reason why anymore. Material pools at my feet, and he lifts me, kicking it aside, and leaving me in nothing but a thong, thigh-highs, and heels from the waist down. He sets me back down, his hands cupping my now naked backside, his fingers intimately exploring the crevice between my cheeks, promising much more to follow.

He moves back to my side, one hand squeezing my cheek while the other cups my sex. My lashes lower and I pant, only to gasp as he grips the lace and yanks. I am shocked, and somehow much more vulnerable without that tiny stitch of lace. "Shane, damn it, we're outside." I try to turn again, not sure why this moment sets me off.

He holds me, his hands bracing me front and back. "Easy, sweetheart." His teeth scrape my shoulder, my eyes squeezing shut with the tightening of my nipples beneath the silk of my bra. "No one can see us and we're on top of our city, the day we both reluctantly decided to call it home."

"Home?" I rasp out, that word only one of the nerves he's hit. And I say it. I don't know why but I do. "I hate that word and I'm not like you. I had no choice."

He turns me, pressing me against the railing, his big body in front of mine, his legs pinning my legs. "Why am I different? Because I have family? Because you don't?"

"I do. I have an asshole brother just like you."

"Then you know that having family that doesn't give a shit about you *is* being alone."

Damn it, my eyes prickle, and I look skyward. "Yes," I whisper, turning my head, and wishing I'd kept my mouth shut.

He cups my face, forcing me to look at him, his thumb wiping away a stupid tear that makes me weak. "I don't cry," I say. "This is your fault. I don't know how you made me feel this. I don't even know what 'this' is and I don't know you. We're strangers."

"Not anymore we aren't."

"*Yes.* We are."

"You always have a choice," he says, sideswiping me with the change of topic. I am shaking from yet more stupid adrenaline and whatever "this" is that I still don't understand.

"No," I all but hiss. "I don't have a choice."

"Why don't you?"

"Everything or nothing, Shane. I said nothing. Stop trying to get into my head when I want out for just one night."

His eyes glint, a mix of hard steel and more of that blue fire. "You want to forget everything else?"

"That was the whole point in *this*."

He reaches down and grabs the top of my shirt and before I have any clue what he intends, he yanks, and the buttons fly here and there. I gasp, my hands flattening on his shoulders. "What are you doing?"

"Making you forget." He reaches around me and unhooks my bra, dragging it from my shoulders, and tossing it aside. I am left all but naked, when he is not. This realization shakes me. *He* shakes me and exposes pieces of me I don't want exposed. I try to hug myself but he gently catches my wrists.

"Emily," he says softly, and again he's made it sin and seduction.

"Shane," I whisper, and somehow the rest of the world fades, and he's grounded me in the moment. All of my old demons fade into the darkness of my past.

He seems to know when it happens. Maybe it shows in my face. Maybe he feels it in my energy, but then, and only then, does his gaze lower, raking over my breasts, a touch that isn't a touch. My body reacts, nipples tightening, breasts heavy, and the dampness that was on my panties is now slick on my thighs.

"You're beautiful," he murmurs, more gravel to his tone, and when he looks at me, I see the gray steel of demand and dominance, but there is also enough blue fire to burn me inside out. "And so damn sweet," he adds. "It's sexy as hell."

"Sweet is not what I want to be," I say, translating it as being called the pushover that got me into this mess I'm in. "It's not what I am."

He leans in close and inhales deeply. "You smell sweet." He

cups my face, and he caresses his lips over mine, once. Twice. His
tongue flickers past my teeth, a quick tease that has me wanting
more before he adds, "You taste sweet." He presses my hands to
the railing behind me, holding them there, his cheek settling
against mine. "I want you, Emily. And I'm going to have you.
On my lips. On my tongue." He nips my earlobe, sending a shiver
down my spine as he adds, "On my cock, riding me and thinking of nothing else but me."

His words, his promises, ripple through me like a whisper,
my fingers curling under his touch, around the bar. I am wet. I am
aching in every place he is not and I want him to be, and I reach
for him, only to have him catch my hands and hold them over
the railing.

"Don't move your hands from that railing unless I tell you
to or I will stop whatever I'm doing no matter how good it feels.
Understand?"

"Yes," I whisper, and just like that, I've given him what I
swore I'd never give a man again: control. But it's unexplainable
when I have been conditioned to believe my control is what protects me, and my lack of control is responsible for every one of
the many mistakes in my life. It's not just what he wants. It's what
I want too.

There are three sides to every story. Mine, yours, and the truth.

—*Joe Massino*

CHAPTER SIX

SHANE

Emily's agreement is all about one thing. *Trust.* Something I don't give or take lightly. Nor am I a stranger to the need to escape, and I'm not sure Emily is either. I just don't think she's as good at it as I am. And normally for me, that escape is fucking hard and fast, and getting it out of my system. But nothing about this night, or Emily, has hit the spots I know as familiar. They are simply the spots I need.

Still holding her hands on the railing, I spread my arms until they align with the railing, forcing her grip farther, my body draped over her, intentionally allowing the heavy starch of my shirt to tease her nipples. I linger there, building the anticipation intended to force her to think of this, and me, and nothing else. Seconds tick by, my blood pumping, my body cradling hers, the thick pulse of my erection aligned with her hips, the sweet scent of her drowning my senses in all the right ways. When I am certain she has waited long enough, I nip her shoulder. She yelps, and I lick the offended area, my lips curving against her skin at the moan that follows. She leans her head forward, the only part of her I don't have pinned, resting it on my shoulder. A breeze lifts around us, slightly chilled.

She shivers and I press my cheek to hers. "Don't worry. I plan to heat every chilled spot on your body." I seal that promise by dragging my lips over her neck, to her jaw, then settling a breath from her mouth, promising a kiss I don't deliver. I want to taste her, but I don't. I linger there, teasing her and me, waiting for the reach of her lips and I pull back, my hands flexing over hers.

"Don't let go," I warn, dragging my palms up her arms to settle on her shoulders, and when I look at her I know she doesn't mean for me to see the fear in her eyes or the sweetness that she rejects because she thinks it makes her weak. "Close your eyes," I order, forcing her to let go of her control and give in to me.

"What?" she asks, a hint of panic in her voice and expression that tells me I've made her feel exposed and vulnerable, an extreme reaction considering all she has to do is open her eyes if she so pleases. It only drives home how on edge she is, and how much she needs a safe place to let go of her control.

"You want me to fuck you?"

"What? Shane—"

"Do you want me to fuck you?"

"Yes."

"Then close your eyes, Emily," I repeat, pushing the words with a harder command this time.

She inhales sharply and lowers her lashes. "Are you happy now?" she challenges.

My lips quirk with her feisty remark, further convincing me that she's a fighter that won't let fear win. "Not yet," I assure her. "But we both will be soon."

"How soon?" she asks, more of that breathless sexiness in her voice. I feel it in my groin.

"When we're both ready."

"I'm ready."

Now I'm smiling, and once again, I wonder how that is even possible this night. I lightly stroke my mouth over hers, a tease that is barely there. "You're ready," I murmur, letting my breath fan over her lips, "when I say you're ready."

I step away from her and her eyes pop open, but her hands remain on the railing. "What if I just grab you and kiss you and—"

"You know the answer."

"You'll stop what you aren't even doing yet."

"And I won't either, if you don't shut your eyes again."

The look she fixes me with is fierce, as are her words. "I hate you right now," she declares, and she shuts her eyes.

"Angry sex," I approve. "Sounds good to me." I loosen my tie and walk to a table, folding it and setting it on top, reaching for the top button on my shirt, but a master at forcing my own control, I decide not to undress.

Instead, I grab a chair and carry it with me, setting it in front of her. Close. Really damn close the way I want her body to mine, but I don't touch her. I want her to feel me looking at her, wanting her, planning every place I intend to lick and touch. Her breasts, with her sexy, rose-colored nipples puckered into tight balls. Her flat trembling belly. Her naked sex that will know my tongue sooner than later and then finally, her lovely, heart-shaped face, where her teeth worry her bottom lip. And what I see in her is exactly what I'm after. Nervous excitement. *Arousal.*

"Shane," she whispers, telling me I've taken her to the edge, where I want her.

"Open your eyes," I order, and the moment she blinks and finds me sitting in front of her, I cup her backside and lift her into my lap, straddling me, the angle forcing her weight onto the railing.

"Shane," she hisses, panic in her voice. "Damn it. What if the glass breaks?"

It's the reaction I'd expected, and it ensures she is one hundred percent here with me. "Easy, sweetheart," I murmur, my hand flattening on her belly. "It's reinforced and there's horizontal steel bands supporting it." I look her in the eyes, letting her see the certainty I instill in my voice. "But I have you and I won't let you go."

"You're sure."

"One hundred percent." I soften my voice. "*Relax.*"

She inhales and then exhales, and with that breath, I feel the tension in her body ease. I lean over her and press my mouth to the spot between her breasts, cupping one of them, and I have no doubt my stare smolders as I pin her with it. "Trust me."

Now she shuts her eyes of her own accord, as if that word is not one she can process as a possibility. She confirms much of what I've pieced together about her life. Someone hurt her. Someone made her vow not to trust. Holy fuck, I get it. Too well and I understand fully that my path to trust with this woman is earned. What I don't understand is why it matters so much to me. I could be fucking her now. I could have fucked her five times over.

I finger her nipple, softly at first, and then rougher, tugging and teasing. Soft sounds of pleasure slide from her parted lips, her body arching toward my touch. She is all but panting, telling me she is as on edge as I am. My mouth finds that spot between her breasts again, trailing over the curve of her breast, toward her nipple. Her head tilts back into the light wind, with no regard for her weight on the wall any longer. Holding her between the shoulders with one hand, the other anchoring her hip, I lower my head to lick one nipple, and then the next, sucking in the same order.

"Shane," she pleads again, and damn if I don't like how my

name sounds on this woman's lips. What I want now is her quaking uncontrollably.

Caressing down her hips, my hands glide over her belly, to the V of her body, my index finger flicking her clit. More of those sexy sounds slip from her throat and I move lower, exploring the slick, wet seam of her body until she is squirming. Then, and only then, do I slip two fingers inside her and maneuver the chair and our bodies to bring my mouth to her belly, and lick a path toward my fingers.

My mouth lingers where she and I both want it to be, one second, two—

"Shane, damn it," Emily breathes out.

My lips curve and I lick her clit and then suck deeply, losing myself in the sweet, salty taste of her, licking here and there, and everywhere, my fingers pumping against the rocking of her hips. Too soon, she stiffens, her body tightening around my fingers, trembling a moment later. I ease the licks into soft caresses, my fingers to gentle strokes, until she collapses, the tension in her body turning to soft, limp satisfaction.

That is until reality has her eyes going wide. "The glass. I'll fall."

I answer by flattening my hand at her back and lifting her from the wall to sit fully on top of me, my palm moving to the back of her head to drag her mouth to mine. "Now I taste like you," I proclaim, my lips slanting over hers, my tongue stroking deep, letting her taste my hunger mixed with that sweet, salty mix of her arousal.

Her hands come down on my shoulders, and I know the moment she realizes she can touch me now, her fingers flexing, her tongue stroking more fully against mine. She leans forward, and one of her hands finds my hair, gripping it, not teasing it. "You have to get undressed," she announces, and suddenly she leans back, grabs the top of my shirt above my buttons, and yanks, to zero result.

She pales, and looks appalled, blood rushing to her otherwise pale cheeks. "In my mind that went much differently."

I stare at this woman who truly defies everything I expect from a woman, a smile playing on my lips. "Not as you planned?"

"My secret's out. I'm not exactly what anyone would call a seductress."

"I like you just the way you are," I say, the rage of my body wiping away my smile. She turns somber.

"You don't even know me."

"But I'm about to," I assure her, dragging her hands to my neck. "Hold on." I stand, cupping her backside, and start for the door, ready to be inside this woman. Her legs wrap my waist, exactly where I want them and plan to keep them, and as much as I want her in my bed, I just want her, and settle for the living room. Once there, I bypass the cold leather couch, and set her gorgeous bare backside on top of an oversized ottoman with soft faux fur on top. She grabs the edges and kicks off her shoes.

"I'll do it this time," I say, reaching for the buttons on my shirt, and working them free. She reaches forward to help me and I take one look at her mouth, and cup her head and kiss her. A deep, drugging kiss that I end far too quickly, and in a rare moment where impatience wins, I tug my shirt over my head and toss it on the coffee table. And her hands are already on me, one flat on my chest, the other on my arm.

It's then that I realize she's tracing the tattoo on my right arm, and I have no idea why I don't just kiss her again and get on with fucking her. Instead, I kneel there, and I let her trace the lion with an eagle perched on its head, the bird's wings spread, and pieces of a day I don't want to remember coming back to me.

She glances up at me, her hand closing over my arm, her attention on me, not now. "What does it mean?"

My mood darkens instantly, and I don't even consider dismissing the question. "The eagle is knowledge, strength, and leadership. The lion is cunning and vicious. He'll rip your throat out if you give him the chance." Her lips part in shock, exactly my intention, and I twine my fingers in her hair, dragging her mouth to mine. "That's why you never turn your back on the lion."

"And your father's the lion."

My fingers tighten in her hair at the assertion that stuns me, and seems to infer she knows more about me than she should. *She* is the one who sees too much and *she* has unleashed my raging emotions. I turn her away from me to face the couch, my body framing hers, my hands cupping her breasts. "I'm the man who's wanted to fuck you for hours and it's time for me to be inside you." I wonder what the hell has taken me so long in the first place. "Don't move."

She covers my hand over her breast. "Shane—"

"Talk later. Fuck now." I lift off her, my hands on her waist, and as on edge as I am now, I do not want to scare her, or stir her demons because mine have decided to come out and play. I lean into her again, softly saying, "Right now—"

"I know," she says. "So what are you waiting for?"

What am I waiting for? Again, she surprises me, but I'm not going to analyze her, or my reaction to her at this very moment. Not when I could be inside her, feeling her instead. "Don't move."

"Don't take too long," she counters, and that remark manages to bring me down enough to play her game. I press my hand to her lower back and gently, but not too gently, smack her backside.

She sucks in air, arching her back, that pretty backside lifting, my hand caressing. I bend down and kiss her spine. "I'm not sure what I think about that," she says, glancing over her shoulder.

"Don't think and I won't either."

I release her, and don't even consider standing to undress. In all of thirty seconds my pants and underwear are down and I've rolled the single condom in my wallet over my hard-as-fuck cock, and I grab her hips, slipping between her thighs. At that moment my phone rings from somewhere on the ground, and I grimace, not about to let her go to fling the damn thing across the room the way I'd like to right now.

I stroke my cock along the seam of her body, preparing her, and then, I'm done waiting. I press into her, driving deep, and reaching around her to cup her breast again, my already ridiculously hard cock now officially harder. "I'm not sure you could feel any better than you do right now," I say, pulling back, the sound of her erratic breathing only making me hotter. I drive into her and she gasps, spurring me to do it again. And again. I need more of her. I need to be deeper, to drive harder. I just need more, and still cupping her breast, I raise upright, and take her with me. She grabs my hands and holds on tight, and she can't move like this. I know that, but she doesn't have to do anything but hang on.

I free one of my hands to press it between her legs and stroke her, thrusting as I do. She leans back into me, trying to arch into my touch. I lean back to drive at another angle.

"Oh," she cries out. "Shane I—"

She stiffens the way she had on the balcony and this time when she spasms, it's around my shaft, not my fingers, and holy hell, it rocks me. *She* rocks me, and I pull her against me, that final hard collision of our bodies sending me over the edge with her. I shake, and she trembles, and everything is white space for I don't know how long. I come back to the present, and I don't want to let go of her. She isn't just some new fuck buddy. She's a drug I could easily call an addiction when I don't have addictions, and at a time I'd be nothing but poison to her. That's a problem for her and me.

EMILY

Shane is holding me from behind, still buried inside me, the aftermath of my orgasm leaving me with goose bumps all over my skin and a strange warm spot in my chest. Not ready for this night, or even this moment and the next, to end, I don't want to move, but Shane leans us forward, and I catch myself on the ottoman with my hands. He pulls out of me and I am instantly awash in a cluster of emotions that have me spinning around only to find his hands on the cushion on either side of me, his strong arms caging me.

And he is stone, his expression is unreadable, his jaw set hard, proof that the nerve I hit over that tattoo is still raw and present. "There is nothing about you," he says, "or this night, that is uncomplicated or what I expected."

"I don't know what that means," I whisper. "What are you saying?"

"Think about it. You'll figure it out." He runs a hand through his dark hair, leaving it a sexy, tousled mess. "I'll be right back." And just like that he's on his feet, pulling his pants that he never even took off, up. I've been naked on top of the damn city, and he *never even undressed.* He turns away and I watch as he crosses toward the fireplace and then disappears down a hallway.

I force out a breath that seems to be lodged in my throat. *Think about it? You'll figure it out?* Okay. Well. I'm all over the place here because the way I see it one of two completely opposite things just happened. Either I was just given a nudge and space to leave or he no longer plans to make this one night. I don't have time to analyze his meaning or why I'm in a million tight knots right now. My feelings and his intentions, don't—no, *can't*—matter. This is a reality check for me. The bottom line is that I should never have been here. *Thinking done.* I hop to my feet, snatch up my shoes, and run for the balcony door for my clothes, in hopes of departing before Shane returns. Exiting to the now dark balcony again, the lights flicker on, and I drop my shoes by the door to free my hands.

Scanning, I locate my skirt pooled on the ground by the railing, and rush forward. Grabbing it, I step into it, and tug it into place, leaving the zipper open while I hunt for my bra. Instead I locate my blouse under the chair Shane had been sitting in. Shoving aside memories of me spread wide with his mouth in intimate places, I snap it up. One look at the thin material and absent buttons and I know I need that bra. At least if I have it on, I can hug my shirt shut, and be covered if I have a mishap. On the hunt, I rotate and gasp as I bump into Shane.

"What are you doing?" he demands softly, his hand shackling my wrist by my side, while I pull my blouse in front of my naked breasts.

"I need to go," I say, thinking maybe he didn't want me to leave. And I swear my arm is tingling from his touch. "We both have . . . stuff . . . tomorrow. Early. I need to get up early."

"I have an alarm," he counters.

"You said we're complicated, Shane."

"Whatever we are, or are not, neither one of us wants you to leave. I know I don't want you to leave."

He doesn't want me to leave. I don't know what to say or do.

"I called Susie and she's sending over ravioli," he adds.

I blink. "What? You did? It's late."

"Ten o'clock. They close at eleven." He indicates a black T-shirt in his hand I haven't noticed until now. "I brought this for you." He steps to me and tugs the shirt over my head. Responding automatically, I drop my blouse, shoving my arms through the holes, and let the shirt fall to my knees.

Shane gives me a quick inspection, his eyes lighting with approval. "Did I mention I like you in my clothes? And out of yours." I don't have time to respond before he drags me to him, lifts the shirt, and slips his hands inside the band of my skirt. "I took this off of you for a reason," he says, sliding it off me, the material pooling at my feet. He grips my waist and lifts me, kicking it aside. "How about some wine?"

I stare up at him, and something unnamable expands between us, and that something is what he'd meant when he said *think about it*. It's also exactly why I was going to leave and why I can't. "Will you let me drink it this time?"

"Cognac isn't wine and I didn't want you to pass out on me. But now, as long as it's in my bed, feel free." He laces his fingers with mine, and it's somehow the most intimate thing we've shared, as is the way we just stand there for several seconds before he says, "Let's get that wine."

"Let me bring in my clothes," I say, tugging my hand free, and grabbing my skirt and blouse. Shane picks up my shoes and I do another sweep of the area. "I can't find my bra anywhere."

"You don't need it," he promises, ushering me to the door before I can argue that I will tomorrow. Or later when I really leave but I let it go, entering the apartment first, and rotating to face him only to have him take my clothes from me. "I'll put those in the bedroom." He motions to the minibar. "There's wine in the cabinet. Take your pick."

He's already walking and I'm staring after him. The man just kidnapped my clothes, which is kidnapping me. I wait for the panic to set in, but it doesn't come. Shane doesn't know the truth about me and there is no reason he ever will.

It's better to live one day as a lion than a hundred years as a lamb.

—*John Gotti*

CHAPTER SEVEN

EMILY

Now with the excuse of being Shane's captive, I turn toward the minibar, fully intending to enjoy the wine and the man, when Shane's phone starts ringing from the living room again, reminding me about my phone. I take a step toward my purse, and think better. If I didn't get the call I'm expecting I'll be upset. If I did, I'll be freaked out that I missed it, and it's not like I can have yet another heated phone debate in front of Shane. I turn back to the minibar, but Shane's phone has not only stopped ringing, it's started again. Concerned about the late hour and a possible emergency, I walk to the living room and grab it, but I'm not sure what to do from here. Should I call out to him? Should I hunt him down?

Sighing, I just take it with me in hunt of the wine, setting it next to the cognac. It starts ringing again and my gaze catches on the name "Seth" by accident. Regretting ever going after his phone, I quickly squat and open the cabinet, counting the rings until they go silent. Then and only then do I stare at a dozen bottles of wine, shifting one here and there to stare at labels, concerned I'll pick the most expensive bottle on the shelf. I have a fleeting memory of how romantic I'd thought my parents trying a new bottle of wine every Friday night had been. She never had a glass again after he died.

"Having trouble?"

I jump at the sound of Shane's voice to look up and find him towering over me. "You surprised me," I say, popping to my feet to discover he's changed into a snug white T-shirt and a pair of navy sweats and still manages to look *GQ*.

"You must have been really concentrating on the wine."

"I was thinking of——" His phone begins to ring where it sits on top of the minibar, and his brows furrow in confusion.

"I grabbed it for you," I explain quickly. "It keeps ringing and I was going to bring it to you but I felt weird about it. Then I felt weird about calling out to you or ever touching your phone." It stops ringing again. "Then I felt even weirder when I saw the caller ID like I was snooping. I should have just left it where it was. I'm sorry."

He studies me, his expression unreadable, several beats passing in which I wonder what he's thinking, before he says, "You're fine. Did you pick a bottle?"

"I don't know much about wine and I was worried I'd pick an outrageously expensive bottle." I go back to what seems important. "Shouldn't you deal with those phone calls? It's late. What if something's wrong?"

"For the first time in a year, I'm not taking calls."

"Don't you want to know who it is?"

"I know who it is. You want a sweet wine, I assume?"

"I want a cheap wine."

"I don't have any cheap wine."

"Then I don't want any."

He squats down, grabs a bottle, and stands again. "This one it is." His phone starts to ring and he ignores it, motioning toward the kitchen. "Let's sit at the bar," he says, already moving that direction.

"I don't drink much," I call after him, his shoulders especially impressive under the stretch of the cotton tee, a hint of the dreaded tattoo peeking from one shoulder. "I'll waste the bottle."

He rounds the bar and appears on the other side in the kitchen, reaching above him to a cabinet. I grab his phone, and join him, claiming a high-backed leather barstool at the same moment he sets two crystal glasses on the counter. I, in turn, set his phone in between them.

He ignores it and fills both glasses. "Try it and make sure you like it."

I fight the urge to push him to take the call. He knows who it is. He knows it's not an emergency. Unless he doesn't. "It's Seth," I say.

He picks up the phone and hits the button on the side that I can only assume is the volume, then rests his hands on the other side of the bar. "Try the wine, sweetheart."

"I was just worried—"

"I know."

Okay. He knows who it is so all is well, only his energy says differently but I don't get the chance to press him. The doorbell rings. "That will be the food," he says. "And once again, I'll be right back." He disappears on the other side of the bar and I stare at the phone. Oh God. Is Seth his father? Some people call their parents by their names. It's odd, but so is his father having sex in the kitchen with his friend's mother.

Almost too quickly it seems Shane reappears but this time on my side of the bar. "Your phone's ringing," he says, surprising me by offering me my purse and setting the bag of food on his stool.

My gut knots and I accept it, forcing myself not to react.

"Well since no one offering me a job would be calling now," I say, hanging it on the back of my stool, "I'm not taking calls either." I inhale the rich scent of spices. "And I swear that ravioli smells better this time than last."

"You can take the call, Emily. It's really okay."

"I don't want to take the call." And I don't want to invite questions. I scoot off my seat. "I'll get silverware if you tell me where it is." I dart around him before he can stop me.

"By the refrigerator," he calls out. "And we don't need plates."

I pull open the drawer, and stare at the expensive silverware, glad for the short retreat that's giving me time to shove aside the worry threatening to take control of me. It can't have control. I can't survive that way. I grab two forks and shut the drawer again, turning to face Shane. "Do you want water?"

"I'll take a bottle."

Turning to the fridge, I open it and note he has hardly any food. Okay, no food. Just protein shakes and water. "Do you eat at home ever?" I call out, grabbing him a bottle, and heading back around the bar to find our take-out containers still sealed, and in front of our places, the bag set aside.

"I work a lot and order room service."

I claim my seat and set the water next to him. "I guess that explains why you chose to live in a hotel."

"This place is my father's," he says. "We have a family business I chose not to join, but they needed my legal expertise short term so it was convenient."

"And now they convinced you to stay long term."

"I convinced myself to stay, and I told a realtor to find me a place today."

"Wait," I say, forcing myself to bite back my questions that will lead to *his* questions. "Please tell me this isn't where he brought his woman."

He freezes. "Holy fuck, that's not what I want in my head when sleeping in my bed, but thank you for that motivation to get the hell out of this place." He reaches for my wineglass. "And a good reason to drink. Try it. If you don't like it I'll grab another bottle before we start eating."

I accept the glass and our hands collide, my eyes lifting to his, the connection I feel stunning me with its force. "Don't pretend to like it if you don't," he warns.

"I wouldn't do that, but we aren't opening another bottle no matter what." I tilt the glass up and sip, a really yummy sweet explosion of flavors finding my tongue. "It's quite possibly the best glass of wine I've ever had and please tell me it doesn't cost as much as your suit."

"You know how much my suit costs, but not the wine."

It's an observation meant to invite information, which I don't give. "You learn wine by being around someone who actually knows wine. Or taking a personal interest beyond an occasional drink."

"And you know how much a custom suit costs by being around money."

"Or arrogant attorneys that wouldn't dare shop on the bargain racks."

My quick rebuttal earns me the tiniest hint of a curve to his lips. "I think you just called me arrogant."

"Of course you're arrogant, Shane." I pick up the glass. "But you manage it with a fair amount of grace."

Now he laughs, disbelief lacing the deep, sexy sound. "Arrogance can be handled with grace. I had no idea."

I take a sip. "I didn't think so until I met you. But maybe you're on your best behavior."

His lips tighten, his mood darkening. "Yes. Well. Therein lies the problem."

He's not talking about me, and he doesn't offer more detail, instead reaching over and removing the lid from my container, like he needs to take care of me, and it's kind of an amazing feeling. Knowing I said the wrong thing isn't.

He shifts to his container and lifts the lid. "Let's see how you like it."

We both pick up our forks and somehow we look at each other at the same moment. "I'm good at hitting the wrong nerves, aren't I?"

"I could say the same to you."

He noticed but that doesn't surprise me. "Then why are we sitting here together?"

"Because we want to be."

Because we want to be. It's such a simple answer when nothing else in my life, and I suspect his life, is simple. "And we're hungry," he adds, using his fork to indicate my plate. "Try it."

I turn my attention to my plate and take a bite, and I can't help it. I moan. "Holy wow. This is my new addiction. It's way too close to my apartment for my waistline. I'll be running double in the morning."

"You run?" he asks.

"I do. It's kind of my sanity. But I guess in the winter here I'll have to try a gym."

"I'm a runner too and I can attest to that fact. In the winter, you'll want a gym. There's a great one attached to the Ritz a few blocks away."

"I'll check it out." We both take a few bites, the short silences actually remarkably comfortable, though I can almost feel him thinking. And I'm thinking about what he'd said about being on his best behavior as he opens his water, slugs a drink, and offers it to me.

I glance at the bottle, and then at the water on his bottom lip, deciding that if I had more courage, I'd kiss it away. But I don't, and my gaze inches upward to his, the air seems to charge around us, and I forget to breathe. Oh yes. There is something far more intimate about us, and this moment in time, than sex, and I can't seem to convince myself that it's bad. I reach for the bottle, tilting it to take a deep swallow, before offering it back to him. He leans my way, his thumb stroking away the remnants of water from my lip, his head lowering for a kiss that doesn't come.

His phone vibrates and he freezes, his lashes lowering, tension in his mouth inching toward mine. "Fuck," he murmurs. "I should have turned it off." He glances down at the phone. "Now my mother's calling me."

"Do you think she found out about the woman?"

"I hope like hell not." He grimaces at the caller ID. "And now Seth is calling again."

"Take the call, Shane. Get it off your mind because I know it is."

He gives me an agreeable nod, and punches the answer button. "Is this about my father or the security feed?"

I'm appalled to realize I can hear Seth reply. "I'm on my way home to go through the security footage."

"So this call is about my father," Shane assumes.

"He took the woman to the Four Seasons."

My jaw drops at this outrageous act by his father while Shane laughs without humor. "Of course he did. Who's the woman?"

"I'm working on it."

"Then why call me repeatedly rather than leave me a message?"

"I was about to come over there before your mother does."

"What?" Shane asks.

"She called me when she couldn't reach you, insisting that it's imperative she talk to you, and indicated she might go to your apartment."

Shane runs a hand over his face. "Why?"

Why is right. Why am I listening? I try to get up. Shane catches my arm, and gives me a look along with a shake of his head, while Seth answers. "She wouldn't tell me."

I mouth, "I can hear everything."

Shane nods his understanding but seems to dismiss any concern, turning his attention back to his call. "Of course my mother wouldn't tell you what she wants," he concludes to Seth. "That would be too simple. I'll deal with her."

"I'll have a report on the security feed by morning."

"And the woman," Shane amends. "We're paying enough people to get me an answer by morning."

Woman? Does he mean the one he saw his father with tonight? Surely not.

"Until she goes home," Seth replies, "I have no way of tracing her."

Damn. That sure sounds like he's talking about the woman his father is with and it's a slippery slope he's headed down.

"Try," Shane orders, ending the call to look at me. "I need to deal with my mother. It'll be fast."

"I could hear every word of both sides of your conversation," I quickly say, "not just your part. I should go to the balcony."

"I want you right here."

"No you don't, because I'll tell you that you shouldn't be looking into that woman, Shane. And yet I know it's none of my business."

"What it is, is more complicated than a simple affair."

"Like I said, I should go to the balcony."

"Stay," he says, and while he says it like one of his commands, which I've come to realize are simply second nature to him, I sense an undertone of a plea I don't believe he'd ever issue.

I give a choppy nod and resettle on the barstool. He wastes

no time punching a button on his phone and almost instantly says, "What's going on, Mother?"

"I heard you saw your father tonight," I hear her reply.

"I see him daily," he says, obviously treading cautiously.

"At the *restaurant*, Shane. Susie said you obviously were not pleased."

He's silent several beats, as if weighing his reply. "Did she tell you why?"

"I know your father's having an affair. It's you I'm worried about."

"You know he's having an affair?"

He sounds incredulous. Been there, done that, and I never came to terms with why my mother accepted my stepfather's affairs.

"Of course I know," his mother confirms. "It's fine."

Shane looks at the ceiling, seeming to rein in whatever emotion she's stirred, before saying, "We'll talk tomorrow." His tone is short and absolute.

"Son," she begins. "Your father—"

"I have company, Mother."

"Oh. Well. Good. You need to fuck some of your frustrations out. We'll talk tomorrow."

Okay. Talk about embarrassing, and from his mother of all people.

"Tomorrow," he bites out, ending the call, and for a moment he just sits there, his spine stiff, his gaze fixed forward. I wait, giving him space and time.

He scrubs his jaw, no doubt trying to shake off a mire of emotions I know pretty well, but I doubt he hopes to share with me, or anyone. "I'm sorry you heard that," he says, shoving his phone in his pocket, and standing to press his hands on the back of his stool.

"I'm thick-skinned," I say, rotating to face him, finding his stare fixed on me, his expression unreadable, but that is expected from a man who makes a living hiding his reactions to things.

There are a million things that come to my mind that I could say—like how people have coping mechanisms—but he'd said this was more than a simple affair and anything I say could negate me respecting the implications of that claim. And I don't have time to weigh the smartness of that decision as he steps to me, his hands coming down on the back of my chair, his arms caging me. "This thing between us is not about two kids, PTA meetings, and four dogs in our future."

"Four dogs. That's a lot. I do want *a* dog though."

"Emily."

"I don't need PTA meetings. This thing, as you call it, is a one-night stand, Shane."

"That's not happening."

"What's not happening?"

"This is not a one-night stand. Neither of us will be done with each other that fast, and we both know it."

"You can't decide what we are on your own."

"You're running, but not from me."

"Let me up." I shove on his unmoving arm to try to break free. "Damn it, Shane."

"Do you want this to be a one-night stand?"

"I'm not capable of more right now."

"We're keeping it simple. We're going upstairs to my bedroom to fuck."

"And tomorrow?"

"We'll fuck some more."

It's just sex and he's upset right now. Come tomorrow morning, he'll be over this. "Fine," I say. "Then why are we talking?"

His eyes glint and the next thing I know, he's lifted me off the stool, scooped me up, and is crossing the living room to carry me up a long set of wooden steps. Heading, I assume, to his

bedroom, a man on a mission, to fuck everything out of his system, and no matter what he just said, I'm pretty sure that includes me. There's no reason to worry he'll see too much, or
want too much. He is just reacting to his family drama, and no
one understands that more than me.

At the top of the stairs, we enter a room shrouded in shadows and he doesn't turn on the lights. He sits me on a bed, and
then he's gone, leaving me to eye the one thing I can make out
clearly in the room. A giant wall of more windows, the sky now
black, as if clouds have wiped out all light. The way Shane and
I both want to wipe away the darkness. *You're running,* he'd said,
and it hadn't been an accusation, but rather a statement of fact.

The sound of a condom package tearing has me twisting
around to find him standing at the edge of the nightstand,
naked—like the way he makes me feel inside. He comes back to
me then, joining me on the bed, and my shirt, his shirt, is gone
in a flash, his hands replacing it. His tongue and mouth are everywhere. And when he finally turns my back to his front, and he is
inside me again, his body wrapped around mine, our pleasure
colliding, our bodies collapsing in release, he holds on to me and
he doesn't let go. And he doesn't hurry away, nor do I try to
move. We just lay there, in the darkness, together, and therefore
we are not alone.

I blink awake from a now familiar nightmare, jerking to a
sitting position, my hand at my throat in the midst of panic and
terror. Forcing air into my lungs, I become aware that I am in a
bedroom and in bed alone, but it's not mine. It's Shane's bed, and
the autumn scent of him is everywhere around me, even on my
hair and skin. A chill runs down my spine, reminding me that
my nightmare is a product of the reality I'm forced to hide from,
when I just want to face it and make it go away. That, and I'm
naked. I grab the blanket, tugging it to my chin, the sound of

rain splattering on glass calling my attention to a wide expanse
of windows hugged by curtains to my left. The room is cozy, my
memories are not.

"Stupid nightmare," I murmur, glancing at the clock on the
nightstand, noting the time as six thirty, which must mean Shane
is already up and getting ready for work. I'm shaken by the idea
that I hadn't noticed he'd left the bed when I can't afford to be
that oblivious to my surroundings, but then last night comes
back to me, and good lord, I'd fallen asleep with him still inside
me. And now I'm here and he's not and it's the awkward morning after. Unless . . . he's not even here. That would certainly
wipe out the awkward part and I both hate and love that idea.
Whatever the case, Shane isn't here, and that means I need out
of this bed and into my clothes.

Scanning the room, I take in the details I couldn't see last
night: An oversized dresser made of heavy gray wood sits directly
in front of me with a flat-screen TV above it. A door I think leads
to a closet is to my right. And to my left are the giant window
and a chair where I am relieved to find my clothes. Of course,
there appears to be nothing in view to cover myself with so I'm
going to have to run across the room naked, most likely at the
exact moment Shane walks into the room. And the longer I sit
here, the more that becomes a possibility.

Decision made, I throw the blanket aside, climb out of bed,
and dash for the chair. I snatch my skirt, quickly stepping into
it, tugging the zipper as I step into my high heels. Frustratingly,
my bra is missing and then I give my blouse a woeful inspection
that tells me I'll be walking home with my breasts hanging out
if I don't steal one of Shane's shirts. The one lying on the chair
will work just fine, and I snatch it up to realize it's my size, and
reads FOUR SEASONS. Shane obviously hit the gift shop for me,
proving he might be giving me a silent good-bye, but he did so
with some gentlemanly class. And really, I'm glad to avoid the

face-to-face meeting that would only make me wish for what I can't have.

I tear off the tag and pull it over my head, more than ready to grab my purse, check the two phones I carry inside it for calls, and head home. One step toward the door, though, and I stop myself. There is no way around it. I have to pee so badly it is a physical ache. I rotate and head for a door I think is the bathroom. I pass through the doorway, I flip on the light, and I shut the door. I take a step and once again stop, my lips parting in stunned appreciation for the gorgeous, all-white bathroom, with an oversized oval tub framed by another giant window as the centerpiece.

Memories of a time when I lived like this stir in my mind, followed by a whirlwind of emotions I don't have time to endure in Shane's bathroom. Shoving them away, I hurry forward to do what I came in here to do. Once I'm done, I stop at the mirror and good lord, my hair is so puffed up it looks like squirrels played in it when I was sleeping. I hunt for a brush and find it in a drawer next to a razor, and waste no time taming the wild affair on my head. That's when I notice the new, unopened toothbrush sitting beside a tube of toothpaste. Shane left this for me and since I stupidly fell asleep, I have no gauge on what this means. Probably it's like the shirt—he's being a gentleman. And he'll probably have a car waiting for me, which I'm not going to take because that means the driver will have my address.

Whatever the case, I brush my teeth, toss the brush in the trash, and then face the door. Now, I'll leave. He's not here, so why am I nervous? I'm just going to grab my purse and head out the door. I reach for the knob. What if he is here? He's not. He's not here. I open the door and yelp as I find Shane standing in front me, already dressed to kill in a black suit, royal-blue tie, and starched white shirt.

"You're really good at scaring me," I accuse, balling my fist at my racing heart, elated that he's still here when I should be welcoming a quick departure.

"Not my intent. I was going to knock and make sure you found the T-shirt." His gaze lowers and lifts. "And I see you did." He drags me to him and gives me a fast, quick, but oh-so-drugging kiss, the taste of man and rich, strong coffee, exploding in my senses. "Minty fresh," he says softly. "Looks like you found the toothbrush too. Unless you used my toothbrush."

"No," I say, appalled. "I'd never do that. Has someone actually done that?"

"They never get the chance since I don't invite women to my apartment."

"What?" I ask, stunned yet again by this man, and by the fact that my hand has found its way to his chest, right where I want it.

"I never invite women to my apartment and damn sure don't curse the phone call that got me out of bed with them."

My heart is thundering, but so is his under my palm, and that crazy, addictive energy that charged the air around us last night is back. "What are we doing, Shane?"

"Figuring it out as we go."

"I'm not . . . I can't . . ."

"We'll figure it out."

"No. No, we can't. We said——"

"No PTA," he supplies. "Just a lot of fucking and whatever else we decide to let happen."

"Shane——"

The doorbell rings. "And that will be the coffee I ordered. I was afraid mine would put hair on your chest and I like you how you are." He kisses me fast and hard. "Meet me downstairs." And just like that, he's leaving and I'm staring after him, once again with my fingers on my mouth where his lips just were. I can't do this. Can I? Maybe just another night or two won't hurt. I can do that. I want to do it. I *am* doing it.

Charging forward before I change my mind, I exit the room, and hurry down what in the light of day is truly a stunning bamboo staircase attached to the wall. At the bottom level, Shane is nowhere to be found. I hurry to the bar to grab my purse and check my phone. The minute I reach the bar, I find him on the opposite side. "White mocha," he says, setting a Starbucks-style cup in front of me. "That's what they recommended downstairs."

I reach for the cup. "Thank you." This man is too charming for my own good. "It's my favorite." I take a sip. "And it's excellent."

His eyes light up. "Then I owe Tai an extra tip."

Really too charming. "He didn't mention a bra randomly falling on someone's head did he?"

He laughs. "No. He didn't, but that would be good for a laugh."

"That would be humiliating."

"They'd never know it was yours." He lifts a bag. "Bagels. They make them here."

"Don't you have to be at work?"

"Eventually."

One of my phones rings and I bend down to grab my purse and somehow it's unzipped and I end up pouring the contents everywhere. I squat and scramble to pick everything up, reaching for one phone, and then the other, but it's too late. Shane is on a knee in front of me, and he's got the second. He glances at it and at the one in my hand. "Two phones."

Unease ripples through me. "I bought a new one when I lost mine."

I can see his mind working, perhaps remembering me telling the guard the phone I'd lost was new. "Two new phones," he says, confirming that's exactly what he was thinking. "Talk to me, sweetheart. Let me help you."

A ball of emotions tightens in my chest. "We're sex, Shane. This isn't your problem any more than I should have commented about you looking into your father's date last night." I shove the phone, as well as my compact, back in my purse, holding out my hand. "Can I have that please?"

He stands with my phone and I follow him to my feet, slipping my purse over my head and across my body. We stare at each other, and those gray eyes study me, intensely gorgeous. I hate that I met him now, this way. "Shane—"

He steps to me, taking my hand and pressing the phone into it, holding on to it and me. "You're right. It's none of my business. Yet. But I plan to change that."

"I don't want you to change that."

"Yes. *You do.*"

He's wrong. Because I like him. Really like him and he'd most likely hate me if he knew the secret I'm hiding. "You don't understand—"

"Make me understand."

"It's complicated. We both agreed we aren't doing complicated."

"I'm good at complicated, sweetheart. Try me."

If only it were that simple. My phone starts to ring in our hands. "It could be about a job," I say, grasping at a chance to breathe and think.

"Of course. We'll talk when you're done."

Talk? I can't talk to him about anything remotely close to the truth. He releases my hands and his own phone starts ringing. I glance at mine to discover a local number and quickly answer only to miss the call that had to be about a job. I'm waiting for the message to beep when I hear Shane say, "You got to be fucking kidding me. There's a big tip for you keeping him in the lobby. I'll be right there." He ends the call, pocketing his phone. "Stay here. My father is trying to pay us a visit."

"Oh my God. Why would he do that?"

"Because he's my father." His hands come down on my arms. "I'm sorry about this. Let me get rid of him before we leave."

"I'll be here waiting," I say, wanting it to be the truth, but knowing it can't be.

He steps around me and the voice mail on my phone beeps. I stare at it, waiting for the sound of the door shutting. The minute it does, I punch the button and listen to the call, letting out a sigh of relief. At least one of my problems is solved. I squeeze my eyes shut, rejecting the idea that Shane is officially another problem, but I can't. I open my eyes again. I know his father showing up downstairs is my escape. I know I have to leave before he gets back, but I don't want to be gone. I dig the second phone out of my purse, and punch in the only number I ever call on this phone.

SHANE

Watching the elevator floors tick by, I am certain of two things. I'm not letting Emily get away and I'm done playing my father's games. The doors open, and I step into the hotel lobby to find my father leaning against the wall, his arms crossed in front of his black pin-striped suit, his red power tie in place and his white shirt starched, which can mean only one thing. He has a room in this hotel that he maintains, including a change of clothes. And damn it, I am as pissed at him as I am at that piece of shitty news; among other things, I still notice how thin he is, probably one eighty when he'd been two hundred pounds when I'd arrived last year.

I stop in front of him and he smells like perfume. "Good

morning, son," he says, not the least bit irritated that I wouldn't allow him upstairs to an apartment he owns. But then, why would he? He dictated my presence.

"Your message is loud and clear, Father."

"Do tell, son," he says, a slight rasp to his voice I've never noticed before now. "What exactly is my message?"

"You'll do what the hell you want and approval is the last thing you give a damn about."

"Is this where you threaten to go back to New York again?" he asks, not denying or confirming my statement.

I give him an assessing stare. "I backed you in a corner over Derek and the pharmaceutical branch and you didn't like it."

He pushes off the wall and stands toe-to-toe with me. "That was a gift and consider it the last one you'll get. Control your brother or go back to New York because somebody has to run this company when I'm gone." He starts to turn and stops. "You're wearing your weak spot like a badge of honor."

He starts walking and I follow his progress, watching as he rounds the corner and for a moment after he disappears, I stare after him, a tight ball forming in my chest that I try to reject, but it just keeps getting bigger. I turn and jab the elevator button, the doors opening instantly. Stepping into the empty car, I hit the code to return to my floor, and I'm quickly sealed inside, that ball now a hot spot expanding in my chest. *Son of a bitch.* That wasn't my father playing one of his head games. It was him, in his demented way, telling me the cancer is getting worse. Bringing that woman here was about pissing me off to avoid any pity I might throw his way.

Facing the wall, I press my fist against the wood, hanging my head, damn glad I have a few minutes alone to grapple with the razor blade of emotions cutting through me. I hate him and I love him. How is that even possible? The hate is justified, guilt-free in the past, but death, *fucking cancer,* changes everything.

I dig through my mind for a source of my love for him and I can't even find a memory to cling to. And yet, I'm still in knots, still wearing guilt over my hate like a weighted glove.

The elevator dings and I shove off the wall, stepping out into the hallway, a mix of emotions driving my long strides. Anger. More guilt. More fucking anger. I'm at my door and I barely remember the walk. The very idea of the woman inside, her smell, her taste, and the way she feels in my arms, calms a bit of the beast that is my emotions raging inside me. I enter my apartment—no, my father's apartment, a matter I need to remedy now, not later—discovering Emily absent from the bar where I expect her to be waiting. Her coffee is there though, and I reach for it, finding it untouched since I left.

Scanning the kitchen and lower level, I see no sign of her presence. A bad feeling rolls through me and I glance toward the balcony, the rain splattering the window ruling out the idea she might be there. Listening, I look to the steps, but there is silence encasing me, and I know she is gone. And I know I'm going after her. I head for the door, exiting into the hallway, and I don't stop until I'm at the elevator, inside the car, and punching the button for the lobby level. Perfectly still, I stand there, staring ahead, shoving that beast born of my emotions into a mental box to be analyzed at a more appropriate time. Right now, I have one agenda. Emily, who beyond reason, is important to me. Maybe it's the timing of meeting her. Maybe it's the hope and optimism in her eyes and her words that defy whatever she thinks has beaten her but I know has not. Whatever it is she does to me, I need it, which means I need her.

The elevator dings again, and I step to the doors, exiting the car the instant they part, and striding toward the front of the hotel.

"Good morning, Mr. Brandon," someone murmurs.

I lift a hand, my gaze scanning for Emily, my approach to

the front of the building never slowing. Finally, I reach the double glass doors, and they part, and I exit to find Tai just outside to my right, rain pounding the awning above us, splattering the ground beyond.

"Did you see Emily leave?" I ask him.

He looks baffled. "No sir. Should I have?"

"Did anyone else?" I ask, ignoring his question.

"I'm certain she didn't come through the front of the building. Considering the weather, she'd have needed a car and I would have handled that for her."

"If she didn't come through here, where would she be?"

"This is the only exit other than the garage. She must still be in the building."

The garage. *Fuck me.* "If she shows up, stall her and call me."

"Of course," he says, but I'm already giving him my back and entering the hotel again, my legs quickly eating up the space between me and my intended goal. I reach the elevators and opt for the stairs, heading down a level to the only floor allowing access to the street. Entering the garage, I scan and find no signs of Emily, and considering she'll be walking in the rain, I head for my car, fully intending to search for her. Clicking the locks, I'm about to open the door, when I spy a note on the front window. I grab it and find the delicate scribble of a woman's hand.

I'm too complicated. I can't do that to you. I'm sorry.

Don't let your tongue be your worst enemy.

—*John Franzese*

CHAPTER EIGHT

SHANE

I tell myself to let Emily go, but the idea of her being battered by the storm has me driving the nearby streets, ensuring she's not in need of aid. But I don't find her, and she's made it clear she doesn't want my help. The problem is, I can't seem to shake the idea that she needs it, nor can I dismiss her as a passing fuck. Shoving the note she'd left into my pocket, I reluctantly accept that for the moment, my search is over, and I drive toward the office. My father's words *when I'm gone* run through my mind, and I quickly detour to the highway, heading toward my parents' house with the full intent of finding out what is going on with both of them.

The next twenty minutes have me stuck in hellish traffic, wishing for a Manhattan subway to cut the time that is money, all the while in my own head, and not my father's. I don't need to consider what he'd meant with his accusation of my "weakness." That was about me hanging on to New York and a career I'd busted my ass to create. But I'm past that now, and my focus is Derek's weakness: his lack of morality, which he hates in me, paired with his greed. By the time I navigate the elite Polo

Club neighborhood where my parents live and turn into the driveway of their sprawling fourteen-thousand-square-foot tan stucco mansion, I know that somehow, some way, I'm going to have to turn those things around on him.

Pausing at the gate, I'm glad the rain has stopped, allowing me to key in a code. Once it opens, I continue past the brick paved gardens in front of the house, my gut twisting at the sight of the giant birdbath with a lion spraying water. My father is everywhere and the idea that he will soon be nowhere but our memories is unfathomable. Shaking off that idea, I pull to the back of the property, parking outside the five-car garage my father keeps filled with toys he never drives, and kill the engine. Shoving open the door, I'm about to stand when my cell phone rings. A glance at the caller ID confirms it's Seth, and I hit decline, needing answers to certain questions from my mother before I'm presented with more problems or questions.

Stepping out of the car, I'm almost to the back door when it opens. My mother, who normally sleeps until at least nine, appears in the doorway fully dressed, her raven hair puffed and sprayed, her lips painted red. "I expected I'd see you this morning," she says, greeting me with a hug, which I return before pulling back to eye her black skirt and matching silk blouse scooped a little too low for my approval.

"I know you didn't dress like that for me."

"If you aren't going to look good, why bother to get dressed?" she asks, motioning me forward. "Coffee's ready." She enters the house, calling out, "I figured you'd need it after your all-night company."

Following her inside, my shoes scraping the limestone tile, I forget her remark, and stop in the doorway, my gaze scanning the giant foyer that is more museum than house. But I don't see the intricate design on the rounded ceiling, the expensive art on the walls, or the massive winding mahogany stairwell to my left. Memories of my childhood and teen years erupt in my mind, clawing at me in a less than kind way.

"Shane?" my mother calls out.

"Coming," I reply, shaking myself and pulling the door shut behind me.

Cutting left, I walk directly into an L-shaped kitchen larger than most Manhattan apartments, the centerpiece an island lined with pale wooden drawers and topped with a brown slate counter. My mother pours coffee into two cups. I round the island and take one of them. "Just how you like it," she says. "Too strong for everyone else."

"And yet you're about to drink it."

She walks to the fridge, opening the door. "With half a bottle of vanilla creamer in it." She grabs the bottle and carries it to the island and fills her cup, while I step to the other side, directly across from her.

"Why are you up so early?" I ask. "And don't say for me. We both know I'm worthy of a robe and bad hair."

"Because you give unconditional love, honey. And you do remember that I do interior design work, right?"

"Not at this time of the day."

"Some jobs inspire me. And this one is for the mayor, who in case you don't recall, is highly thought—"

"To be a future presidential contender. You do aspire big, don't you, Mother?"

She laughs. "You came by it naturally."

"You're acting like nothing happened last night."

"Your father has always had affairs."

"Always?"

"You find this hard to believe?"

I grimace. "No. No, I suppose I don't. And you're fine with it?"

"I've had a lot of years to be fine with it, son."

"Do you have affairs?"

"Yes. I do." She sets her cup down. "And before you judge me—"

"I'm not. I know who he is and what he is." I hesitate. "He brought that woman to the Four Seasons."

"I know."

"What do you mean, you know?"

"I hired her."

I lean on the counter. "Mother, what the hell did you do?"

"He's going to have someone in his bed other than me until the day he dies. I want to know if he's sick—"

"We know he's sick."

"He won't tell me what the doctors are saying. Besides. I need our empire protected and that means I need you in charge, not Derek. This potentially allows me to access information you may need." I give her my back, running a hand through my hair, in a rare display of frustration I don't even try to contain. "Shane, look—"

"No," I say, facing her again. "Every time I think this family can't get more fucked up, you all prove me wrong."

She leans on the counter. "I'm protecting us both. I'm helping you."

"There's nothing about this that helps me. And why was this mistress you hired seen with Derek?"

"Your brother works fast. She spent one night with your father and he tried to milk her for information."

"Like I said. There's nothing about this that helps me, or any of us. I need to go." I start to leave and force myself to stop. "Why did Father allow Mike Rogers onto the board? Why would he give away that kind of power?"

"Mike's a good man, Shane."

"You say that like you have personal knowledge."

"He was your father's first major client. He's been with us since almost the beginning. He put us on the map."

"And I'm supposed to expect that justifies father trusting him with twenty percent of the stock when he trusts no one else?"

"We gave him stock for putting us on the map."

"You know *your husband,* my father, would not allow him to stay. He's too greedy and cautious for that. Either he has some kind of leverage over Mike to control him or the opposite is true."

"Mike's a billionaire, son. That's a lot of motivation to your father, not to mention he's high profile and good for the brand. But of course, your father has ammunition on everyone involved with the company."

"What does he have on Mike?"

"He doesn't tell me these things, Shane, but if that's what you need to know—"

"I need to know what he has on every member of the board."

"I'll dig around his private files, but Mike isn't a problem."

"Mike's a twenty-percent stockholder," I repeat. "He's a problem for me."

"And an asset when you take over. He's not like the others."

"Exactly my point," I say. "Who's the woman you've placed in Father's bed?"

"A med student who needs some help paying the bills. I thought she'd be an asset in evaluating your father's health."

I'm not sure I've ever fully appreciated my mother's cunningness until this moment and I'm glad I didn't. If I'd known how screwed up both my parents were as a child, I might have ended up more like Derek. I don't even bother to tell her my suspicions about my father's health. I turn and walk away.

"Shane," she calls out, but I don't stop or reply, heading for the door and exiting into a light rain that reminds me of Emily's probable departure by foot.

I climb in the Bentley that also reminds me of her, but unfortunately also drives home the many flavors of my father's manipulation. What I've failed to see until now is my mother's equal skill. I'd known she was smart and fiery enough to stand toe-to-toe with my father, but in the past twenty-four hours my eyes have opened to what I didn't want to see. At some point, she became like him to survive him, just as Derek did.

Starting the engine, I shift into gear and head down the driveway, idling as the gate opens, my brother's words repeating in my head. *I know who's in my corner. I wonder if you do.* My mother is telling me she's in my corner, but I wonder. Is she telling him the same? And does she have any side but her own? I pull through the gate and the rain erupts again, a prelude it seems to the battle brewing in the heart of the Brandon family empire that I intend to win. I'm just not sure there will be a family left to back the name.

Once I'm on the highway, with my phone attached via Bluetooth, I dial Seth. "The woman's name is Ashley Johnson," he informs me. "She's twenty-four—"

"And a med student," I supply.

"Yes. How did you know that?"

"My mother hired her to keep an eye on my father."

He whistles. "Every time I think your family can't get more fucked up, they prove me wrong."

"That's what I told my mother, who assures me my father has blackmail material on every member of the board. She's working on getting it for us but I'm not counting on her."

"Like I said, I have dirt on everyone to push them out, should you so choose, with the exception of Mike. I'll have those files to you today."

"The security feed?"

"A few concerns I'm not ready to voice yet. I'll have answers this afternoon."

We're about to hang up when my mother's remodeling job comes to mind, followed by my own words yesterday. *Blood divides as easily as it unites, especially when money and power are involved.* "My mother's cozying up to the mayor," I say. "I need to know if he's got any connections to Brandon Enterprises other than her, especially my brother."

With the realization that my briefcase is at my apartment, I decide that the plan is to hole up there with my files I still haven't finished reviewing and a pot of coffee. In other words, far away from the family drama distracting me from my focus on building BP profits by way of creating the strongest team of experts in the industry. Only that drama feels front and center as I arrive at the Four Seasons, hand off my car to be parked, and enter the hotel, my encounter with my father ever present in my mind. As is him being here to fuck a woman my mother hired to sleep with him. The many ways that is insanity can't be counted, but of major concern is a woman who will sell herself for money, having intimate knowledge of our family, which she can then sell as well.

By the time I step off the elevator on my floor, I've vowed to shove all of this aside for a few hours of work, except my phone rings. It's Jessica. My said "family drama" proves it will hunt me down with a damn hammer in its hand.

"Your father is in a mood," she announces. "I mean the man is terrorizing the entire building. Not just our staff. He went off on Karen at the coffee bar for getting his order wrong. He is such an ass."

If this were anyone else, I'd suggest it were cancer- or medication-related, but this isn't my father's first attack on everyone around him. Not by a long shot. "What do you need from me?" I ask, suspecting my father's wrath has turned in my direction, most likely to punish me for this morning, when he's the one who instigated it.

"He's having a conniption over a deal memo he wants reviewed," she says.

"Tell him to e-mail it to me," I say, entering my apartment and shutting the door.

"He doesn't have it on e-mail. He says he needs to know if he's being bent over before he's screwed, not after."

"He said that to you?" I ask and quickly add, pressing fingers to the bridge of my nose, "Never mind. Of course he did." I unbutton my jacket and settle my hands on my hips. "If I go there, it's not going to end well. Bring it here."

"I'll be there in half an hour," she says, ending the call before I can change my mind, clearly just wanting out of that office for a while.

Sighing, I walk to the coatrack, shrug out of my jacket, and hang it next to the one that smells sweet like Emily, who's still lingering in the back of my mind. A welcome distraction from my father's bullshit or the complications that could arise from my brother handing an FDA inspector a bribe. I walk across the living room and stand at the window, watching rain splatter the glass, frowning at something I spy on the patio. Opening the door, I glance out in the storm and start laughing. Emily's bra is hanging on one of the dangling lights. I laugh harder. Even when that woman isn't here, she manages to break through the crap around me.

An impossible smile lingering on my lips, I leave the bra, shutting the door, and walking into the kitchen, I take a barstool with me, and set my briefcase down on the island. Next I get that pot of coffee started and power up my MacBook with my files ready to view beside it. Once I have my cup of coffee, I sit down and take a sip, the strong bite of cinnamon in my favorite blend exploding in my taste buds, and I wonder if Emily would once again grimace. I set the cup down and reach for my files, organizing my four top candidates for the pharmaceutical division. Two executives and two of the top scientists in the pharmaceutical industry—I've spoken to one of each. Recruiting them won't be an issue, but in light of the FDA bribe, I have to think about human corruptibility and them becoming my brother's targets. Building BP to win over the board is no longer the plan. They won't be around to impress if the plan I hatched yesterday morning works.

I've just finished cup number one when the doorbell rings. I'm about to stand when the door opens and I hear Jessica call out, "I let myself in. I hope you're decent." She doesn't wait to find out, because of course she knows I am. She rounds the corner in a one-piece black suit dress, running her fingers through her spiky blond hair, and stops on the other side of the island.

"The deal memo," she says, setting an envelope down. "He wants you to call him within the hour." She snorts. "Like bossing you around ever works. I really love that about you by the way." She eyes the coffeepot. "Why yes, boss, I would like a cup of coffee."

"Help yourself," I say, but she's already headed for the pot, and aside from filling her own cup, she refills mine.

"Do you actually have creamer?"

"Cabinet above the pot," I say, my phone buzzing with a text where it lies next to my computer. I grab it and glance at the message from Seth. *Your father leased room 751 for six months. Confirming, but I do believe the "other" woman is living there.*

I set the phone down, precisely, slowly, reining in the anger burning through me, and not quite sure if it's more directed at my mother or my father.

"Do you want your twenty or so messages now or never?" Jessica asks, appearing in front of me.

"If never is actually an option, then you can handle them."

"I already did. I just wanted you to remember how efficient I am." She sits down in front of me. "In case you leave and I need a reference."

"I'm not going anywhere. Correction. I'm leaving this

apartment. If you do your job. Get in touch with my realtor and find me a house."

She blanches. "You want me to find you a house?" She holds up her hands. "I mean that's good. It's job security for me, but Shane. A house is a big thing."

"Narrow it to the top three."

She looks like she wants to argue, but says, "Fine. Okay. Any specifics?"

"Close to here."

"Apartment?"

I think of my apartment in New York. "House." Then I think of convenience. "Apartment. Just not in the Four Seasons."

"Price range?"

"Whatever it takes to be in something comparable to what I'm in now."

"What about Cherry Creek? It's ten minutes away and it has gyms, food, and shopping. There are new high-rises going up, but the house prices are on the rise too. In other words, if you buy now, you're going to have great resale potential."

"Cherry Creek works. Top three, Jessica."

"All right then. Top three it is."

"Soon."

She gives me a curious look. "Of course." She sips from her cup. "I should get back. I'm one of the only people who'll stand up to your father."

"Before you go." I close the folder and hand it to her. "Inside you'll find two executives and two scientists I've shortlisted for BP. None of them is local. I've put calls into each of them and flagged the ones I spoke with. They'll be e-mailing you official résumés, but I don't want them run through human resources. Talk to their references and work with Seth, and his private security team, to look into their backgrounds."

"Operation 'keep your family from screwing up a good thing

before it happens.' Check." She runs her fingers through her spiky blond hair again and randomly changes the topic, feeding me information she believes is of interest. "Your brother hasn't been in today."

"Good for everyone dealing with my father. Like you."

"Message received. Go back to the office." She stands and rounds the counter to set her cup in the sink before leaving without another word. I like that about her. She gets when to talk and when to just not.

I reach for the envelope holding the deal memo that caused so much hoopla, pulling it out. It takes me all of two minutes to know this isn't about bending him over. It's an investment in a nonsense business that has to be a bribe of some sort. Considering this new business is located in Boulder, where our trucking division is, it's a good bet it's related to that. I don't even want to know what that means about what is going on there. I've had enough of this crap to last a lifetime. I text Jessica. *Find out if there was, or is, a Nina Thompson working for the trucking division in Boulder.*

I don't wait for her reply, dialing Seth. "I need those files on the stockholders, yesterday."

"I have them and more I need to talk to you about. Where will you be in an hour?"

Working in this apartment clearly isn't a success. I stand up and start packing my briefcase. "I'll see you at the office. Before we hang up, I need you to have your security people run the name Nina Thompson in Boulder. I'll explain later."

We end the call and I make my way to the hallway, pausing to put on my jacket before I head toward the elevator. Once I'm there, I start to push the lobby button and instead punch the seventh level. My phone buzzes with a text from Jessica. *Ex-employee who left abruptly a month ago.* Confirmation that the deal memo is a front for a payoff. I pocket my phone again as the elevator jolts to a halt. I exit, quickly locating my father's new rental, and knock on the door. It opens almost instantly and I'm faced with a woman in her twenties with long dark hair wearing jeans and a tank top. She's also a younger version of my mother with features way too damn similar, and my stomach rolls with the certainty my mother chose her for that reason. My mother, who is far more manipulative than I've given her credit for.

"Can I help you?" she asks.

"You're fucking my father because my mother's paying you to. So here's what's going to happen. I'll double your money, but I want reports on everything you tell my mother and don't tell her. Understood?"

She barely blinks. "Okay. How will this work? How do I reach you? How do I get paid?"

"Seth Cage, my right-hand man, will be your contact. He'll be in touch. And if you make a deal with anyone else, and I find out, which I will, I'll go to the med school, and give them proof of how you're paying your tuition."

I turn and walk away, heading for the elevator. Now, time to deal with my father and this deal memo.

EMILY

It's nearly one o'clock in the afternoon, and I'm still chilled to the bone from this morning's run in the rain, not to mention that my feet in high heels didn't appreciate it. Just to leave a man I didn't want to leave, but all is not lost. I have a job now and I've made it through human resources and a tour, and my new boss has already given me work, despite never even looking up from his desk to acknowledge that I'm his new assistant.

So here I am at my new desk, a list of things to do and some comfort in knowing I'm beginning again. Of course, the job comes with the complication of my one-night stand working in the same building, but I'm not going to think of that now. I grab the file in front of me and proof the document that needs to be taken to the courthouse for all the appropriate signatures.

I start jotting down everything I've been told about Brandon Enterprises because writing things down is what my mother said would keep me from missing things. It's control for me. It's organization. It's something I can manage. And right now, things I can manage feel really good. The intercom on my desk buzzes. "Call Shane until you get him to answer."

I can almost feel the blood run from my face. *Shane.* He said Shane. I grab the receiver and pick it up. "I'm sorry. Who is Shane?"

"My youngest son. He's in the Rolodex on your desk or he damn well better be. If you can't get him yourself, walk over to his office and stand at his assistant's desk until she gets him on the line."

"Yes. Yes, sir. On it." The phone shakes in my trembling hand and I press the receiver to my forehead, squeezing my eyes shut. Oh God. It can't be *my* Shane. Actually, how can it not be him? I met him here in this building but I was sure he worked in the law firm, five floors down.

I lower the receiver to the desk, suck in air, and will myself to calm down. I grab the Rolodex, and I turn right to Shane's contact information, but I can't dial him. Tabbing forward, I find his assistant and punch her extension. She answers immediately with, "This is Jessica."

"Hi. I'm," I hesitate on my name considering the circumstances, and settle on, "Mr. Brandon Senior's new secretary. He's trying to reach . . . your boss."

She snorts. "Of course he is. Shane's not here. Tell him he has the deal memo and he's reviewing it."

"Oh. Okay. Learning how this works."

"I'll find you later and give you some survival tips."

"Thank you. I'd really appreciate that."

The line goes dead and I buzz my new boss's office. "Shane has the deal memo but he isn't in right now."

"Fuck! Go to Jessica's desk. Find him." The intercom goes silent.

"You just found him."

My breath lodges in my throat at the oh so familiar voice. I set the receiver down and look up, finding Shane towering over me, his blue suit fitted to perfection over a body I've seen naked. His expression is pure fury.

"Shane, I can explain."

"Follow me," he commands. "And don't even think about refusing."

"Emily," Mr. Brandon says over the intercom.

Shane shakes his head, silently forbidding my reply, and my stomach rolls. I need money. I need this job and I'm about to lose it. He turns and starts walking. I squeeze my eyes shut and swallow hard before jumping to my feet and following him. I glance down at my outfit, confirming my simple light blue dress, paired with a black jacket, is conservative enough for church. No cleavage. No clinging to the wrong places. No wrong message. Well. Except that I slept with him and he thinks . . . I don't know what he thinks. And oh yeah. I left without a good-bye when he wanted me to stay. I wanted to stay but I can't show that and I'm really not sure it matters anymore. And I can't even explain why I left without lying.

We pass through the lobby and I don't even consider looking at the receptionist. I just stare ahead and keep tracking behind him, traveling a hallway that feels eternal. At a fork, Shane cuts left, assuming I'm following, and of course, I do. Almost immediately we're headed toward a corner office with a striking blonde I assume to be Jessica sitting at a desk outside the entrance. I catch her curious look and quickly cut my gaze.

Shane doesn't speak to her, walking directly to what I assume to be his office door. He disappears inside and I follow, hesitating a step before the threshold to steel myself for what is to come. The instant I'm inside, his hand comes down on my arm, and he shuts the door. I blink and I'm against it, and his big body is framing mine, legs trapping my legs, both of his hands now on my shoulders.

"What kind of game are you playing?"

"Game? No. No game. I had no idea—"

"Bullshit. You're working for my brother."

"What? No. It's your father—"

"Is that why he showed at the restaurant? Is that how he knew we were there? You told him."

"Shane, I don't know what you're talking about."

"Don't fucking play coy, Emily. What's the endgame here?"

"I'm really confused."

"I'm not. They want you to get inside my head. Well, it won't work. They're in it and they've pissed me off. Tell my brother or my father I'm taking over this company and they can't stop me."

"Shane, I really—"

"You're a good actress. Because I bought all that innocent, sweet bullshit, and thought you were actually honest. I thought you needed help."

"Let me go," I hiss, shoving at his chest, furious now myself.

His hands settle on my rib cage just beneath my breasts, scorching me inside and out. "I'm not done with you yet."

"I didn't know who you were."

"And yet, as you pointed out, you just happened to be at the security desk when I came downstairs."

"I *didn't know* who you were," I repeat. "And I needed this job."

"How much did he pay you to fuck me? Do you get a bonus for doing it again?" His hands slide to my breast.

"Stop!" I shove at his hand, punching his chest. "Stop it damn it, or I'll shout."

He steps back from me, holding up his hands. "Whatever, sweetheart."

"Don't call me sweetheart." I hug myself, feeling violated by a man who had made me feel special last night. "And you're the good actor. I actually thought you were charming and sexy and now I just think you're an asshole." I turn and reach for the door handle. He's behind me in an instant, his hard body pressed against mine, my hands flattening on the wooden surface. "Stop," I whisper, and damn it, I flashback to us naked, touching, kissing, and how good he'd felt. How right when he was obviously very, horribly wrong.

His hands settle at my waist, one finding my belly and flattening.

"I read you so wrong."

"If you say so," I choke out, emotion balled in my throat.

He turns me around and worse than touching me, he isn't touching me. His hand settles on the door, above my head, and those gray eyes I've seen blazing with heat are now pure ice. "I do say so."

"I'm not what you think I am, Shane, and I need this job, but if I'm fired, just say so and let me start looking for another."

"Mr. Brandon to you. Remember that."

"Then you remember I'm not your 'sweetheart.'"

"Until you're paid to be, right?"

"Like I said. How did I not know you're such an asshole?"

"The same way I didn't know you're—"

His intercom buzzes and Jessica says, "Seth is here and he says it's urgent."

Shane squeezes his eyes shut, the lines of his handsome face all sharp edges and anger.

"I was what?" I demand.

His lashes lift, his eyes hard, and even colder than before. "Like everyone else. And this conversation isn't over. Meet me at seven o'clock tonight in the parking garage." He pushes off the door, grabs me, and turns me so that my back is to his front, his hand back on my belly, his head lowering, intimately close to mine as he orders, "Be there." Then he reaches around me and opens the door.

A moment later, Shane is no longer touching me and a tall, intimidating blond man in a suit is standing in front of me, blocking my path. "Excuse me," I say. And damn it, he doesn't move, his hard stare fixed on my face.

"You're Brandon Senior's new secretary."

I have no idea how he knows this and right now, I really don't care. "And I need to get back to work," I say, and then repeat, "Excuse me."

"Emily," Shane says, his voice radiating along my spine. "Make sure you *do* go back to work."

I don't turn. "Yes, *Mr. Brandon.*"

The man in front of me eyes him over my head and several beats pass like hours, before Shane gives the okay for him to release me. Finally, he steps aside and I am free to go. Only I'm not free at all. Not even close.

I don't wanna be a product of my environment. I want
my environment to be a product of me.

—Frank Costello

CHAPTER NINE

SHANE

I watch Emily round the corner, adrenaline coursing through me
like liquid fire and acid, and I slowly become aware of Seth and
Jessica staring at me. Forcefully, I shift my attention to them. Seth
is arching a brow at me while Jessica stands at her desk, holding on to it and looking confused and concerned. Obviously, I
haven't been discreet and I have no option but to offer an explanation. "She found herself inserted between me and my father,"
I explain, and I'm really damn ready to know the details.

"Oh no," Jessica says. "Shane, she's new and I promised to
help her learn her boundaries."

"A little late for that, I'd say." I'd laugh at the irony of that
statement if every muscle in my body wasn't clenched thanks
to the scent of Emily's perfume clinging to my clothes.

"Should I—" she begins.

"No," I supply. "My father wants his deal memo. Tell him I
read it and he can go fuck himself."

She blanched. "Shane, not even I can—"

"Tell him I'm still reviewing it." I motion to Seth and walk
into my office, making a beeline for the window, where I stand,

arms crossed, and will the adrenaline coursing through me to calm the fuck down.

Silent seconds tick by, and I can feel Seth at my back, just as I can feel Emily's presence in this building, like she were standing right here next to me.

"What just happened?" Seth asks.

Yes. What the hell just happened? I've made a career out of reading people, and I don't know how I got it wrong with Emily—unless I didn't get it wrong and I was just a total dick. Whatever the case, there is too much on the line for me to be a fool with this woman, and yet, when I turn to face Seth, I go another direction. "I went to see the 'other woman,' as you called her. I offered her double what my mother's paying her to give us the same information she's giving my mother, but my mother isn't to know."

"What's to stop Derek from doing the same?"

"I told her I'd ruin her medical career. She's expecting your call."

His eyes sharpen. "Gloves off. Now we're playing like New Yorkers. Good thing." He lifts a folder. "You aren't going to like this."

"Just get to it," I snap irritably. "I can do without any more dramatics today."

He drops the folder on my desk and flips it open to yet another photo of my brother, this time with a very young, pretty, dark-haired woman. "Teresa Martina," he says. "He's quite friendly with her."

"And I care why?"

"Because she's the daughter of Roberto Martina, the kingpin for one of the largest cartels in existence. And while Roberto favors Mexico, her brother Adrian runs the U.S. operations from right here in Denver."

Anger rips through me and I press my fists to the desk. "Has he dragged the BP division into the cartel?"

"He has a relationship with Adrian, though I don't yet know the extent."

"In other words, if he hasn't, he's working on it. He has to have someone inside BP involved in this."

"Agreed," Seth says, crossing his arms in front of his chest. "William Nichols, your head of research and development, had some activity on the surveillance footage I find of interest, but nothing I can say is related to this."

"What kind of activity?"

"Taking calls outside while pacing and appearing on edge, but the man could be going through something personal. We're putting him under watch."

"I know this security team we've hired signed the contracts I drew up, but make damn sure they aren't for sale to the highest bidder."

"I know the owner personally. I promise you. We're golden." He narrows his gaze on me. "You don't just walk away from a cartel, Shane. I dealt with these people when I was with the CIA. And if that's where we're at, our problems are far bigger than the police."

"I'm aware of that." I push off the desk and turn to the window, unbuttoning my jacket and settling my hands on my hips. Seth joins me, both of us staring at the thick, black clouds. "What I don't understand," I say, "is how the hell Derek isn't." My mind tracks back to my father's office yesterday. "Derek made a point of reminding me that BP is my acquisition and I'm linked to anything that happens there."

"A threat," Seth says wryly, leaning a shoulder on the steel beam running along the window. "You could walk away, Shane. Get the hell out of here."

"If I do that, my father and brother will end up dead. And my mother could end up collateral damage."

"What about you? What happens when they ruin your life?"

"I'll take my chances." I turn to face him, hands still on my hips. "At this point, we don't know anything. Derek aspiring to work with the Martina family and *doing it* are two different things. And as much as I'd like to take the direct approach and bulldoze him for answers, he won't be honest and it will only alert anyone who might be helping him to stay off our radar."

Seth gives me a disapproving look. "There are a lot of things I could say to you right now, but I won't."

"Good decision." I glance at my desk where the envelope Jessica brought me lies, realization coming with cold, hard clarity. "Son of a bitch. My father just gave me the proposed paperwork for an investment that's an obvious cover for a payoff."

"That Nina person," Seth assumes.

"Yes. That Nina person, who left the trucking division abruptly a month ago and is suddenly worth the hundred and fifty thousand dollar investment my father wants to make."

"And the trucking company is a perfect target for running drugs. It would be easy to come to the conclusion there's already activity happening there."

"Whether there is or not, if we are thinking about this, then Martina will be thinking about this." I scrub my jaw. "I need to shed that division."

"Not only will that send up red flags to your brother, and your father if he's involved, but it'll risk a potential rift with Martina that you don't want to go into blindly, if at all."

"Which means I need to control them instead."

He reaches into his pocket and offers me a flash drive. "That has enough damning information on Riker Ward, the CEO of that division, to do that and more. It also has equally invasive information on the rest of the board, aside from Mike, and therefore, offers you the power to command them all."

"Unless my brother, or father, beat me to the punch," I say, accepting it.

"Derek's too busy paying everyone off to know how to really control them."

"Don't underestimate Derek, and since my father handled this payoff for the trucking division, I lean toward his involvement. And he is all about control. Which brings me back to my questions about Mike. But the highest priority right now is finding out if we're already in bed with Martina."

"Which, in turn, brings me back to the transportation division. Send me to Boulder, and I promise you, with the dirt I have on Riker, he'll tell us exactly what's going on up there and what that payoff is for as well."

I lift the flash drive. "Spare me the reading time," I say, placing it in my pocket. "What's the dirt you're referencing?"

"Riker's gay," he says. "Which wouldn't be a problem except for a few important details. He's not only in the closet, he's married to a woman, has three kids with her, and a father who's a conservative politician. And yes, I have proof. The man is in bed with so many men I wonder how his wife doesn't know. And before you ask, I'm thorough. She doesn't."

I suck in a breath and let it out. "I don't want to be the person that screws up this family's life."

"He'll never let me tell her," he assures me. "And I wouldn't without your approval anyway. You know that. But for the record, this family's life is already screwed up and it's fucked up that they don't know it."

I hesitate all of two seconds. "Do it." The truth is, my fleeting moment of guilt was wasted on a man who revels in breaking the law.

"I'll leave tonight then," Seth replies. "Right after I pay the 'other woman' a visit." He motions to the desk. "Need me to do anything about Nina?"

"I have it handled."

Still he doesn't leave, an expectant few beats of silence pass-ing before he asks, "Anything else?"

Translation: he wants to know about Emily, and while I have every reason to get him digging around about her, some-where in the middle of this conversation, I've decided I'm not done with her myself quite yet. "Nothing," I say.

He narrows his gaze a moment, clearly weighing my reply. "Very well," he says, heading for the door.

"Don't shut it," I call after him, grabbing the envelope with the deal memo and staring down at it, clear on how to handle it, but Emily is another matter. Creating a distraction to keep me from finding the Martina connection would be smart. And yet, I'm foolish enough to want to believe Emily is telling me the truth. She's either the only woman who's ever rocked my world, or she's a source of information I can, and will, use.

I round the desk and the instant I'm out the door, Jessica says, "Your father—"

"Handled," I say, and I don't stop walking, passing my brother's closed door and dark office before cutting down the hall-way and through the lobby, where Kelly is greeting a visitor I don't know.

Continuing on, I enter the next hallway to my father's office, not sure if I should expect to be requesting Emily's phone num-ber through human resources after visiting with my father or if I'll find her still present and accounted for. I round the corner, bringing the empty desk in front of my father's office into view, and the idea that Emily's run again is actually a relief. If she was a game piece my father and/or brother placed in an attempt to distract me, or throw me off my game, she'd still be here.

I walk to my father's open office door and enter, finding him behind his desk on the phone. I shut the door and he glances up. "I'll call you back," he says to whoever is on the line, clearly not waiting on a reply before hanging up to direct his, "About damn time," at me.

Stopping in front of his desk, I toss the envelope down as I had the photo of Derek and the FDA inspector. "I know that's a payoff." I know I can't cave too easily or he'll suspect something is wrong. "Which is exactly why you asked me to bring it to you on a thumb drive or hard copy. You didn't want it proof of our file transfer. What's it for?"

He leans back in his seat. "Must you always try to prove why you earned that Harvard law degree?"

"You expected me to be the best and I am," I reply. Pushing for any piece of information I can get, I ask, "What does Nina Thompson know that she shouldn't?"

"Does it matter?" It's my turn to offer a deadpan look, and after two beats he scowls and snaps, "Riker had an affair with Nina. When he tried to break it off, she threatened to go to his wife."

Riker, who is gay, had an affair with his female employee? I'd laugh at the blatant lie if I wasn't concerned about what's really going on, and how my father's involved. "Why didn't you just tell me that?"

"Your skills are better used for bigger things. I handled it. *Like I always do.*"

Like he handled the Feds, but I let it go, pushing for a way inside this deal's origin instead. "If I call Nina's lawyer, what will I hear?"

"I convinced her not to hire a lawyer."

Of course he did. "If I call her, then?"

"What do you think?"

I consider him. "I'll pay her off. Consider it handled."

"I'll deal with the conclusion of the agreement."

"Part of my employment contract requires my signature on all legal agreements. *I'll* handle it."

"Not this time," he says, his tone absolute. "Riker's a friend and he's worried about his family."

I shake my head at the absurdity of him having friends. "Of course, Father, and fucking around on his wife certainly proves that concern." I pick up the envelope. "An investment is the wrong packaging for a gag deal. I'll rework it and you'll have your contract by morning."

I turn and walk away to hear him growl into his intercom, "Come to my office, Emily."

Tension ripples down my spine and I open the door to come face-to-face with my sweet-smelling potential liar. She physically flinches at our standoff, a reaction that hits me in a variety of ways. One: she's fucking gorgeous and I still want her. Two: no one trying to rattle me would be this rattled by me—not unless she's a good enough actor to fool someone who makes a living reading people.

"Shane," she says. "I mean . . . Mr. Brandon."

I step to her. "Not 'asshole'?"

Her cheeks heat. "That would be unprofessional and I'm trying hard not to get fired. Unless you just made that happen."

"In other words," I say, "calling me an asshole is an appropriate term. Just not at the office."

"I plead the fifth. I'm not incriminating myself to a man who could fire me."

"A little too late for that, sweetheart." I step around her.

"No," she says from behind me and when I face her she steps closer, lowering her voice. "I didn't know who you were and no matter how many ways you infer or say I did, it still won't be true. And I'm not your sweetheart, *Mr. Brandon.*" She whirls around and charges into my father's office.

I stand there, fighting the urge to go after her. Whether she is telling the truth or not, there is one thing for sure. It's game on, and if I win, she'll be telling the truth and back in my bed, where I most definitely want her. If I lose, she's lying, but she's still ending up back in my bed.

EMILY

Trying to garner some semblance of control, I make a mental list I don't dare write down, deciding a number of things quickly. Number one: I don't have the luxury to leave this job if I'm not fired. Number two: in order to survive in the middle of a company, and a family, at war, I can't be the gazelle outside the lion's office. I have to be me, *the real me* that my nightmare of a secret has suppressed, and that means holding my own with all of the Brandon men. It's a task I take on with Brandon Senior, from the moment he barks his first order and I spout back with knowledge, not fear, an act that earns me a long, hard glower, before respect flints through his stare.

By six thirty, only a half hour before Shane's demand that I meet him in the garage, I've continued to hold my own with my new boss. On the other hand, I'm concerned that meeting his son, who had me naked and submissive last night, in private, isn't the best way for me to keep my job. The intercom buzzes for about the twentieth time this afternoon and Brandon Senior barks, "I need that document I asked for before you leave."

"Finishing it now," I assure him, only to glance up in shock to discover Shane's brother has snuck up on me and is standing in front of my desk.

He leans forward, resting his palms on my desk, his eyes the same gray as Shane's, but his are cold and cunning while Shane's are intelligent and calculating. "Yet another new secretary," he observes.

The ways I don't care for that description are too many to count. "And you're Derek Brandon."

"And you know this how?" he asks, a predatory tone to the question that reaches beyond its simplicity and is meant to intimidate me.

"Because," I say, stamping the paper in front of me to assure him he does not have my full attention, "I've met your brother and you look like your father."

His reply is a long, intense stare, another attempt to stir unease in me because he clearly thinks I'm the gazelle outside the lion's office. I laugh after a few beats. "Do you not like to be told you look like your father?" And before I can stop myself I say, "Would you rather I say you look like your brother? Or do you prefer to hear that he looks like you?"

I've earned an instant scowl and he shoves off my desk as if pushed. "Good luck with the job. I hear there's a betting pool for how many days you'll last." And with that fear-mongering remark, he walks into his father's office. And that's when my skin prickles and I feel Shane before I even see him.

My gaze jerks to the hall, and there he is, far better looking and intimidating than Derek could ever hope to be, leaning on the wall, just watching me, his expression all hard lines and shadows. Seconds tick by like hours in which I wonder if he thinks me still being here is a sign of guilt rather than necessity. I wonder if he knows his concern over my possible betrayal made him act like the true spawn of his father. Or maybe it wasn't acting at all? Worse, I wonder if he thinks the way Derek was leaning over my desk infers intimacy and my guilt. Another couple of seconds pass by, and he turns and walks away, and I swear he takes all of the air in the room with him.·

I shake myself, my decision about tonight's meeting made. Grabbing the Rolodex, I find Shane's number, surprised his cell phone is on the card, and I key it into my phone. Next I grab the file on my desk and walk toward the office, only to have the door shut, but I still hear Derek say, "I told you Shane would buy the Nina Thompson story."

I grimace and turn away, walking to the desk and punching the intercom. "Yes, Ms. Stevens?"

"I have your document. Shall I bring it in to you for your review?"

"Leave it on your desk."

My list for the day complete, I ask, "Do you need anything else before I leave?"

"Just an answer to a question."

"Of course."

"How many days?"

I blink and then I grimace at what I know is a reference to my conversation with Derek. "However long I stay," I reply, "won't be determined by an office bet or by delicate sensibilities I don't have."

There is silence. And more silence before he says, "Good night, Ms. Stevens."

I pop to my feet and grab my purse, shoving it over my head and across my body, and all but run through the now dark lobby. Punching the elevator call button about ten times, I will it to produce a car. The door to the offices opens and that prickling sensation is almost instantaneous. I whirl around and he is walking toward me, and why, why, why, does he have to be so stunningly male when he was so stunningly an ass-hole?

I lift my chin, refusing to be that gazelle. He takes his time, torturing me with his approach, until he towers over me, too close. So very close, and I can smell him, all spicy, and mascu-line, wonderful, in the way that he defines and owns. I can almost feel him. That is how much, despite him being an asshole today, I want this man.

"Running again?" he asks softly, his voice a low, raspy taunt that somehow still manages to be a seduction.

"I'm not running. And I'm not quitting a job that pays double what it should to compensate me for tolerating your father. I was going to call you when I got downstairs."

"Call me how? I'm not at my desk."

"Your cell phone number was in the Rolodex. I was going to tell you I can't meet you someplace private."

"Why?"

"Because you think I slept with you for the wrong reasons and therefore you think I'll do it again."

"Why *did* you sleep with me?"

"I told you my reasons last night."

"Tell me again," he orders.

"No."

He arches a brow. "No?"

"No," I repeat firmly.

"How do I know this isn't a game?"

"If this is a game, I'm losing. Fire me if you're going to fire me, Shane."

"I'm not going to fire you."

"Does that mean you're the one playing games?"

"I don't play games, but we both know you're in some kind of trouble."

"You're my trouble," I say defensively. "You're the one who has me fearing I'll lose this job."

"And people in trouble," he says, as if I haven't spoken, "make mistakes. But I wasn't a mistake."

My throat goes dry. "If you're saying I knew who you were, I told you, I didn't know."

"That's not—"

The door behind Shane opens and my gaze lifts and jerks back to Shane's. "Your brother," I warn softly, quickly putting two steps between us.

"Tell my father," Shane says instantly, as if we're holding a conversation we weren't, "nothing has changed. I said the contract will be ready in the morning and it will be."

"I'm sorry, Mr. Brandon," I improvise. "He's just pushing me to get it right away." The elevator doors open. "Thank you again," I say and quickly dart inside the car.

Turning, I face forward and find myself pinned by Shane's intense steely gray stare, the connection jolting me. There is something going on between me and this man. Something I don't understand. And that is my last thought before Derek steps to the side and the doors shut. It's over. Shane is gone. I slump against the wall, unsure of what just happened. I have my job but absolutely no clue if Shane still believes I've betrayed him. He said that sleeping with him wasn't a mistake. He never said he was sorry or wrong about anything that happened in his office. So there is my answer. He believes I betrayed him and he *is* playing games with me.

It's nobody's business but mine who put these slugs
in me!

—*Owney Madden*

CHAPTER TEN

EMILY

I give up on sleep at five in the morning, pulling on leggings, a
tank top, and a warm hoodie, and pause to finger the dainty silver bracelet on the counter that my mother had given me when
I graduated high school. She'd changed those last few years. Become someone I didn't recognize, someone with no dreams of her
own, who existed to survive rather than to embrace life. Because
of *him*, I think. He is the root of every choice I've made. In fact,
if I made a list of how I got where I am now, he'd be at the top of
the list, the catalyst to everything. It's not a pleasant thought and
I shove it aside to turn my attention to tying my hair at my nape.
Bypassing makeup, I brush my teeth, and attach my headphones
to my cheap phone, which actually has a music app. From there,
I exit my apartment, lock the door, stuff the key in my bra, and
with the full intention of running Shane out of my system, I
start jogging. It's not a great plan, but it's better than hours of
willing my eyes shut for sleep, only to see him, and darn near
taste him, in between my fury at his accusations.

By the end of block number one, the night chill I'm coming
to know is common year round here is almost gone, and I shove

down my hood, crank up a familiar song in an effort to mute out the conversation with myself I keep having in my head, and step up my pace. But instead of escaping into the music, I find myself replaying every thought that kept me up last night, starting with one that is especially bothersome. If Shane believes I am working for his family, he's keeping me around to prove some point or pick my brain for things I don't know. That means I could be gone any second. I have to find another job. And it hurts and makes me angry all over again.

The more my mind tries to play with me, the harder I run, and I'm a good six blocks from home when I look up and jolt at the sight of a man in sweats running toward me. A tall, familiar-looking man. Oh God. This can't be happening. It's Shane and he's almost on top of me. I turn and launch myself in the other direction, but it's too late.

I make it all of a few steps before he shackles my wrist and rotates me to face him. "We need to talk," he says.

"No. No, we don't. This is my private time and I don't work for you right now. Not here."

"Come with me," he orders, and the next thing I know he's leading me into a coffee shop and through the rows of seats, and the only way I can stop him is to make a scene. And since technically he is still one of my bosses, that doesn't seem smart. It's an assessment that seems good until he's leading me into a bathroom, locking the door, and crowding me into a corner.

"You can't do this," I hiss, and I don't know what to do with my hands, flattening them on the wall behind me.

"It looks like I can."

"You're a bully and now you're using my job against me too. This is wrong. I didn't even know I'd gotten the job. Human resources called me yesterday morning."

"I told you I am not firing you. Your job is between you and my father."

"And yet I'm shoved against a wall in a bathroom. With you." I try to duck under his arm. He steps closer, completely pinning me, and this time my hands can go nowhere but his chest. That I've seen naked. And *I* feel naked right now. "Let me out of here."

"I was a total ass yesterday, Emily. I'm sorry."

I blanch, momentarily stunned by the unexpected apology that none of the powerful men I've known in my life have offered, not sure what to think. Before I can figure it out, he presses again. "Why did you leave without saying good-bye?" This time his voice is softer, more seduction than demand.

Because he sees things I can't let him see. But I can't say that. "I didn't want the awkward morning after. It was a one-night stand."

"That wasn't a one-night stand."

It's the answer I both want and can't accept. "We said—"

He drags me to him, his hand at the back of my head, and before I can so much as breathe, his lips cover my lips. My hand flattens on his chest, my arm firm, and I try to resist, but his tongue strokes against mine, and the taste of him, hunger, and male perfection, assaults my senses. Another stroke, and my elbow softens, my fingers are curling around his shirt only to have him tear his mouth from mine to declare, "Now we've ensured it's more than a one-night stand. It's here and now and whatever we decide it can be. Come back to my apartment with me."

"No," I say quickly, flattening my hand on his chest. "I have to go to work, Shane. Your father won't like me being late. And this is very complicated."

He cups my head again and kisses me, deeply, passionately, until his forehead rests against mine. "Does that feel complicated? We'll work it out. Together, Emily." And for several seconds we just breathe together and I think, *Maybe I can do this.*

Maybe he's the light at the end of what has been a dark tunnel. He leans back and looks at me, and what I feel in that moment is something I do not understand. Something warm, and ripe, and undiscovered, that I want to know. "Let's get some coffee and sit down and talk," he says, brushing my messy hair from my eyes. "Okay?"

"Yes. Okay."

A loud knock sounds on the door and I jolt. "Are you done in there?" a woman calls out.

"Just a minute!" I shout back before I whisper to Shane, "This is so embarrassing."

He leans in and presses his cheek to mine, his lips near my ear. "Hold your head high when we exit and act like it's normal." He nips my lobe, sending a shiver down my spine, before lacing his fingers with mine and leading me to the door. Glancing over his shoulder, he gives me a questioning look.

I reply with a choppy nod and he exits the bathroom first, with me doing just what he said, holding my head up and never looking at the woman waiting just outside. We are almost at the end of the hallway when a thought has me tugging on Shane's arm. He turns to face me, a question in his expression. "How did you go from accusations to this?"

"I heard you meet my brother for the first time and I heard you taunt him over me. No one who was with them would speak that way to him."

"But after that, by the elevator, you said me sleeping with you wasn't me making a mistake, inferring that it was calculated."

"No. I simply said it wasn't a mistake and I would have come to your apartment and said as much last night, but I had an ex-firm call me about a case that reopened. Anything else?"

"No. Nothing else. The time?"

He glances at his watch. "Six thirty."

My eyes go wide. "I can't sit and have coffee. I have to shower and dress and walk to work."

"We'll get it to go and I'll walk you home and come back and give you a ride."

He's already leading me toward the counter, and I'm repeating the word "home" in my head. As in my shell of an apartment that I can't let him see without him asking questions I can't answer without lies. And he deserves more than lies, but if I tell him the truth, he'll hate me.

"What was that sweet concoction you were drinking when I met you?" he asks as we stop at the counter.

"White mocha," I say and he glances at the woman behind the counter.

"White mocha and a large triple-shot latte."

My mind flashes back to our dinner, and how he'd nailed my personality off my coffee, and I off his. I can't do this and not just because I work for his father, which is a whole other kind of complicated. I'm quickly falling hard for this man and I will destroy him in the process. I have to end this and there is no halfway about how. This man goes for what he wants and unless I'm brutally clear, that will be me. Even quitting my job, which isn't an option until I find another, won't be enough. We both live downtown and I can't afford to move.

He pays for our drinks and the minute he faces me, I say, "I can't do this."

His hands come down on my arms, warm and strong, right and wrong at the same time. "What are you talking about, Emily?"

"You all but called me a whore, Shane. You were an asshole. You *are* an asshole and I don't accept your apology." I shove at his arms but he holds on to me the way I want him to, when he cannot. "Let go, Shane," I hiss.

He studies me, his expression unreadable, hard. "What are you doing?"

"I'm going home to change and do not follow me. Don't be such an asshole that I have to quit a job I need. Don't do that to me after what you did to me in your office."

"Emily—"

"You touched me like it was your right in that office, Shane. Touched me. We're done." I turn and rush for the exit when all I want to do is turn back around. Darting past a couple holding open the door, I cut right, instead of left toward my apartment and immediately cut into an alcove in front of a closed office, sinking into the dark corner, and waiting. And waiting, but he doesn't come, a reality that delivers both relief and regret. Sinking into a squat, I press my face to my hands, hating what I just did.

By seven fifteen I've showered and left a message for every job I applied for, and two temp services, and needing some semblance of control at least, I make a list of their companies and phone numbers. A lesser salary somewhere other than Brandon Enterprises isn't ideal, but a paycheck is what matters. By seven thirty I've dressed in a navy skirt with a matching jacket, paired with a matching scoop-neck silk blouse. My hose are black. My heels are four inches high. My hair is flat ironed to a rich brown shine and my makeup is done in pale pink hues. I reach for the bracelet my mother gave me, but set it down. It's too me and that's exactly what I can't be right now. And when eight o'clock arrives and I walk into the fancy Brandon Enterprises offices, I look like that someone else I'm forced to embrace. Like I belong here, even though I'm pretty sure at least one Brandon male is ready to disagree.

I stuff my purse in my desk, after taking out today's to-do list, and I poke my head into Brandon Senior's office, finding him behind his desk, scowling at his computer. Delicately clearing my throat, I say, "Good morning." His head pops up, his eyes narrowing on me, and I add, "Would you like coffee?"

"What I'd like is the contract Shane promised I'd have this morning."

"I'll call Jessica right now."

"Don't call. Walk over there and get it."

I can almost feel the blood drain from my face. "Yes. On it."

I step away from the doorway, drawing a calming breath that isn't calming at all. I knew I'd have to see him today. I just didn't think it would be right now. I glance at the clock on the wall beside my desk. Eight ten. If I'm lucky he won't be in yet and I can get Jessica to pass along the contract to me the instant it's ready.

Spurred by that possibility, I hurry down the hallway, waving at the pretty, happy blond receptionist, barely remembering a time when I was like her. I steel myself for the potential of seeing Shane and round the corner. Jessica is behind her heavy mahogany desk, looking stunning in an emerald-green dress that contrasts with her striking light blond hair, while Shane's door stands open. His lights are on but there is no stopping now.

Her eyes land on me. "Happy day two. That's longer than some of Brandon Senior's former secretaries made it."

I stop in front of her desk. "I have thick skin and a history of working for assholes," I assure her.

"And you're visiting me early."

"I offered Brandon Senior coffee and he commanded me to present myself here to pick up a contract he's waiting on."

"It's right here."

At the sound of Shane's voice, my gaze lifts to find him standing to the right of Jessica in his office doorway, his suit a dark gray, his tie light blue, his expression impossible to read, and a folder in his hand. "Is it ready for me to take to him?"

"Yes," he says, and I am certain he will punish me for this

morning with a power play, forcing me to walk to him, so I step around the desk. At the same time, Shane pushes off the door-jamb, and before I can prepare for the impact, he's not only strid-ing toward me, he's radiating that dark energy I'd noted after his meeting with his brother. That's where I rank now.

Too soon, and not soon enough, he's in front of me, too close considering Jessica's watching us. For several beats, we just stand there, him towering over me, big, broad, and intimidatingly in command in ways beyond who he is in this building.

He offers me the folder. "It's all yours," he says, his voice low, terse.

I reach for it and he doesn't let it go, holding my stare as he adds, "And now we're done here, Ms. Stevens."

Ms. Stevens. I didn't even know he knew my last name. The formality, along with the certainty that his statement has noth-ing to do with the contract and everything to do with him being done with me, cuts like glass, despite that being my necessary goal. I tell myself to politely say thank you, but I just can't. I nod and he releases the folder, allowing me to turn and walk away. And somehow I manage to do just that: walk, calmly and pro-fessionally, even though the explosion of emotions inside me has me ready to launch myself forward and get to the bathroom be-fore they get the best of me.

I exit the hallway to the lobby, wave when the receptionist greets me, and keep moving, exiting the offices, to the exterior section of the floor. I cut to the bathroom to the right of the ele-vators. Shoving open the door, I pass three empty stalls and en-ter the final larger one, and lock myself inside before sinking against the door. My chest is tight, the ball of emotions I've been suppressing for months building there, threatening an eruption I can't have now. This has to wait until I'm out of here, but really, it's so appropriate that secrets and lies have forced me to Denver and now they're tearing me apart while I'm here.

Pressing my hand to my face, I shove hair from my eyes, only to have the folder fall to the ground, the contract slipping out. I squat and grab it and my gaze catches on the name "Nina Thompson" and the conversation I overheard last night comes slamming back into my mind. *I told you Shane would buy the Nina Thompson story.*

The exterior door opens, jolting me into shoving the paperwork into the folder and standing. Footsteps sound and I move to the back wall to avoid being seen.

"Emily."

I squeeze my eyes shut at the sound of Jessica's voice. "I'm in here," I say, but make no move to open the door.

"You okay?" she asks, now at the other side of my stall.

"Yes," I lie, because if she believes it, maybe I will too. "Of course."

"I don't believe you."

Okay. That went well.

"I buzzed Brandon Senior," she continues. "I told him he'd have the contract within an hour to buy you some time. Open the door."

"Not yet."

She's silent a few beats. "How do you know Shane?"

"I . . . What?"

"Obviously there was something between you two and it didn't start here."

She's direct and in a world wrapped in lies, I actually respect that about her. I inhale and open the door. "I don't know how to answer."

"He trusts me. You can too."

"Has he told you?"

"He said it's none of my business."

She's honest again. God, I like this woman. "It's complicated."

She snorts. "When is anything not around this place? How about we go to lunch today?"

"No," I say quickly and when her eyes go wide I quickly add, "I mean, thank you but Shane will misread it. He'll think Brandon Senior has me nosing around for information."

She smirks. "No one in this place believes they can get information from me. We'll do lunch. I can try and get details from you and you can keep dodging my questions. I enjoy the challenge."

"Shane won't like it."

"I'll take care of my boss. How's noon?"

"Jessica—"

"Noon it is." She turns and exits the bathroom, determined to get her way. She won't. I'm not antagonizing Shane after what happened this morning. I glance down at the folder. *I told you Shane would buy the Nina Thompson story.* I need to tell Shane, but he might think coming from me that it's a trick. I could tell Jessica, but I don't know if Shane really trusts her. E-mail could be hacked and so could internal phones. That leaves only one option.

Decision made, I rush for the door, and I don't stop walking until I find the security of my desk, relieved to find Brandon Senior's door shut. Hurrying to my desk, I sit down and slip the contract into my top drawer before removing my cell phone and clicking Shane's number. Not sure it's really him, I pull up the text message option and type: *This is Emily. It's urgent. About a work thing. Are you there?*

Him. I think. *I'm here.*

I study it and type: *Please prove it's you.*

Him again. *Your bra is hanging on a light above my balcony.*

Impossibly, I laugh, quickly shaking it off to type: *Before I give this contract to your father, I overheard Derek say quote: I told you Shane would buy the Nina Thompson story.*

There is a long electronic silence before he replies with: *Give him the contract.*

That's it. I stare at it. And stare at it some more and then finally it beeps again with: *Thank you, Emily.*

Emily. Not *Ms. Stevens.* I stare at the screen all over again, and I type: *I'm sorry.* Then I erase it. I type it again, but I don't hit send. The truth is, even if I could open that door with Shane again—if he'd *let me,* which I doubt—I can't. And I really hate the reality that creates that certainty. I erase the apology and put my phone back in my purse, shutting the drawer, and with it, the short chapter of my life that was me with Shane Brandon.

> If a man is dumb, someone is going to get the best of
> him.
>
> *—Arnold Rothstein*

CHAPTER ELEVEN

EMILY

The rest of the morning, my cell phone does not ring with even one single call about a job, but the phone on my desk rings incessantly. It becomes abundantly clear that the primary business Mr. Brandon is involved in is the investment side of the company. Presently, he's packaging a high-dollar hedge fund that has tensions elevated between him and his potential investors, and I'm getting the brunt of it all. By midday, my list of things to do is a mile long, I've been yelled at by him and at least three other people, I've coordinated two conference calls, both with groups of complete asses, and I'm pretty sure I've started to grow horns of my own.

It's nearly noon when the intercom buzzes and I hear a loud cough. "Get in here, Ms. Stevens."

Unfazed at this point by his barked orders, I walk to his office, entering at the same moment he bursts into more coughing. Then he scowls at me as he demands, "Why do I not have Mike Rogers on the phone?"

"His secretary says he's at a team meeting," I say, wondering how I've turned my low profile into calling NBA team owners who will actually answer.

"I don't care where the fuck he is," Brandon Senior snaps. "If I don't have him on the phone in fifteen minutes, you're fired."

I bristle at the threat, and my first instinct is to retreat, which angers me for my reaction more than at him. I will not allow these damnable circumstances to turn me into that person. If he really intends to fire me, he's going to do it no matter what, and if not, my response sets a tone for the future. "If you fire me," I say, my voice firm and confident, "who'll put up with your crankiness? And arrange your conference calls? And find Mike for you?"

"Well, you haven't found him, now have you?" he asks, the challenge in the question sidetracked when he hacks a few more times.

"I *have* found him," I retort when he settles down. "He just refuses to be interrupted."

"When he's on the phone with me, *then* you've found him. Get out of my office and shut the door until then."

I'm not fired, apparently, and I don't get out of his office, watching as he obviously chokes back more coughing. "Can I get you something hot to drink and some drugs to go with that cough?"

"Mike Rogers is the only drug I need."

"I respectfully disagree."

"You're pushing your luck, Ms. Stevens."

Resigned to his stubborn arrogance, I exit the office, pulling the door shut, and then claim my desk, immediately searching my Rolodex for Jessica's number, and hitting that extension. "Jessica," I say when she answers. "It's Emily."

"I was about to head in your direction for lunch."

"I told you, I can't go with you," I say, and quickly change the subject, "but I have a question. Is there a drugstore that delivers nearby? It's for Brandon Senior."

"Not that delivers. What's wrong with him?"

I open my mouth to reply when a gorgeous woman in a sleek black pantsuit breezes into my workspace, her long, brunette hair a shiny veil touching her shoulders. More than a little shocked that I wasn't warned of her entry first, I quickly say, "I need to call you back," to Jessica and replace the receiver on the cradle. "Can I help you?"

"Honey," she purrs, stopping in front of me, and shifting her Chanel purse from one shoulder to the other, "if you're sweetening my husband with that sweetness you ooze, you've already helped."

My eyes go wide. "You're—" I almost say *Shane's mother.* "Mrs. Brandon." And good grief, she looks too young to be Shane's mother, her pale skin more porcelain than most twenty-year-olds.

"And you're the newest target for my husband's wrath." She claims a chair in front of my desk and a bit to the left. "How are you handling him?"

"His wrath isn't so bad," I say. "Some of the people he does business with are fairly hateful, but I'm no delicate flower."

"Has he threatened to fire you yet?"

Obviously this is a thing for him. "We just did that about five minutes ago."

"And you're not in the bathroom crying. I approve. If you're still here in two weeks, I'll take you to the spa to celebrate." She stands up, and I turn in my chair to watch her walk to her husband's door, open it, and walk right in. Oh God. Is she going to get me fired? Or . . . not? What does a man who brings his mistress to his son's hotel expect of me where his wife is concerned? And officially, I've decided Shane's family unit is as screwed up as mine.

"Lunchtime!"

At the sound of Jessica's voice, I whirl around to find her hurrying toward me, her purse on her shoulder. "Snap, snap," she commands. "Let's head out."

"I can't go, Jessica. I told you that."

She stops in front of my desk. "I talked to Shane. It's fine."

"No," I say. "I appreciate it. I really do, but I'm not going."

"He said—"

"It doesn't matter what he said. It matters what he'll think."

"Wait in the lobby, Jessica."

My lips part in shock at the sound of Shane's voice and Jessica whirls around to face him, her body blocking my view. Blood rushes in my ears. Brandon Senior can't rattle me but his younger son can. I count three seconds and ten of my heartbeats, before Jessica steps aside to let Shane pass and heads for the lobby.

Shane is instantly in front of me, leaning forward, and his hands are on my desk, much like Derek's were. But he's not Derek, and this is nothing like that encounter. "Go to lunch with Jessica, Emily."

"I'm not going."

"You can trust her. The woman won't break a promise, or your trust, not even to me. I *want* you to go."

"Shane—"

"You can't work here, or live in this city, without anyone. Okay?"

My chest tightens with the memory of him asking me that in the bathroom. "You're sure?"

"I don't say anything I'm not certain about."

I am instantly reminded of him telling me that we're good together, and I wonder if he questions that now. "I'll go. Thank you."

He doesn't move. I don't move and that something indescribable I felt in the bathroom, and the restaurant, and every time I'm near this man, is happening again. I can't escape it. I don't want to escape it and I wonder how I can work with him and how I can leave and never see him again. "Have a good lunch," he says, pushing off the desk and disappearing around the corner, and I swear he takes all the air in the room with him.

My shoulders slump. How is it possible that my nipples are tight and aching? How can any man affect me this intensely? My mind goes back to the two men in my life, both extreme opposites; both had seemed right because they were so wrong, and turned out to be just wrong. And painful. But Shane is right and still wrong, and there seems to be nothing I can do about it.

"You ready?"

I glance up to find Jessica standing just this side of the hallway. Holding up a finger, I punch the intercom button. "I'm going to lunch with Jessica unless you need me to stay?"

"What I need is Mike Rogers."

"I'll keep trying him on my cell phone."

"Oh good grief," I hear Mrs. Brandon say. "Let the poor girl go to lunch before you run her off too."

My eyes go wide and Jessica, who's now standing in front of me, lifts her brows, her expression ripe with amusement. "Go to lunch," Brandon Senior commands, giving me two of the Brandon men's approval.

I open my drawer, snatch my purse, and point toward our escape path before he changes his mind. We flee for the front and I stop to talk to the receptionist. "Hi, Kelly," I say. "I'm going to lunch. If Mike Rogers calls, it's crucial he talk to Brandon Senior. If we miss him, we might both get fired."

Her eyes go wide. "The last thing I want is that man angry at me. I'll be careful not to miss the call."

"Great. Thank you."

Jessica and I head to the elevator but I'm not feeling good about this decision. "I'm worried about leaving."

"We can stay close," she says, as one of the cars opens. "There's a fancified pizza place downstairs."

" 'Fancified'?" I laugh. "I'm not sure that's a word."

"It is because I say it is."

"You are a match made for Shane." I cringe at the telling statement and quickly attempt a recovery. "Pizza it is," I say, dashing into the elevator.

She follows, punching the button and scrutinizing me. "Match made for Shane? I'd ask you how well you know him again, but I've seen how he looks at you. I already know."

I don't fall into the trap of asking what that means. "What I know is that not only is he a Brandon, he's a winning attorney. You seem to hold your own well."

"He called you Ms. Stevens earlier today and just now he called you Emily. And you call him Shane."

"You call him Shane."

"I'm his direct secretary."

"Jessica—"

"I'm not being nosy. I have a point. If you both want to be discreet—"

"There's nothing to be discreet about."

"Then get the formality right," she finishes as if I haven't spoken. "Communicate and decide how you're going to handle it and stick to it."

She has a point. "Thank you, Jessica."

"None needed. I protect Shane and he is very protective of you, which means I protect you too." She doesn't give me time to digest that tidbit before adding, "Maybe one day, not this day, you'll trust me enough to tell me about it." The elevator doors open and about five people are ready to crush us. We clear the car and fall into step.

"Has Brandon Senior threatened to fire you yet?"

"You're the second person to ask me that in half an hour. And yes. He has."

"And you said what?"

"He's trying to find Mike Rogers so I asked him, if he fired me, who was going to find Mike Rogers for him."

She laughs. "He must really want Mike Rogers, and, truth be told, so do I. He's rich, sexy, and actually has a personality." We enter the line at the pizza joint.

"Well, that will be a change," I say, "considering everyone else involved in the hedge fund Senior has going is an ass."

"Money does that to people," she says before turning her attention to the cashier to order a slice of pepperoni and water. I do the same, both of us paying and moving to the end of the bar.

One of the six round wooden tables comes free and Jessica points. "Grab it. I'll grab our food."

I take our waters and quickly dart forward and claim our spot, then grab a stack of napkins. About the time I'm fully settled, she joins me, and I take a bite and give a thumbs-up. "This is good and way too easy to grab considering how fattening it is."

Jessica finishes a bit and dabs at her mouth. "I get it to go sometimes, usually on those lonely Friday nights. My love life sucks, probably because I'm always working."

"Shane's a slave driver?"

"To himself. I try to help and force him to go home, but I fail mostly."

"How long have you been with him?"

"Almost a year. I worked for an attorney that almost beat him in court a few years back. He figured that meant I had to be good."

"And you are."

"I am," she says, and somehow it's confident, not arrogant. She unscrews her water. "I need to tell you something. Shane doesn't know about that hedge fund and he should. He has to sign off on all contracts. It's part of his employment agreement."

"I don't think it's a secret. I wasn't told it is."

"And yet Shane wasn't told at all, which means I have to tell him and I don't want you to think I did it in an underhanded way. I'll make sure he makes them believe he found out on his own."

"I'm not worried about Shane, or you, throwing me under the bus and I appreciate you being forthright."

"Always," she says. "Look. One of the reasons I wanted to go to lunch was to make sure you understand this family is at war and Shane is the good guy."

"I know Shane's the good guy."

She studies me a moment, seeming to weigh my sincerity and then giving me an approving nod. We both eat and she gives me a rundown on the staff, ending with Anna, Derek's assistant. "She's new. I don't know her. I don't plan to know her and she spends plenty of time behind closed doors with Derek."

"Oh," I say, reading between the lines.

" 'Oh' is right." Her phone buzzes where she's set it on the table and she grabs it and looks at a message. "I'm helping Shane find a house or an apartment to buy and a hot one just hit the market. I need to run and look at it before someone scoops it up."

"You're picking his home?" I ask, surprised he would hand over something so personal.

"I didn't want to, but he says he's too busy to deal with it and he has a sudden urgency to move."

Because of his father showing up at the Four Seasons with his mistress, I think, but would never dare say.

"He wants my top three recommendations," she continues, "and I really want to find the perfect choices." She touches my hand. "Come with me. You know him well enough to say he and I are a perfect match. I need help."

"No way. That would be highly inappropriate."

"Not if it's helping me," she argues. "He doesn't have to know."

"I'm not going, Jessica."

"Fine. Fine." She grabs her purse. "I hate to leave you."

"I'm fine and I need to get back to work."

She stands. "Let's try again tomorrow."

"Yes. I'd like that." And I mean it. I like her. I trust her. *Shane* trusts her and I get the feeling there aren't many people he does trust, most certainly not me at this point.

She darts away and I stare after her without really seeing her, my mind on Shane and the hedge fund. Why wouldn't Brandon Senior tell him about something like that? Surely, word would spread. Is it just a power play?

"Imagine meeting you here, Ms. Stevens."

I barely contain an outward jolt at the sound of Derek's voice, recovering as he sits down in front of me, his navy suit complemented by a yellow tie.

"I'm sure this place is popular for busy people who don't want to leave the building."

He narrows his eyes on me, and while they are the same color as Shane's, Derek's are two shades colder. "I'm surprised my father let you leave at all."

"Your mother influenced him," I say.

"My mother has a way of influencing everyone. You too will be in a place of influence by my father's side."

"I'm not by his side. I'm outside his door and hardly influential considering everyone is betting me out of the door."

"I'm not."

I don't bother pointing out his inference otherwise, nor do I like the sense of being the gazelle with yet another lion. Narrowing my eyes at him, I seek to set a tone with this man as I did his father. "You have no food, Mr. Brandon."

"Derek."

"Why are you here?"

"You work for my father, which means you'll be handling sensitive material for both myself and my brother. It's good business to know more about you. Clearly he's already made that point. I'm late to the party."

Unease slides down my spine. Does he know about me and Shane? Could he have seen us? We were together in the building and near here. I laugh and manage to sound amused. "He must be good then."

"Good?"

"More like amazing if he's already assessed me, considering I've had about five minutes in total conversation with him."

His eyes glint. "Instead, he sent Jessica to get to know you and learn all your secrets."

That hits a nerve I don't want to exist, but logically I know he's trying to make sure I'm not in their camp and crossing enemy lines. For all I know, his father warned him I was at lunch with Jessica. "My secrets," I say, leaning closer, "are very interesting."

He studies me, his attention piercing, his presence as commanding as Shane's but with a cutting edge that makes one feel trapped rather than spellbound. "Are they now?"

"They are," I say, stepping out on a tightrope. "I once told my boss's son he was an asshole. He wasn't happy. He even threatened to fire me."

"And why was he an asshole?"

I sit back. "I guess he was just born that way."

His lips curve and he laughs. "You're entertaining, Emily." And with that, he gets up and leaves, and I follow his path, confirming his departure, watching him turn left toward the building's exit. That's when my skin prickles and I cut my gaze to find Shane standing near the entryway of the restaurant watching me, his expression unreadable, but that dark, edgy energy is back. He stands there—just stands there—with me as his sole focus. I fear he thinks he just saw proof I'm colluding with his brother. I'm not sure what to do or not do, but before I figure it out, he turns and walks away. I start to go after him, but Jessica's warning about discretion rings in my head, and I sit back down. I'll tell her what happened. That's appropriate, as Shane is my boss's son. *Just* my boss's son and if I keep treating him like more, I'll become a tool Derek can use against Shane.

The strength of a family, like the strength of an army, lies in its loyalty to each other.

—*Mario Puzo*

CHAPTER TWELVE

SHANE

It's nearly seven o'clock and I have six contracts to review—all of which legal says they need by tomorrow—and I can't help but think the inundation of work is an effort to hide something I need to find. And what the hell does it say that I have to think that way to survive in a family-run business and I'm part of the family in question? I toss my pen down and lean back in the chair, tension stiffening my body. Pushing away from the desk, I stand and walk to the window, staring out at the sky, lightning ripping down the path of darkness, seeing another storm brewing. My mind travels to where it has been many times the past few hours: Emily. Then my brother. Then Emily again.

A knock sounds on my door. "Come in." I turn to find Jessica in the doorway.

"Can I look at some of those contracts for you?" she asks. "I *am* a paralegal, you know. And you actually pay me to help you with your workload."

"I'm good," I tell her. "Go home."

"You go home."

"Find me one and maybe I'll be more eager."

She narrows her stare on me. "Something happened."

"Something always happens," I say, dismissing her dig for information. "Go home."

"I mean with the apartment and your father. That's why you're pushing me to find you a new place."

"Just get me the hell out of there, Jessica."

"I tried to get you to look at one today and we lost it. You can't delay with a hot property."

My cell phone rings and I fish it from my pocket, confirming it's Seth with an update on Boulder, and eyeing Jessica, who holds up her hands. "I'm going. I'll shut the door behind me."

I give her my back and answer the call. "Talk to me."

The door shuts behind me as Seth says, "I'm going to need to stay a few days."

"What the hell does that mean? I thought you had the ammunition to control things down there, namely the CEO of that division."

"Yes. Riker." There's disdain in his voice. "He claims Nina found out he's gay and threatened to go public."

I scrub a hand over my jaw. "*Fuck*. That's possible."

"He was lying and I went to see Nina and her place is packed up. I called accounting and her check is to be hand delivered to your father. So wherever she is, he knows. You were right about not underestimating your father."

"What do you propose?"

"For starters, I fly in a guy I know and the two of us wire the warehouse and Riker's house. And I get a few guys in the warehouse on our payroll. Approve those things and I'll get you control over this operation."

"I don't see how I have a choice, but we need a backup plan with the rest of the board members." I end the call and stuff my phone in my pocket, looking skyward and asking myself why I'm here. Really? Why is this important to me? Derek would throw me under a bus in a heartbeat. If I open my mother's eyes and she doesn't walk away, then it's on her. *Fuck*. This isn't just about jail with a cartel in play anymore. It's about life and death. I can't leave. Besides, truthfully, the challenge of cutting through all this crap and making us great is one I revel in.

Shoving the contracts into my briefcase, I hook the strap over my chest and shoulder, when a knock sounds on the door. *Why is she still here?* "Come in, Jessica."

The door opens and I freeze at the sight of Emily. "I need to talk to you," she says, and before I can object she's inside and shutting the door.

"Are you insane?" I demand, rounding the desk and stalking toward her.

"You're angry," she says as I stop in front of her. "I should have called or texted you after you saw me in the restaurant. Derek showed up out of the blue and just sat down. That wasn't what it looked like."

"I'm not angry at you," I say, fighting the damnable urge to touch her. "And that was *exactly* what it looked like and it was a reality check for me. You were right. We can't happen. My brother clearly knows, or suspects, something between us and he will ruin you to ruin me."

"I can handle myself."

"You already did. You shut me down when I was too selfish to know it had to be done. Don't come into my office at this hour. It gets us attention we don't need. And don't come to me at all if you don't have to."

"No one else is here," she says. "Your father's sick. I thought it was just bronchitis, but now I think it's more. I thought about calling your mother, but I've only met her briefly and—"

"When did you meet my mother?"

"Today, and I have no sense of how he'd react to me calling her. That's why I'm here. He's really sick."

"Define 'sick.' Why do you think it's more than bronchitis?"

"He's coughing up blood, Shane."

Blood. The word punches me in the chest. "You're sure?"

"Very and that can't be good."

I run my hand through my hair. "I guess we all forgot to tell you he has cancer." I reach for the door at the sound of her intake of air, yanking it open. "And he gets angry when he's reminded that he does." I leave her behind, stalking down the hallway and through the now dark lobby, not slowing until I'm at my father's closed doors.

I'm about to knock, but my father erupting in a coughing fit sounds on the other side. Knowing how he despises seeming weak, I wait and wait some more, but he continues to hack eternally. A blade of pain slices through me and I lower my forehead to the door, telling myself *this is bronchitis* or something other than the cancer traveling from his brain to his lungs. Sometimes I pretend he isn't dying. *Most of the time* I pretend he isn't dying. It's how I cope, perhaps because it's how he copes, but there are moments of reality like this one that gut me and turn me inside out. To hell with knocking.

I open the doors to find my father sitting behind his desk in profile and hunched over. Mindful of his privacy, I shut us inside the office, rounding the desk to find he's leaning over a trashcan. My gaze lands hard on the blood tingeing the napkin in his hand, the sight driving that proverbial blade of dread a little deeper. So does the way he avoids looking at me and the next bout of coughing that leaves his lips stained red.

Desperate to help him, though I doubt he would do much but kick me if our positions were reversed, I grab the bottle of water on his desk, and hand it to him. "Drink," I order.

He accepts it and damn if his hands don't shake, a sign of weakness he's never shown, not even during chemo. I watch him tilt the bottle up, choking as he tries to swallow, but just when

I'm about to take it from him, he starts gulping. Half a bottle later, he's wiping his mouth and straightening. "This didn't happen," he orders.

"It did happen," I say. "Mom——"

"It *didn't* happen," he growls, rotating to face his desk, and I can almost see that invisible wall, which he habitually slams between us, fall into place, about ten feet higher than normal.

I inhale and let it out, standing and rounding the desk, arms crossed as I stare down at him. "The cancer has spread," I say and it's not a question.

"I'm being treated."

"That's a 'yes.' "

His gray, bloodshot eyes meet mine. "Yes. What did you want when you came in here?"

"More chemo?"

"Yes."

"When?" I press.

"Starting Monday, which is why I'm trying to get my goddamn work done. Why are you here?"

I ignore the question. "Does Mom know?"

"No one knows. That's why I said this didn't happen. Keep your mouth shut."

"She deserves to be told."

"Why? So she can worry more than she already does?" His expression tightens, his fingers laced in front of him on the desk as he leans forward. "Back to business. What are you here for?"

The cold reserve of his tone matches the look in his eyes that tells me that wall is now a block of ice. Anger starts to form in my gut. "Why," I say, "when you're dying, would you help Derek take this company into deeper, darker places, rather than help me secure a different future for him, and for everyone involved? Why, Father?"

"Son, I'm on the sidelines keeping score with one agenda.

This company has to survive, and thrive, in my absence. You want to restore its ethical virginity, do it. Make it happen."

"You're as on the sidelines as a quarterback and apparently you're going to go into your grave lying to me." I lean forward, pressing my hands on the desk, challenging him. "Do we amuse you, Father?"

He stands, mimicking my position, all signs of his sickness fading into the hard man that built an empire on secrets and lies. "I assure you, nothing about handing over the reins to Brandon Enterprises amuses me. If you can't second-guess your brother, you can't handle this company."

"I'm not competing with my brother and we both know it. I'm competing with you. It doesn't have to be this way. You have the power to change everything. Help me get us free of all this dirty money."

"Help you? Who'll help you when I'm gone? If you can't take what you want, then someone else will take it when I'm gone."

Our eyes connect and hold, a silent war between us, and while I pride myself on control, the absolute ability to contain what I feel, I am tested by this man who I both love and hate. He is destroying us, as cancer is destroying him. "Do the right thing before you die," I bite out. I turn and start walking, making a fast path to the door, my hand coming down on the knob.

"Shane." I pause, but do not turn as he adds, "Everything is not black and white, son. If you want to defeat those walking in the gray, you have to go there with them."

He's so beyond the gray, it's laughable, and with this budding cartel connection I'm certain he's involved with, it's more like black sludge. He will never repent his sins, and I'm done trying to convince him to change, let alone convince myself he's really on the sidelines. I'm not just at war with my brother. I'm at war with my father.

I turn the knob and exit the office, immediately aware of Emily at her desk. "Is he okay?" she asks.

"He's himself," I say, continuing on to the lobby, away from my father and away from Emily. I can't see her right now. Not with my family gutting me, and her pushing me away, no matter how smart she is for doing it. Because one touch from that woman, and I'll be selfish enough to fuck her until she forgets why she left that coffee shop without me. I know whatever she's running from can't be as lethal as the Brandons and the Martinas forming a partnership.

Passing through the lobby, I exit the offices and walk directly to the elevator bank, punching the call button. "Shane."

Emily's voice carries from the office doorway, radiating through me like silk and sandpaper and I do not look at her. The elevator doors open and I grind out, "Not now, Ms. Stevens," stepping into the elevator and leaving her behind. Inside, I face forward—and fuck me—she's standing in front of me.

"Shane."

My name is a plea on her lips and I have just enough time to get lost in her big, gorgeous blue eyes and her wounded expression before the doors shut between us. And somehow, some way, I remain aware of the cameras and don't react. I stand there like stone, waiting for the car to reach the garage, my mood throwing rocks around inside me. From one nerve to the next, I am bruised and beaten when the elevator finally jolts to a stop.

I step forward, a steel barrier preventing the escape I'm once again impatient to make. I'm on edge, in need of an outlet that allows me control. I need to run ten miles or fuck this hellish rage of emotions out of my system, but the only one that sounds right to do that with is Emily. Just Emily, who has come into my life and turned it a little more upside down. Finally the doors part, and I step outside to find Derek once again making an odd late-night return to the building. And once again, we meet in the middle of the garage.

"Ah, baby brother," he begins, reaching up to loosen his tie. "All these long hours and all for naught."

"Not now, Derek," I snap.

He narrows his gaze on me, his attention sharpening, and he seems to sense the foreboding in the air. "What is it?"

"The cancer has moved to his lungs. He's coughing up blood."

He inhales slowly, seeming resigned in his reaction. "Translate that to an outcome."

"He won't say much and he hasn't told Mom at all. Chemo starts Monday. That's all I was able to pry out of him."

"How do you know he's coughing up blood?"

"I saw it," I say, not about to bring Emily into this. "Which is why he had to tell me."

"Holy fuck," he curses, running a hand through his hair, and gives me his back, his face tilted toward the ceiling, struggling with the news that our father might pretend he doesn't have cancer, but he indeed does.

Seconds tick by and he faces me, laughing without humor, and scrubbing his jaw. "How can I hate that man so much and be gutted by the idea of him dying?"

"How can you hate him and want to be him, Derek?" I demand, the question setting me off. "Look at yourself. Look at what—"

He lets out a low growl and shoves me against the wall, concrete grinding against my back, his hands clutching my jacket. "You fucking bastard," he hisses. "Shut up. Shut the fuck up. I am not him."

"Right," I say dryly, my hands balled by my sides, his anger muting mine, driving me into courtroom mode. "And the sun doesn't come up every morning."

"I am *not* him," he bites out again, a charge barely contained just beneath his surface.

"No," I say, and not ready to tell him I know about the cartel, I settle on, "You're headed to much darker places and we both know it. Translation; dead or in jail, and one of those has no return."

He glares at me, his emotions pushing against mine, wanting a reaction, but it's in moments like these, when someone else loses it, that I excel and win. "What now, Derek?" I challenge softly.

"What indeed," he replies, his voice practically vibrating, before he abruptly releases me, putting several steps between us. "Wherever I go," he says, tugging his jacket straight, "if you stay here, you're going with me."

"I'm not going anywhere, *brother*, and mark my words, I'm not following you where you're headed, nor is this company."

His lips twist and he lets out a tight rasp of laughter. "You amuse me, *brother*. If our father dies tomorrow, I have the vote, and you'll be gone. And I'll do anything to make sure I keep that vote. *Anything*. And we both know you don't have the backbone to stop me."

He heads back to his car, and I'm not sure, but I think he just told me that he'd kill our father to ensure that vote happens when he wants it to happen. Or maybe he meant he'd kill me. I have no idea who Derek is at this point. He's damn sure not the brother I grew up idolizing. I'm halfway to my car when he speeds past me. I stop and stare after him, and the whirlwind of emotions I can't even name, which I've been suppressing not just today, but this whole damn year, begin a slow boil. I need the hell out of here. I need everything I can't have.

EMILY

An hour after Shane disappeared onto that elevator, shutting me out, I am still at my desk working on one edit after another to the deal memo his father is using for the hedge-fund recruits. Brandon Senior, on the other hand, busies himself rejecting every version I give him, in between hacks and phone calls. And being here is making me crazy, when all I can think about is Shane and the torment I'd seen in his eyes moments before that elevator had shut. Finally though, I think I've nailed it and I carry the memo into Mr. Brandon's office.

"Here you go," I say, setting it on his desk, noting the white ring around his lips and the ruddy look to his skin.

He glances down at it, scanning for several seconds before looking at me. "Finally, Ms. Stevens."

"I'm sorry, Mr. Brandon."

His brow arches. "Feisty this morning to submissive this evening. You know, don't you?"

"Know?" I ask cautiously. "Know what?"

"About my cancer."

"Yes," I say. "I know."

"Who told you?"

"You," I say, dodging a direct answer. "With the bloody cough."

"Who told you?" he pressed.

"Does it matter?"

His lips thin. "I suppose it doesn't. You may go, Ms. Stevens." I don't move, unsure I should leave him alone. He might be an asshole, but he's coughing up blood and he is Shane's father. He arches a brow at me. "Something you need, Ms. Stevens?"

"I'm not sure I should leave you."

His eyes glint hard. "If I drop dead, I'm sure you'll clean up the mess tomorrow. Get the fuck out of here."

The outburst jolts me and I rush across the room, exiting the workspace, having learned a big lesson. Concern pisses him off. I grab my purse and I don't bother to say good-bye, nor do I stop walking until I'm at the elevators, punching the button. The car to my left opens and Shane's mother exits.

"Mrs. Brandon," I greet, facing her, and she's still in her same black pantsuit, her hair and makeup still perfect.

"Emily," she greets me, finding her way to the space directly in front of me. "I was hoping to catch you. We should talk."

"Talk? About?"

"Are you aware my husband is sick?"

"Yes."

"Of course, you are. You're bright." She crosses her arms in front of her chest. "It's cancer and it's terminal."

" 'Terminal,' " I repeat. The word rings with a grimness I'd not quite fully digested until this moment. "Is it manageable?"

"He did a clinical trial and has done well, but I understand he's hiding worsening effects from me now. What do you know about that?"

"I know today was a bad day," I say, cautiously.

"That's a carefully weighed answer I can't afford." Her hands go to her hips. "Stick it out with him and I'll pay you a fifty thousand dollar bonus."

My eyes go wide. "Fifty thousand dollars?" Alarm bells go off in my head. "Why would you pay me that kind of money?"

"I need someone close to him I can trust and who won't leave."

"That you can trust?"

"That's right. You'd simply call me once a day and give me an update on his medical condition and the projects he's working on."

" 'The projects he's working on,' " I repeat. "Why would I do that?"

"I have to tidy things up if he suddenly crashes."

"No," I say quickly, not sure whose side she's on and not sure it matters. I'll protect Shane directly, not through a third party. "I can't do that." I punch the elevator button again. "I won't."

"It's *fifty thousand dollars.*"

"It's me becoming a spy in this war going on in this family. Who are you going to pass the information to? Derek or Shane?"

"You know more than I thought."

"It doesn't take much to figure out the obvious."

"This is for me and him."

And him. That seals the deal, because Brandon Senior sure as hell doesn't have Shane's best interest in mind. "No," I say. "And if this means you're going to fire me, I'll live with that."

She studies me several seconds, her expression unreadable, but there is a tiny quirk to her lips. "To be clear. Your answer is no."

"No," I repeat. "So if you're going to—"

"You're not fired, Emily. Have a good weekend." She turns away and walks toward the offices. I watch her until she disappears behind the glass doors, baffled by what just happened. The elevator dings and I give myself a mental shake before hurrying inside the car. Facing forward, the steel doors shut me inside, and I'm still thinking, *What just happened?* Was that a test to see if I can be bought? Or did she really mean to have me spy for her? I am still clueless when I step out of the car into the lobby.

At the front doors, I exit to a gust of wind laced with a chill us Texans call winter, while Coloradans seem to call it year-round. Vowing to buy a light jacket with my first paycheck, I find my way to Sixteenth Street, where I stop, my gaze finding the towering building that is the Four Seasons. Where Shane is and where I was with him. Where I want to be now, and suddenly, every reason I have for pushing him away feels small compared to the reality cancer delivers. Life can be short, a reality I've learned the hard way and I know he's faced with now himself. I can't stay away. I start walking and the next thing I know, I'm standing at the entryway of the hotel and Tai is greeting me.

"Emily. Good to see you. Do you want me to call upstairs and tell Mr. Brandon you're here, or is he coming down for you?"

"I'll call him from inside myself," I say. "Thank you."

"Of course. Let me know if I can do anything for you while you're here."

"I will. Thank you."

He steps aside, giving me a grand wave forward, and that's when my nerves kick in. Shane isn't expecting me and he told me he'd had second thoughts about us, going so far as to tell me to stay away from him. And I should. I know that, but I just . . . can't. Not tonight. I move through the lobby, digging my phone from my purse, and it hits me that at any moment, Brandon Senior could appear. It's not likely, after his wife joined him at the office, but it's possible. That has me double-stepping and rounding the corner to the elevator bank and punching in Shane's number, each ring radiating through me with a new push of nerves.

"Emily," he says when he answers, his voice sounding raspy.

"I'm downstairs, by your elevators, and I'm really nervous about your father returning and seeing me. Please come get me."

"You're here."

"Yes. I'm here."

Silence follows, stretching eternally it seems, before he says, "Don't move." The line goes dead. He's on his way down and I'm not sure if it's to tell me to go or ensure that I stay.

You weren't supposed to walk away no more . . .

—Tommy Agro

CHAPTER THIRTEEN

EMILY

The elevator door opens and Shane appears, dressed in black sweats and a black T-shirt, his tennis shoes unlaced as if he'd thrown on clothes to come and get me. My eyes meet his and the connection is a charge that lights up my body. What this man makes me feel is simply indescribable and I suddenly can't breathe for the impact of seeing him.

"Come here," he orders softly.

I don't hesitate, crossing the small space between us and stopping in front of him where he holds the doors open. "Why are you here?" he asks, and he doesn't reach for me or touch me when *I want* him to touch me. And I want to touch him perhaps more than I have ever wanted to touch anyone.

"You know why," I reply.

His response is no response. He stands there, towering over me, searching my expression, looking for something I hope he finds. Sincerity maybe? A lie I'm not telling this time? I do not know but I am certain whatever he finds will decide if I go upstairs with him. "I *couldn't* stay away and the truth is, I didn't want to."

There is a flicker of emotion, or perhaps a glint, in his eyes, and then he's dragging me to him, inside the elevator, and he's keying in his floor. Another quick maneuver later, I'm in the corner of the elevator, his powerful legs pinning mine, his hands on the wall above me, instead of on me.

"*Why* are you here?" he repeats, that dark energy I'd felt in him the first night he'd fought with his brother back tenfold.

"I told you. I couldn't stay away. And . . ." I hesitate a moment on a confession, a piece of myself I'm supposed to deny now, but I can't. Not with him and what I know of his father now. "And because," I continue, "my father killed himself and I know what it's like to love and hate a parent at the same time. And I know how that guts you and fills you with guilt."

I have barely said the words and his hands are framing my face, and again, he is looking at me, but not with a question this time, but rather with shock that fades into heat and desire, and then he is kissing me, deeply, completely. And he lets me taste the guilt I've proclaimed to understand. The anger, which I know and expect, is there too. Hot. Fierce. Intense and barely contained. It is raw, the way I know his emotions have to be as well and I am certain he wants to drive them away, at least for now. For a moment in time that lets him forget what will never truly be gone.

The elevator dings and he tears his mouth from mine, lacing our fingers together and leading me into the hallway without stopping. With purpose in his steps, he walks toward his apartment, and I am right there with him. I am ready to be alone with him, to revel in every second I have with this man. I know it can't last. And I am ready to be the way he escapes and finds just a little peace in the war that rages in his reality.

By the time we are at the door my heart is racing and my knees are weak, not from nerves, but from the pulse of energy radiating between us. He opens the door and we are inside his dark apartment at almost the same moment. He releases me then, leaving me chilled in all the places he'd made me warm, which is pretty much everywhere. The door shuts behind me, sealing our deal to spend this night together. A moment later, maybe two, Shane's hands settle on my arms, and before I know what is happening, I'm facing the wall, my purse clattering to the floor, my hands pressed to the hard surface in front of me. He steps into me, his big body cradling mine, wrapped around me, hard where I am soft. Right in every way that nothing could ever make wrong.

"We're going to fuck. Just fuck and I need you to tell me you know that."

"I'm the one who said—"

"*Say it.*"

"I understand."

"*Say* it."

"We're just fucking."

He leans in closer, his breath a warm tickle on my neck, his voice a firm demand. "You do what I say. You trust me. Without question." *Trust.* It is not something I give easily, and yet, I sense that this isn't about just wanting my trust. It's not even really about trust, but rather the control death steals from you.

"Emily—" he begins.

"Yes," I say. "You can have the control."

"I asked for trust."

"Same thing," I say, and he must not disagree, as he unzips my skirt, letting it fall to the ground, and already he's dragging my jacket down my shoulders, his fingers caressing my skin and leaving goose bumps in their wake. I shiver and oh so easily, I am lost, not in worries or fears, but in this man, a thunderstorm of emotions and sensations assaulting my senses. There is no time for anything else but him, no room, and already my shirt has fallen to the ground, my bra is unhooked. Another blink, and

Shane is on one knee, his fingers twining in the lace strips at my hips, dragging my panties down to my ankles. I have an instant to realize just how naked I am, inside and out, before his teeth scrape my backside, and I moan with the tightening of my sex and nipples. I've barely recovered from a rush of pleasure, before he's standing again, lifting me, and kicking aside my clothing, my shoes lost in the process.

And then he is turning me to face him, tearing away my bra, his hands bracketing my waist, eyes lowering to rake over my breasts, then lifting to my face. "Trust has to be earned. Control can be taken and if you think control and trust are the same thing, you've been with the wrong man. I'm not the wrong man. At least, not tonight."

"No," I agree. "You are not the wrong man."

"No, I am not, but right now, I just need to fuck. Hard and fast, and then we'll do it right."

"Hard and fast is right, if that's what you need."

"What do *you* need?"

"You," I say, repeating what he'd said to me that first night we were together. "Just you."

His eyes darken and he tugs his shirt off over his head. Before it even hits the ground, my hands are on his chest, fingers nestled in the springy hair there, heat seeping from his body, to mine. He cups my head and kisses me, and I sink into him, melting . . . Oh yes, I am melting into one big puddle of lust and desire, free in a way with this man that is indescribably different than with the men of my past. The way everything is indescribably different with Shane. And he is touching me, caressing me, pinching my nipples one moment, his fingers in the slick wet heat of my sex the next. We are wild. We are ready for more and more and more, but he pulls back, pressing his hands on the wall behind me. "Holy fuck. I don't have a condom."

"I'm on the pill," I blurt out, and quickly add, "I don't do unprotected sex. I just . . . I'm on the pill. I swear to you. The last thing I want is to get pregnant."

He cups my face. "For who?"

"What?"

"Who did you go on the pill for?"

"Me. I did it for me."

"Are you running from a man who's going to show back up?"

"No. God no, Shane. And if we're just fucking why does it matter anyway?"

"Don't talk," he says, his voice low, gravelly, his mouth slanting over mine. And then he is kissing me, and there is more than guilt on his lips now. There is hunger, lust, *demand*. And I answer him, holding nothing back, wild, frenzied, and everything is a whirlwind of sensation that burns through me until there is nothing but my hands on him and his on me. Somehow, his clothes are fully gone, and I'm against the wall, or the front door I think, and he is inside me, cupping my backside and lifting me. I respond instantly, my legs automatically wrap around his waist, and I don't know how, or why, but we still, our bodies locked together, our breathing heavy whispers, coming together as one. *We* are one in this moment, two people lost and found in each other, both of us fighting a battle the other understands in ways no one else can.

Seconds tick by, and he whispers, "What the hell are you doing to me?" but I never get the chance to ask him the same. He lifts me off the wall, one hand pressing between my shoulder blades, molding me to him, the other cupping my backside as he pulls me down on the hard thick ridge of his erection, and thrusts into me again. I pant, curling forward and holding on to him, burying my face in his neck. And then we are moving, swaying, a grind to our hips, a raw urgency to every glide and pump, the sounds he is making, low, guttural, and oh so sexy, driving me to the edge. Tension builds between us, and in my sex, that sweet spot spiking my nerve endings, and pushing me to that place of no return. My sex clenches like a vise around his shaft; every muscle in my body tenses with it. He groans, his hands flexing into my back and bottom, and he starts to shake. I think I am shaking too, and everything fades into bliss. I don't know how much time goes by until I come to the present. And he is back too. I feel it like I feel him.

"Hold on," he murmurs, carrying me deeper into the darkness of the apartment. I don't know where he is taking me, and I don't care. I want more of him, wherever that takes us. Turns out, that's the bathroom off the living room, where he flips on a light, and sets me on the counter by the sink. He grabs a towel, offering it to me before he pulls out, and snatches another to clean himself up, before tossing it into the hamper. "Stay right here," he orders, already disappearing into the other room.

I glance around a bathroom similar to the one upstairs, in that it's all white, but this one is smaller with an egg-shaped tub. My mind is on how completely naked I feel right now, and how unsure I am about what to expect next. Shane returns, his sweatpants back in place, a T-shirt in his hand that he slips over my head. "Your uniform of my choice," he says when it's in place, resting his hands on either side of me. "I'm glad you're here."

"You are?"

"Yes," he says. "I am."

"So am I." I hesitate on what I want to say, but only for a moment. "You said trust is different than control."

"It is and I fully intend to show you how."

"And trust is important to you because of your family."

"Right again."

"Then I really need to tell you a few things."

I expect some sort of reaction, perhaps withdrawal in anticipation of what I might say, but he simply settles his hands on my waist. "I'm listening."

"I know you said we're just fucking, but——"

"Because I needed, *we needed*, to 'just fuck,' not because we're the equation of a few random fucks. Be clear, sweetheart, for my part and I am sure yours, I could have called any number of fuck buddies tonight. I didn't and that was because they aren't you, and therefore they aren't what I needed."

It's everything I want to hear, and yet . . . "I'm confused, Shane. At the office, you said we are a problem, because your family is a problem."

"Trouble doesn't begin to describe my family, but I'll be damned if I want to give you up right now."

Right now. Inferring that he still intends to give me up later, which makes the confession I'd been about to make irrelevant. But I get him and understand where he's at. His father is dying. He needs someone *right now*. Maybe he actually needs that to be me for some reason, and I want to be that someone. I reach up and cup his cheek. "I don't want to give you up right now either."

"Well then," he says. "I vote we order room service and actually enjoy it this time."

"I'd like that," I say, and he lifts me off the sink, setting me on the ground in front of him, but we don't move. We stand there, the way we do sometimes it seems, staring at each other. I know that we've just said we are all about *right now*, inferring later won't matter, but there is something shifting between us, something warm and wondering, I don't understand, but I want and need.

He reaches down, lacing his fingers with mine, his lips slowly beginning to curve. My lips curve too, and suddenly, we're smiling for no reason. He leads me forward, holding on to me as we walk, and I think that is part of what really gets to me with Shane. He holds on to me like he's afraid he'll lose me, when no one else does or cares.

We reach the living room and I sit down on the couch.

Shane doesn't immediately join me, instead handing me a throw blanket before using a remote that ignites a sleek, glass-paneled fireplace in the far right corner. "I'll grab the menu," he says, leaving me feeling cozy and safe in a way I haven't been in a very long time. *He* makes me feel safe, which is probably why I've told him things I shouldn't have. Why I want to tell him everything, but I can't bear the idea he will hate me, or he'll end up hurt.

"Here we go," Shane says, placing the hardcover menu on the table in front of me. "How about a drink?"

"I better not. I'm a lightweight and I might not make it home."

"A drink it is," he says, placing his phone on top of the menu. "Room service is programmed in my numbers. Call down and order my regular egg white omelet and whatever you want. I'll get the drinks."

I twist around to follow his progress to the bar behind me. "I feel like I'm invading your privacy tabbing through your phone."

"If I was worried about it," he says, casting me a sideways look as he opens a glass decanter, "I wouldn't give it to you."

I wouldn't give it to me is the problem. Trapped in a huge lie and falling for a man who is swimming in a sea of those very same monsters, I leave the phone on the table, and wait for what turns out to be his quick return. "Cognac," he announces, claiming the spot next to me, and setting two glasses on the table, before giving me a curious look. "You didn't order the food, did you?"

"Let's just drink," I say, picking up a glass and downing the sweet, potent liquid.

"Emily," he says, softly, setting the glass on the table. "What's wrong?"

I'm lying to you and I need to be honest in every way I can, I think, but I say, "We were talking about trust. Remember?"

"I remember," he says, his tone cautious now.

"Okay then. Confession time. When I said I could never forgive you this morning, I'd already forgiven you. I just thought I had to do that to keep you away."

"And you did that why?"

"There are things in my life I can't and won't involve you in."

He reaches over and strokes a lock of hair behind my ear. "What if I want to be involved?"

"You barely know me."

"But I want to know you." His voice is low, a silk caress on my raw nerve endings. "I'm not going to press you now, but when you're ready, you *can* trust me."

"It's not that simple." And oh how I wish it were.

"I'll make it simple."

But he can't make this simple and I quickly change the subject, before he doesn't let me. "Your mother cornered me at the office tonight."

His reaction is to down his drink, refilling it, and hand mine back to me. I follow his lead, emptying my glass, a fog begging to take over my brain. "Whatever that is tastes good but I better stop before I forget how bad of a drinker I am."

"Tomorrow's Saturday," he says. "And I'll take care of you. Have another."

"I don't need to be taken care of, Shane."

"Tonight, with me, you do. Trust me enough to let that be okay."

"*Trust.* There you go with that word again. You keep saying it."

"I guess I do." He empties his glass again.

Now I give him a curious look. "You haven't asked what happened with your mother."

"What happened is, my father refuses to let me tell her the cancer has moved from his brain to his lungs."

"Brain?" I gasp, setting down my glass. "He has brain cancer?"

"Yes. And after six months of knowing, it still seems unreal."

"How can he have complete mental clarity if it's bad enough to have moved?"

"Complete mental clarity?" He laughs without humor. "That's debatable. What happened with my mother?"

"I don't want to tell you now."

"Nothing can shock me with my family."

"I'm not so sure but okay. She offered me fifty thousand dollars to stick it out with your father through his illness and report to her on all of his activities."

He pauses with the glass to his lips, lowering it to ask, "And what did you say?"

"My answer was no and she thought I was crazy, especially when I told her she could fire me."

"And she said?"

"That I'm not fired and for me to have a good weekend. I'm not sure if she was testing me or really trying to use me."

"Why did you decline? That would have paid for a good portion of law school."

"That's not how I want to pay for school. Unless you want me to help her? Because unless you tell me otherwise, the only person I'm giving information to is you and I'll do that directly."

"Don't give her anything," he says, his statement all but confirming he doesn't trust his mother, but then he turns around and sideswipes me with, "I'll pay you the money."

Insulted and hurt, I'm on my feet in an instant, the blanket falling away, but he shackles my wrist, dragging me down to the couch. "Fuck you, Shane," I hiss, twisting around to face him. "I can't be bought with sex or money."

"I didn't mean it like that. You were loyal to me and I want to take care of you."

"I told you. I don't need to be taken care of."

"And yet you took care of me by texting me that tip about Nina and refusing to feed information to my mother that could go to my brother. How is it wrong of me to want to protect you?"

"I don't want your money."

"All right. I'm sorry. It was just my instinct to give you what you gave up for me." He lowers his forehead to mine. "Forgive me."

The apology tears down the wall I've instinctively erected, my anger sliding away with it, my hand curling on his cheek. "Yes."

Leaning back, he cups my face to look at me. "Thank you for what you did." He leans in and brushes his lips over mine, his hands slipping under my shirt, *his shirt*, to scorch my bare skin. "Thank you for coming here tonight." He drags the T-shirt over my head, tossing it aside, his gaze and fingers instantly on my nipples, which tighten with electric sensations. "I won't bribe you with money," he promises, his sizzling stare lifting to mine, "but sex is another story."

"What exactly is it that you want to bribe me for?"

"I haven't decided yet." He lowers me to the couch, the deliciously heavy weight of him settling on top of me. "But," he continues, "I am certain no answer I'll come up with, including giving you your clothes back, will come to me any time soon." His mouth closes down on mine, his tongue doing a sultry slide past my lips. I think right now I'd give him anything he'd ask for. Even the revelation of my secret, which I know I'd live to regret. And so would Shane.

This is the life we chose, the life we lead. And there is only one guarantee: none of us will see heaven.

—*John Rooney*

CHAPTER FOURTEEN

SHANE

I wake on the couch where Emily has fallen asleep on top of me, the dim lights I never turned off glowing around us. I hear her murmuring, "No. No. No. It can't be true. No!"

"Emily, sweetheart," I say, stroking her hair.

"No! No, I—"

"Emily," I say more firmly. "You're having a nightmare."

She jerks up, her hand pressed to my chest, her naked body draped over mine. "What happened?" She shuts her eyes. "Nightmare. It was a nightmare, right?"

"Yes. Do you have them often?"

"Yes. What time is it?"

I glance at my watch. "Three o'clock in the morning."

"I . . . should go."

I tighten my arm around her waist. "You're not going anywhere, sweetheart." And I'm surprised at how vehemently I say those words and *mean them.* "Not unless you plan on me going with you."

Her eyes flicker with some emotion I want to name but never get the chance. She eases back down, pressing her cheek to my chest. I rest my hand on her head and back, capturing one of her legs with mine. "You want to talk about it?"

"No," she says, her fingers curling in my chest hair. "I most definitely do not want to talk about it."

My nature is to press for answers, and I want to know Emily inside and out, but I read people well, and if I push her too hard, she will run again. I settle for holding her, listening to her breathing slow, reveling in the feel of holding her close, this woman who has taken me by storm and managed to be the cool breeze in the midst of my personal hell. Only when I am certain she's asleep do I shut my eyes and let my mind go to the place it resists. I can only assume that Derek is watching me as I am him, and he'll know Emily was here. The question is, how will he handle that information? My mind starts chasing the possibilities, and I lose myself in my thoughts. They fade into the sound of her breathing and the darkness that transforms into the past.

It's only one week before college entrance exams and I get the flipping flu and then manage to lose my house key. Feeling like absolute hell is not the time to do this shit. I walk around the back of the house where I hope the door is unlocked. It might not be, considering my brother is off at college, my mother is off on some girls' weekend trip, and my father is never home. I reach for the knob, and hell yes! It's open. I enter the house, and head straight to the kitchen for something to drink, stopping dead in my tracks. I blink, not sure I'm seeing what is in front of me. But I am. Our neighbor, and my friend's mother, is naked on our counter and my father's pants are around his ankles while he bangs her.

"You sorry son of a bitch," I growl, turning away before I beat the shit out of him, and leave the house. Fighting the urge to turn back around and pound him, I take off running, and I don't stop until the nausea hits me a good few blocks away. I turn the corner and enter a park. I find a tree to collapse underneath before dialing Derek and hoping like hell he's not in class.

"What's up, brother?" he answers.

"I just walked in on Dad fucking our neighbor."

"Oh shit man. Congrats."

"Congrats? What the fuck is that, Derek?"

"You just scored hush money, or that Mustang Cobra you wanted."

"Hush money?"

"How do you think I got my Porsche? I know something he doesn't want me to tell."

"You think this is okay?"

"It is what it is, Shane. You'll figure that out in time. When something goes wrong, find a way to get something out of it. Take the Mustang and keep your mouth shut."

I come back to the present in a rush of sunlight and the sound of my cell phone ringing. I inhale Emily's sweet scent, and feel the knot of guilt lodged in my chest for never telling my mother about that day. I wonder if she'd have really cared any more than she does today. The ringing stops and I glance at my watch. Seven A.M. That, and Emily's naked body pressed to mine, inspire me to close my eyes and attempt to go back to sleep. The ringing starts again, the persistence upping the chances it's Seth and thus important. Reluctantly, I ease Emily off me, her naked breasts brushing my hand. Her soft moan is pure sex that has my body thickening in uncomfortable demand.

"It's daylight," Emily murmurs groggily, rolling into my spot as I stand. "How did it get to be daylight?"

"Good question," I say, grabbing my phone off the end table, checking my screen to find my caller is indeed Seth, and I've missed him again.

"Waking up to your naked ass is quite possibly the best thing ever," Emily declares, sounding much more awake now.

Smiling, I step into my pants, turning to face her. "You can prove it in a few minutes. I need to make a call." I don't wait for a reply, hitting the redial button and heading for the stairs, only to have the line go direct to voice mail. "Call me back," I say at the beep, stuffing my cell back into my pocket and walking into the bathroom.

Once I'm there, I shut the door, take care of the necessities, including brushing my teeth, and then dial Seth again, and just like before, his voice mail picks up. Intending to return to Emily, I turn and open the door to find her standing just outside in my T-shirt.

"You have to leave, because I have to pee like a Russian race-horse and I already committed to this bathroom."

Laughing, I step past her to enter the bedroom. "I don't think I've ever heard a woman say anything remotely close to that."

"My father used to say it," she calls over her shoulder, before turning to face me. "I forgot it's not really ladylike, but . . ." Shadows cloud her blue eyes. "It was my father's thing." She shuts the door.

Unmoving, I stare at the place she was moments before, remembering her nightmare. With her father on her mind, it seems a good guess that he might have been at its core. And while that might or might not be true, I do believe her claim that she understands what I feel with my father more than anyone, besides perhaps Derek. She gets me in a way I've never allowed anyone to get me, and I don't remember when I ever decided to let her. *Holy hell*, what am I doing with this woman, and why can't I stop? My cell phone starts ringing and I shake off the thought, digging it from my pocket and heading back down the stairs.

"Talk to me," I order.

"The equipment's installed and I've targeted several employees I think can be bought. I should have answers later today."

I enter the kitchen and make a beeline to the coffeepot and

flip the switch I had set to go off in an hour. "I *need* answers today."

"I know it's urgent."

"Today, Seth," I say, pressing my hands to the counter. "The cancer has moved to his lungs. He could fall apart at any moment and right now Derek would claim control. I can't let that happen. And without Mike Rogers on our side, I need to deal with the rest of the stockholders."

"We have a plan for them."

"If it's as good as the one for Riker, we don't have shit."

"Riker and the trucking company are both targets for Martina's operation. That means he was on Derek's radar way before us. The others won't be."

"You don't know that. I told you. Don't underestimate my brother or my father. I can't wait for you to handle this. You need to handpick select people from your security team and get them to the other key stockholders."

"I don't trust anyone to handle this but me. Give me until tonight before you make me do that."

My jaw clenches. "Fine. Tonight." I end the call and set the phone down, rotating to find Emily standing in the entryway. "How much of that did you hear?"

She walks toward me, joining me on this side of the island to lean on it next to me. "Too much, I think."

At least she's honest. "How much of an ass do you think I am now?"

"I don't think you're an asshole, Shane."

I rub the stubble on my jaw. "Then you must not have heard it all."

"I'm pretty sure I did and this is no different than a courtroom brawl. You're at war and war is not pleasant." She glances at the pot. "Please tell me that isn't as thick and strong as car oil."

"It's a Starbucks blend." She moves toward the pot and I drag her to me. "Why are you not asking questions?"

"I don't need to ask questions."

"Because you don't want me to ask you questions?"

"I might be guilty of that at times, but not this time. I've met Derek. I've looked into his eyes and into yours, and you're the better man. You need to win and more so, I understand what you're going through. I know how family can gut you."

"Gut" is a powerful word and I'm not sure if we're talking about her father, or something more, but I stick with one piece of the puzzle at a time. "How old were you when your father died?"

"When he killed himself?" She doesn't wait for a reply. "Fourteen and he was . . ."

"He was what?"

She cuts her gaze away and her fingers flex into my chest, as if she's pushing me away, but she doesn't. "Nothing," she murmurs, not looking at me. "I need that coffee."

I hold on to her, and damn it to hell, I want to push, but I check myself and release her. She is quick to step away from me, moving to the coffeepot. I join her and reach to the cabinet above her head, pulling out two generic mugs and setting them on the counter. There is something about having her here with me in my kitchen that is right in a way I've never let myself—or even wanted to—experience. She reaches for the pot, but I step between her and it, shackling her hips and aligning our bodies. "Remember when I said I don't do relationships?"

"Or two dogs and six kids."

My lips quirk. "Six kids?"

"Six dogs?"

"You're crazy, woman."

"Because I haven't had coffee," she jokes, but then turns somber. "In all seriousness though, Shane. I still get it. No relationship. Just sex. I get that this isn't a good time for you."

"It's never been a good time for me, Emily, and that extends to well before I moved back to Denver."

"I understand."

"No. You don't. I don't do relationships, but I seem to do you, and us, exceptionally well." I cup her face. "Spend the weekend with me."

"What?"

"Spend the weekend with me. I have to get some work done, but I can do it here. We'll hide out, order room service, and stay naked as much as possible."

"Naked. Well, since you put it that way."

My lips curve with approval. "All right then. One more question. Coffee first or sex first?"

Her eyes light with amusement. "I hear coffee makes sex better."

"Coffee it is," I say, releasing her and reaching for the pot to fill our cups.

"Please tell me you have cream and sugar."

"Plenty of both." I open the cabinet and set two boxes in front of her.

"Thanks," she says, eyeing the boxes before emptying several packets of sugar into her cup. "You mentioned work you have to do. I can help you if you'll let me."

"If you don't mind researching drug companies and marketable products, I'd love the extra set of hands."

"I don't mind at all. The whole pharmaceutical side of things sounds interesting, but I do need to run to my apartment and grab some clothes and my flat iron. I can't be a frizzy mess with the same clothes on all weekend." She sets her cup down. "In fact, I should go do that now and get it over with."

"I'll drive you," I offer, certain I can get us in and out of here with more discretion by car than on foot. And I'm damn sure not blurting out a warning about Derek—that needs to be well timed and thoughtful.

"I can walk," she says, her hands settling at the back of her hips. "I'll just run to my place and come back here."

"It makes sense for me to drive you," I insist.

"It makes sense for me to walk and avoid the hassle of getting the car from the garage."

I narrow my eyes on her. "You really don't want me at your apartment, do you?"

Her cheeks flush. "It's barely furnished, Shane. It's embarrassing."

I step to her, my hands settling on her waist, hers on my chest. "You don't have to be embarrassed with me."

"Your world is not my world."

"Considering you're in my T-shirt, that's debatable, but for now, you need clothes." I release her and pick up my phone from the counter to punch the button for Tai. "A problem easily solved."

"Solved how?" she asks, stepping to me, her hands urgently settling at my waist. "What are you doing, Shane?"

"Mr. Brandon," Tai answers. "What can I do for you?"

"Morning, Tai," I say, sliding my hand to her back and molding her close. "Emily needs a weekend wardrobe."

"No!" she hisses softly. "No, I do not."

"Running gear and casual attire," I continue as if she hasn't spoken.

"Of course," he replies. "I can send some things up from our spa immediately. Her shoe size would be helpful."

I eye Emily. "What size shoes?"

"Shane. No."

I cover the phone. "Sweetheart. We're doing this. What size?"

A conflicted look flickers over her face. "Seven."

"Seven," I repeat to Tai, "and she wants a flat iron and whatever you think she might need this weekend."

"Give me a half an hour."

"Perfect." I end the call as Emily shoves away from me, holding up her hands stop-sign fashion.

"I'll let you drive me to my apartment," she declares. "I'm sorry. You were right. I'm a crazy person. Please. Call him back."

"I'm not calling him back."

"I have my own clothes."

I gently shackle her wrist and close the distance between us. "And I prefer you naked. Actually, maybe I should call back and throw the rest of your clothes on top of the lights outside."

"I'm serious, Shane," she warns.

"So am I." My cell phone rings again and I cup her face, kissing her hard and fast, and set her away from me to look at the caller ID. "I wish like hell I could drown this thing for the weekend," I say, punching the answer button. "Why are you calling on a Saturday, Jessica?"

" 'Thank you for working Saturdays, Jessica. Your dedication is commendable, Jessica, and you come through even when your boss is being an asshole.' There's a penthouse apartment that's releasing to the market this afternoon in the heart of Cherry Creek. It's amazing, Shane, and it'll be gone in a blink. You have to go look at it. It has everything. Shopping. Food. A doorman. A balcony to rival the one you have now. I'm trying to convince them to give you a preview showing today."

"Today? That's not happening. Set it up for Monday."

"If I can convince him to do today, someone else can as well. It has to be today. I'm e-mailing you the photos I just took. The realtor can see you in the next hour if you can be there. Call me after you look at it, but I think this is the one. Make the time, Shane."

I grab my MacBook where it's sitting on the island and open it. "If I like the photos I'll go see it."

"I wouldn't be on the phone right now if I didn't know you were going to like the photos."

Of course, she wouldn't. This is Jessica. "I'll let you know," I say, ending the call and setting my phone next to my computer.

Emily offers me my cup of coffee. "I warmed it up," she says, the tiny act of intimacy I've avoided with other women remarkably welcome with her.

I accept it, the touch of our hands electric in a way I'm truly not accustomed to beyond the moment before sex. "Thank you," I say, the air thickening around us.

"Of course," she murmurs, her teeth scraping her bottom lip. "Why are you arguing with Jessica?"

"Because that's what we do," I say, taking a drink before setting the cup down and pulling up my e-mail.

"She's pretty fiery."

"What she is," I say, "is a pain in my ass who's insisting I look at a property today." I find the photos Jessica has sent, download them, and angle the computer so we can both see them. "What do you think?" I ask, tabbing through shots of a blue glass building and an apartment with enough windows to make this one look like it needs light.

"I freaking love it. We both know you want out of this hotel and the ties that bind you here. You have to go look at it."

She's right. I do and I want to take her with me, which I can't fairly do without her understanding that we're under my family's scrutiny. I face her, and she responds by doing the same with me, both of us resting an arm on the counter. "Go with me to look at the apartment." The doorbell rings and I grimace at the poorly timed interruption I should have anticipated. "That will be your clothes." I've barely said the words when my cell starts ringing again and I grab it to glance at the screen. "And *that* would be my mother."

"I'll get the door," Emily says, already moving away, but I catch her arm, cup her head, and give her a deep, fast kiss.

"Now you can get the door," I say, releasing her to answer my call. "You're up early this morning, Mother."

"I don't like it either, but it happens on occasion."

"Well, since it happened and you called me, I hope this means you have information on Mike Rogers."

"I'm working on it, but I thought we should talk about your father's new assistant, Emily."

It's almost comical how fast my family works. "You offered her fifty thousand dollars to be a snitch and she declined," I say, making it clear Emily is more than just in my bed. She's in my ear. I'm claiming her with the intent of backing Derek the fuck off.

"While I commend your innovation, son, your brother knows she's with you this morning. She's no longer your secret source of information and he's already planning to feed her a load of crap to repeat to you."

Derek's words from my dream come back to me. *When something goes wrong, find a way to get something out of it.* And I just did. I can assure Emily that Derek now sees her as a resource, not a target. "Does Father know?"

"You aren't going to comment about Derek feeding you crap for information?"

"He'll never hide everything," I say, and again ask, "Unless Father knows?"

"I don't know, but I assume he does. Derek seems more confident than usual about their alignment and his vote."

"And you know this because he trusted you enough to tell you." It's not a question.

"I'm his mother. He's my son."

"Whom you're betraying by telling me this right now."

"I'm protecting our futures. And I'm protecting you or I wouldn't be on the phone right now."

And yet trusting her is becoming harder. "Protecting us all is about those stockholders. When will you get that information you promised me on Mike and the other stockholders?"

"Chemo tends to weaken your father and loosen his tongue."

"You know his cancer has worsened."

"Of course, I know," she says. "He was a fool to try to keep it from me. Chemo starts Monday morning."

"I know that. You're seriously using his cancer to take advantage of him? Aren't you the one who was worried I'd hurt him if I turned down the Bentley while he was weak from treatments?"

"That was before he used his cancer to pit my sons against each other. A mother's wrath you do not want. And on that note, I'm going back to bed, but a word for the wise that I know you know, but might forget with Emily: everyone is not who or what they seem, and once someone is in your bed, they're dangerously close to you. Watch your back with that woman."

She ends the call.

I can't stand squealers . . .

—*Albert Anastasia*

CHAPTER FIFTEEN

SHANE

I slide my phone into my pocket and wait for my mother's warning about Emily to hit a nerve, my brother's words replaying in my mind: *I know who's in my corner. I wonder if you do.* He'd meant to make me question everyone around me but my distrust doesn't go to Emily for one minute. My instincts are, and have always been, razor sharp, and I trust her. My mother is another story, and her hiring a mistress for my father proves her to be conniving in ways, as a young man, I wasn't willing to see. Whatever the case, Emily deserves to know what she's in the middle of now, not later.

Exiting the kitchen into the foyer, I note she is absent, and I head toward the stairs to find her sitting on the bottom step, her long, brown hair disheveled, as if she's had her hands in it, a collection of mixed-sized paper bags around her. "What are you doing?" I ask, going down on a knee in front of her.

"I can't go with you to see that apartment. Someone could see us who shouldn't and I can't get fired until I have another job. As it is, I was worried your father would be back here with that woman and see me last night. I wasn't thinking this morning, but that could have happened if I left and came back too."

"That's why I suggested I drive you, rather than walk."

"Why didn't you just say that?"

"It didn't feel like the right time, but I was about to talk about this when the doorbell interrupted us."

"The truth is, I *am* hiding from some things in my life, trying to start fresh, and I can't hide from this too. A weekend here, with you, is an escape, but it can't be the reason I lose a job I need. And I can't do this anymore. *We* can't do this anymore."

My hands settle on the bare skin of her knees just beneath my shirt. "You're not going to get fired."

"If your father finds out—"

"He'll be amused," I say.

"Amused?" she asks, her brow furrowing.

"He's intentionally pitted me and Derek against each other and now he sits back and watches, all but holding a bucket of popcorn. Bottom line, if he finds out, he'll think I'm using you to feed me information about his activities and my brother's. In other words, a point on the scoreboard for me. That's what Derek has already assumed."

Her eyes go wide. "Your brother knows?"

"Yes. I knew he would the minute you came here last night. That's what my mother called to tell me."

"*Oh my God.* Your mother knows too." She presses her hand to her belly. "I feel sick."

I reach for her hand, and close mine around it. "This does not affect your job."

"I cannot even comprehend the words coming out of your mouth."

I laugh and she is not pleased.

"This is not funny," she hisses. "This is beyond outrageous."

"My family is fucked up, Emily."

"Won't Derek get me fired?"

"He's planning to feed you fake information about his take-over plans to give to me."

"And you know this because of your mother?"

"Exactly."

"You're right. Your family really is fucked up."

"They are, but there's a light at the end of this tunnel. Frankly, this helps us both."

"I'm back to the part where I don't understand the words coming out of your mouth. Because if this is true, I won't be able to give you proper information."

I blink, stunned at her reaction. "You aren't going to question my motives?"

"Are you kidding me? The more I get to know your family, the more I'm amazed you ever gave me a chance to prove I wasn't working for them."

"The truth was in your eyes," I say softly.

"And yours," she says. In the moments that follow, it is as if trust takes shape in a delicate slice of glass too fragile at this point to be called unbreakable. The fact that this trust is more than I have with my family is bittersweet.

"You wanted to know how this helps us," I say, not expecting a reply. "If Derek, and my father for all I know, think they have me chasing my tail, they won't be watching my moves as closely, or have their guard up as readily. You're an asset they want to keep."

"I thought you said this was a game for your father? You just made it sound like he supports Derek taking over the company rather than you."

"He'll play both sides because it amuses him," I say. "Where his true allegiance lies I have no idea, and I am pretty sure he'll go to the grave without that changing."

"That's how he wants to leave this world?" she asks, incredulously. "Most people try to make amends with those they love."

"I'm sure he has the capacity to love, but whatever his agenda, you and I are simply more entertainment for him. Your job is secure and there is no reason we can't continue to see each other."

"Continue seeing each other," she repeats.

"We're *good* together. I want to know where that goes, but I also want to know you made a choice, not a decision."

"I don't understand."

"Choices come with options, while decisions are too often forced by circumstances. I'm going to give you choices. Piss my father off? He fires you and legally gives you severance, while my brother has no reason to believe you're anything but an informant I lost. You'll be gone and forgotten."

"Forgotten," she echoes, her lashes lowering, a defensive act meant to prevent me from seeing what she doesn't want me to see.

"Not by me," I say.

She looks at me, and anything I could have read in her stare is no longer present. "Is getting fired what you think I should do?"

"I can't give you an objective answer."

"Why?"

"Because the only way we sell you being nothing more than a lost informant to me is if I stay away from you."

"What do you want me to do?"

"Stay. Now ask what I think is smart."

"Leaving is smart," she says. "And that would be easier if you just stop making me feel . . ."

"Making you feel what?"

"Something."

"Something," I reiterate, and I weigh that word on my tongue, deciding it needs no further definition. But whatever it is, it's pure in a way that nothing else in my life is—or has been—in far too long and I'm not letting my brother force her into hiding, when it's clear she's already doing that on her own.

I stand, taking her with me, my fingers lacing snugly with hers. "Come," I command softly, leading her up the stairs, through the bedroom, and into the bathroom, stopping at the glass-encased shower next to the tub.

Releasing her hand, my fingers find the hem of my T-shirt she's wearing, caressing it upward, my fingers trailing over her skin to pull it over her head and toss it aside. It hasn't even hit the ground when my hands are on her slender waist, my gaze raking over her high breasts and pebbled plump red nipples. "You are so damn beautiful," I murmur, and when I look at her, I let her see the hunger in my stare, the depth of how damn much I want her.

"Shane," she whispers. There's no real reason, but she doesn't need one. She just needs to keep saying it, over and fucking over.

I release her, and her lashes lower, becoming half-moons on her pale cheeks. When she lifts them again, I've taken off my clothes, and opened the glass door to the shower, silently inviting her to walk inside. She enters, but not before her gaze flickers over my body, lingering on my cock, and the look might as well be a lick for the way my body pulses and thickens. There is a predatory part of me she stirs, which is about far more than fucking, and when she faces me, just outside the stream of water, I stalk forward, backing her up without a touch until she is in the corner. My hands settle on the wall above her, my cock jutted, thick and hard, between us, but there is more to this moment than sex. "To hell with being objective. You rock my world and I don't get rocked. I'm damn sure going to do my best to make you do this my way."

"Which is what?"

"You stay with me." I lower my mouth a breath from hers. "Stay."

"Yes," she says, sounding breathless. I knew I was right in that coffee shop when I met her. I damn sure like her breathless and I plan to keep her that way for the rest of the weekend.

I brush my lips over hers, a caress and a tease that I follow with a deep, drugging kiss, the sweet, honey taste of her biting at my self-control. But it's her control I want. It's her command of her secrets. I want to tear away her reserve, and that starts now, with me taking her pleasure and leaving room for nothing else. Driven by that intent, I lower myself to my knees, warm water splaying over my back, while I plan to make her warm all over.

My lips find her belly, and her fingers tunnel into my hair, and this time I don't stop her. This time, I am not driving away her demons, and leaving no room for them. I'm tearing down her walls, and sliding into their place, and I waste no time finding her clit and licking it. And licking again, sucking her deeply, using my fingers and tongue to tease and please until she is arching her hips and making soft, sexy sounds of pleasure I feel in the pulse of my own body. I explore, lick, touch, and it is only minutes before she is tugging at my hair, a rough burn that tells me she is on edge where I want her. With only a few more caresses of my tongue, her sex is clenching around my fingers. I ease her into release and back down. When she calms, I stand, cupping her face and kissing her. That sweet honey taste of *all of her* is on my tongue and I want more.

EMILY

An hour after we exit the shower, Shane and I collapse on the bed flat on our backs, one of his legs draped over mine, both of us breathing heavily. "I don't think I need my morning jog today," I pant out.

"At some point in the near future we'll have to eat," he murmurs, the muffled sound of his phone ringing in the bathroom.

"Don't you need to get that?" I ask, rolling to rest on his chest.

His hand flattens at the base of my spine. "I'm ninety-nine percent sure it's Jessica, and I'm not getting out of bed to race over and see that apartment. Not when I have you naked and to myself."

"That apartment's gorgeous. Don't lose it."

"Money talks and so does power. If I want it, I won't lose it."

"And you want Brandon Enterprises."

"Yes. I do."

"But you worked so hard for your law career and were at the top of the food chain."

"I resisted," he says, scooting back to prop himself on the gray cloth headboard, and taking me with him. "But I think you know that's why I'm still in this apartment."

"What changed your mind?"

"The company's going in the wrong direction, and I am certain this will be its demise."

"But it's an empire."

"Empires do crumble. And I don't want ours to be one of them."

"And you think the pharmaceutical division is the key to successfully preventing that?"

"I know it is. It allows us to cut the dead weight that are many of our divisions."

"Well, the financial division sure seems to be booming."

"You base this on what?"

"The powerful, filthy rich people involved in this new hedge fund your father's working on."

"The hedge fund he didn't tell me about," Shane replies dryly.

"Why didn't he?"

"He wanted to bury something I won't approve of before it hits my desk."

"What kind of thing?"

"Nothing good and nothing you need to think about."

"But if I am staying, I should know what to look for."

"I don't want you to look for anything."

"But Shane—"

He slides down to the mattress again and rolls me to my back. "You are not to get involved beyond helping me with my research today. End of topic."

"I want to help."

"I'll fire you myself if you get involved in this, Emily." His tone is hard, absolute, and I believe him, but he softens the blow with a kiss, before rolling away, standing, and in all his naked abundant glory, walks toward a door opposite the bathroom that I assume is a closet.

Grimacing, not sure how I feel about this, I sit up, shivering with my still damp hair and a cold breeze from a vent somewhere nearby. "What are you trying to achieve with your research?" I call out, tugging the blanket to my chin.

He exits the closet in faded jeans, tugging a white tee over his impressively broad chest, giving me only a moment more to admire his defined abs before it falls to the waistband of his low-slung jeans. "I was behind this acquisition but I was too wrapped up in that legal matter I mentioned to dive in fully." He sits down next to me, his dark hair a rumpled, sexy mess that I'm pretty sure my fingers created. "Now, I'm ready to take it to the next level."

"Don't you have staff to research for you?" I ask.

"I do, but I'm not prepared to let my strategy out in the wild."

"You mean Derek."

"Among others."

"What's your strategy?" I ask. "I mean, unless you don't want to tell me."

"You're about to help me research. I'm not exactly keeping you in the dark. As for my strategy, it's pretty direct and simple, at least on the surface. Know everything about this business, my competition, and everyone involved in the industry."

"Everyone? That's a big order, isn't it?"

"Which is why few people are as prepared as I am and that's how I win my battles. I make sure I know everything about everyone I'm in business with."

"And you use that against them?"

"There's a fine line."

"How fine?"

His lips thin, his spine suddenly a little straighter. "I'm starting to believe that depends on who you're dealing with."

"What does that mean?"

His phone starts ringing again. "I better talk to Jessica before she shows up here to get me and I have a few calls to make myself. Room service?"

"Great," I say, and I have the distinct impression he's not as worried about Jessica as much as I've hit a sensitive topic he wants to avoid.

"How about omelets?"

I nod and give him my order before he grabs his phone from his pants in the bathroom and then disappears into the hallway, leaving me with one thought. He always knows everything about everyone. There's only so long before that includes me, which brings me back to what I told him this morning.

"Your bags," Shane says, reappearing in the room, carrying everything the hotel sent me into the bathroom before joining me again. "I'm going to order our food now."

"Great," I say as he heads toward the door.

"Did Jessica set up a meeting?" I ask, not sure how to dress. Okay, I'm not even sure I have clothes that fit.

"We missed it," he tells me. "She's working on it and she's pissed."

"Chocolate," I suggest.

"She's more expensive than that," he assures me and once again he's gone. I'm staring after him, a knot forming in my belly.

What am I doing? I'm crazy about this man. I don't want him to find out the truth about me. I want to tell him, but that doesn't protect him. Damn it, I refuse to accept this situation as unchangeable or unspeakable. Throwing off the blanket and darting for the bathroom, I quickly shut the door and lock it, beginning to scavenge through the items Tai had brought me, weeding through makeup, face cream, clothing, and a flat iron, to finally find my purse, which I'd scooped up by the door and shoved in one of the bags. Grabbing it, I pull the zipper open and grab the two phones, focused on the one I've been willing to ring.

No messages.

"*Damn it. Damn it. Damn it.*" I punch the call button, but after one ring I get voice mail. "You have to call me," I say at the beep. "You have to call me or . . . I am going to be forced to take matters into my own hands." I end the message and rest the phone on my forehead a moment, and the magnitude of one bad decision changing my life doesn't escape me. And yet, I think, resting my hands on the sink and staring at my now wildly messy brown hair and pale skin, had I not made that decision, I wouldn't have met Shane.

Giving myself a mental shake, I stick the phone back in my

purse, and grab the other one, and this time I find a message that amounts to a temp service offering me a low-paying job. In so many ways, Brandon Enterprises is a blessing. A knock sounds on the door and I jump. "Room service said fifteen minutes."

"Great," I say. "I'm starving. I'll hurry."

His footsteps sound and I stuff my phone in my purse, bury it in the bottom of a bag, and remove the toiletries, along with a flat iron I unwrap and plug in. While it heats up, I hunt down Shane's blow dryer to remove the dampness in my hair and dress in a light blue pair of Nike sweats, matching V-neck tee, and tennis shoes. Another ten minutes pass and I've managed to apply light makeup in pale pinks and run a brush through my hair. It smells like some sort of musky Shane-scented shampoo, and is actually a shiny light brown, draping my shoulders. I *like* smelling like him. I like a lot of things about being with Shane.

Setting all of the bags in a corner out of the way, I head for the door, but stop before I exit. I just left a message demanding a returned call. I rush back to the bag and grab the appropriate phone, stuffing it in my pocket, and head back to the door. I'm not sure how I'll handle it if it rings, considering under no circumstances can I take that call in front of Shane. My hand comes down on the knob, and I pause to force myself to make a hard decision. I set a deadline. If I can't come up with a solution that lets me tell Shane the truth by Monday, I have to get fired and stay away from him.

Keep your friends close, but your enemies closer.

—*Michael Corleone*

CHAPTER SIXTEEN

EMILY

Saturday afternoon finds Shane and me huddled inside his office, which is actually more of a library than anything, bookshelves sandwiching a massive pale wooden desk. Us claiming the dark brown leather sofa and chairs nested in a corner. Shane chooses to sit on the couch, while I settle onto the plush brown rug on the floor beside him, both of us placing the two MacBooks he has on top of the wooden coffee table that matches the desk.

Once we've reviewed what he wants achieved, it doesn't take long for us to dive into his research, or for us to get creative and turn the one open wall into a giant bulletin board with a massive amount of data sorted by topic, organization, and people. It becomes evident almost immediately that we are just as good at working together as we seem to be at everything else. And I not only enjoy our sharing of information, but really, truly, get a real thrill out of the case law related to drug-centric lawsuits, but we argue about his risk or reward with certain product choices for the BP division.

One case in particular has Shane ripping a page off the wall, while I insist he leave it in place, detailing the reasons I don't think it's high risk, despite a massive lawsuit ten years ago. He ends up repinning it to the spot on the wall, and when he sits back down, he gives me a scrutinizing look.

"LSAT score," he says.

"I never said I took it."

"*Did you* take it?"

It's a direct question, and I know he'll know if I lie, and the truth is that it matters to me. "I took it. I killed it."

His eyes light with approval. "I had no doubt. You don't need to be sitting outside my father's door. You need to be in law school."

"I'm getting too old."

"When we touched on this the night we met, I had a feeling age was holding you back. Twenty-seven *is not* old."

"Oh come on, Shane. For law school, it is. You know it is."

"We'll agree to disagree on that one. Why didn't you go after you took the test? You had to have had offers."

Regret over the many things that went wrong and can't be shared leaves me with only one answer that I pray he accepts. "It's complicated."

He studies me and I am certain he will press me, but instead he gives me a nod. "Understood," he says, and I don't think he is talking about law school being complicated, but rather, me not wanting to talk about it.

We slip past that moment easily though, and by evening, we've spent more time on work than Shane planned, but I don't mind. I'm also not complaining about our move to the bedroom, where we spend more hours naked than not, and discover we both love *Criminal Minds*, which launches us into a Netflix marathon. We laugh and talk, but I don't miss that after the LSAT conversation he's cautious about pressuring me for more personal details. I'm both relieved and sad at the limits I've placed on us, but still my phone doesn't ring, and the more I think about Derek digging into my background, the more I know where my decision must be headed, and it's not me staying with Brandon Enterprises or Shane. It's a reality that cuts and burns, as hours later, I lay awake in the darkness while he sleeps, his big body wrapped around mine, and I try to chase a way out of trouble that I can't seem to find.

I don't remember falling asleep, but when I wake, it's daylight on Sunday, and Shane is still holding me as if he thinks I'll escape like the first night we met. But I don't want to escape, and he only drives home that point with morning sex, and a suggestion we go for a run together, which I eagerly accept. Both of us dress, Shane in black sweats and a black T-shirt that shows off every perfect line and muscle of his torso. Me in black Nike cropped leggings, a matching tank top, and a hoodie. Ready to go, we head down the hall, and when we step into the elevator and he laces his fingers with mine, it's that moment that I feel us becoming more than the number of amazing orgasms we've shared. The fact that he's proclaimed he doesn't do relationships and that I never intended to do one either shakes me to the core. We *are* more than those orgasms and yet we are still defined by my lies.

The elevator dings at the lobby level, and the instant we step out into the hallway, I am suddenly nervous. "I don't know why I keep thinking we'll run into your father. He was just here one night."

"Actually," Shane says, "he rented a place here for his mistress."

I blanch at the news he's stated as matter-of-factly as he might the weather. "You've got to be kidding me."

"I wish I were," he says, and before I can reply, the double glass doors have parted and Tai is greeting us, diverting us from Brandon Senior to small talk.

Five minutes later, we finally break away from the conversation, but my read on Shane is that the moment to talk about his father is gone, if it really even existed in the first place. We've already moved on to comparing music, and I'm surprised he listens to Jason Aldean, one of my favorite country singers. "I'm from Colorado," he says. "A country boy at heart. You're from L.A. What's your excuse?"

Because I'm from Texas, I think, hating the way the lies circle me like sharks. "Colorado doesn't get to claim Jason Aldean," I say, dashing into a run.

He quickly catches up to me and in agreement it seems, we both reach for our headsets and fall into an even pace together, and even in the absence of conversation, I have this sense of being with him that I've never experienced with anyone.

Forty-five minutes later, he's officially pushed my limits, never easing his pace, and we continue longer than I normally would have on my own, but I like it. "I'm dying," I say, when we finally start walking, my chest rising and falling with heavy breaths. "How far was that?"

"Six miles. Did I push you too hard?"

"It felt like seven," I say, "but no. It was a great workout."

"Next time we'll do seven then."

"Six will do just fine," I assure him, and I have not missed his reference to a future run I really do hope happens.

"Coffee?" he asks, stopping next to one of my favorite chains.

"Yes, but what if we run into someone from the office?"

"It only feeds the idea that I'm using you." His lips quirk. "I am, you know. For sex and coffee. But you can use me too." He opens the door and waves me forward.

I laugh despite my nerves and enter the building, seeing wooden tables, many filled with people, clustered around me. Shane joins me and we head to the counter, both of us ordering coffee and bagels, and he surprises me by draping his arm over my shoulder.

"You aren't being discreet," I whisper as we wait for our order, both holding our pastry bags.

"Am I supposed to be?" he asks, grabbing our coffees, and indicating a free table for two in the corner.

I wait until we claim our seats, sitting across from each other, to reply. "Shouldn't we be at least a little discreet?"

"No," he says, and sets his phone on the table next to him; the way he's monitoring it gives me the distinct impression that even on Sunday, he's working some angle to take over Brandon Enterprises. "We do not need to be discreet."

I consider him a moment and nod, pulling my bagel out of the bag while he does the same. I've just taken a bite of mine when he surprises me. "I want you to stay tonight."

I set down the bagel and grab a napkin, only to have him reach across the tiny table and wipe cream cheese from my mouth, and lick it off his finger. "I owed you," he says softly, and he is close, his mouth a lean away from a kiss, his voice sandpaper and silk on every nerve ending.

"We are most definitely not being discreet," I manage.

"Stay the night again."

Surprised, I lean back to look at him. "I have to get ready for work in the morning."

"So do I."

"I'm not riding to work with you, Shane. That just makes me look like a bimbo."

He arches one dark brow. "A bimbo?"

"If the shoe fits."

"That shoe hardly fits you, sweetheart."

"I am sleeping with one of my bosses."

"Yes. You are, and maybe I should just start ordering you to do things."

"You already do."

"And yet somehow I struggle to get you to do what I say."

"Not at work."

"Then consider yourself at work for a moment, because I'm taking you home early in the morning and you're staying the night. End of subject."

"I'll stay," I say, giving him a tiny smile. "But not because you're my boss. Because I want to stay."

His sexy lips quirk and he reaches for his coffee but doesn't take a drink. He sets it back down, the full force of his attention on me. "I don't wake up with women in my bed."

While he has inferred as much, I am surprised and pleased by this announcement. "I'm no different."

"You went on the pill for someone."

"Paranoia," I say honestly, clinging to every truth I can tell him. "I was afraid of getting pregnant, since becoming a single mom and trying to go to school didn't seem exactly smart."

"But you were in a relationship."

"I thought I was, but I was confused."

His brow furrows. "Now I don't understand the words coming out of your mouth."

I can't muster a smile. "That part of my life is not my shining glory." As with the present day, I add silently before explaining. "He was my college professor and didn't tell me he was married."

"How badly did he hurt you?"

"I found out the day after my mother was killed in a car accident. It was a blow."

"I'm beginning to see you more clearly," he says. And before I can ask what he means, he's already moving on. "What did you do about the professor?"

"Nothing."

"You should have reported him."

"In hindsight, maybe, but I was not in a good place, and I darn sure didn't want to hear I had daddy issues."

"Lots of people date older."

"Yes, but my father was . . ." I catch myself before I say *a law professor* and invite questions I can't answer.

"Your father was what?" he prods.

"Within his circle," I say, avoiding a question about where he taught. "So I brilliantly rebounded with a tattoo artist who was younger than me."

"And yet you have no ink."

"Oh, he tried to convince me to remedy that. But you know, it felt more like a commitment to him, which I wasn't going to make, than a tattoo." I sip my coffee. "I told you my history. Your turn."

"I was engaged to another law student," he says, delivering a bombshell I don't expect.

"Engaged. That's pretty intense."

"Not really. I was young and the pairing fit an image I had formed in my mind of my life and career at the time, which was total bullshit. We ended badly, and after that, I let my career take over, and kept things simple with women."

I tell myself not to ask, but I can't help myself. "Simple how?"

"Women I have agreements with up front."

"Agreements," I say, a bit stunned. "That's cold, counselor."

"Not if it's what they wanted too."

"That never backfired?"

"I never allowed one the chance." He gives me a thoughtful look. "Interesting enough though, with you, I was the one who never had a chance."

"Funny," I say, my stomach fluttering. "I thought the same about me."

Flecks of blue glint in his gray eyes, telling me I've pleased him, and I am surprised how much this pleases me as well. "Then it's mutual," he says, "but actually, there is one agreement I think we should make."

"Agreement," I repeat, the word promising me an escape from the dangers of too much intimacy, while I simply feel like a fool. "I don't need an agreement, Shane. I told you. I understand—"

"Apparently you don't understand, or you wouldn't be about to say what you're about to say." He leans closer. "*Emily.* Let me be clear. I want you. And not just in bed."

"Why?"

"It's indefinable. It's just *you.*"

"But you just said—"

"That we need one agreement. That being, if at any time my brother makes you feel uncomfortable at work tomorrow, you do not stand alone. You text me, call me, or come to my office."

My relief at how wrong I was comes at me far too intensely for the short time I've known this man. "I can handle Derek."

"You're strong, but he's vicious. I know I told you not to come to me at work, but that was before we were outed, and this is now. If you—"

"I will."

"He will trick you and play with your head."

"He's already tried."

"He'll try again."

"He'll fail."

"You come *to me.*" His cell phone buzzes and his gaze flicks to his screen, and he immediately reaches for it. "I need to take this call, but we're not done talking about Derek, or my father, for that matter." He stands. "I'll be right back."

I nod and track his path across the coffee shop to step outside, obviously not wanting me to hear his conversation. He has secrets too, I realize, but that's expected. We've not known each other long, and he's trusted me in ways I believe he reserves for few others. And he has no idea the many reasons I have to trust no one, and yet . . . I want to trust him. But it's not as simple as that, nor is my secret about trust. It's about the damage it could do to him. That *I* could do to him.

Anger at my situation has my hand going into my jacket pocket and grabbing my phone. I check for a message I already know isn't there before hitting the redial button, grimacing as one ring sends me to voice mail. The line beeps and I say, "This is the last call I'm making. If I don't hear from you today, I'm out." I end the call and give myself a mental pat on the back. Let him squirm over the definition of "I'm out." I've just shoved my phone back in my pocket when Shane reappears.

"Jessica got us a viewing of the apartment, but we need to go now. Apparently, the owner still lives there and is out at the moment."

I stand and grab my coffee while he does the same with his. "How close is it?" I ask.

"Ten minutes in a cab if we can find one," he says, and we both grab our bagels and toss them in the trash on the way to the door.

Shane hails a cab quickly, and once we're inside, his hand closes on my leg, and he pulls me closer, aligning our bodies, our legs touching, but already he is glancing at another text message. The next moment, he's pulling up a video he doesn't try to hide, watching what appears to be several men in a warehouse, loading boxes onto a truck. The instant it's over, he releases my leg and punches a call button.

"What the hell did I just watch?" he demands of whoever answers the call, and while I can't hear the conversation, I have a pretty good idea it's Seth based on what I've seen of their inter-actions.

"You're sure?" Shane asks, after listening a few beats. "Son of a bitch, this takes everything to a new level. When do you get back?" He listens again, and then, "I want to meet with the security team as well. Tomorrow." He ends the call, tension crackling off of him, but he contains it, unmoving—every bit of the anger I sense in him well bridled, his control enviable in every way.

Time passes, and still he doesn't speak or look at me, but his hand comes back down on my leg, silently telling me he's still right here with me. I reach down and cover his hand with mine, answering with a silent promise that I'm not going anywhere. I've never wanted it to mean more.

"I had concerns that one of the companies under our umbrella was a liability," he says, turning his head in my direction, "and Seth has confirmed I'm correct."

"Can you fix it?"

"I have to fix it. There's no other option."

The cab stops in front of the blue glass building in the center of what seems to be a high-end shopping district. Shane pays the driver and exits first, offering me his hand, and helping me to my feet, allowing me to discover we're nearly on top of a mall. "I'm no longer objective about this apartment," I say. "It has me at shopping."

He laces his fingers with mine. "I'll bring you back another day and show you around. Unfortunately today, I have some business to attend to."

"I know your family will be cautious with me now, but I'm still close to your father. Tell me what to be looking for and if I can help I will."

"Not this time," he says, draping his arm around my shoulders to put us in motion toward the front door of the building. "I don't want you anywhere near this problem."

Like I don't want him anywhere near my mess, I think, and it's not a good thought. Suddenly, I can't help but wonder if we are the right people but at the wrong time. But how could this ever be the right time in my situation? I wouldn't want to miss knowing Shane and I don't know where that leaves me, or us.

I'm still trying to figure out the answer when we reach the double glass doors of the building. Shane opens the door for me. I step inside the foyer, seeing gray stone under my feet, a capped high ceiling above me, and a luxury seating area outlined by an expensive-looking blue oriental rug. Shane joins me, and I say, "It's pretty, but kind of sterile, where the Four Seasons feels warm and friendly."

" 'Sterile' seems an appropriate description," he agrees, motioning toward the seating area where a man and woman, both in business casual attire, are chatting.

His arm returns to my shoulders.

"I feel underdressed and like I need a shower," I say, as we start walking.

"I'm spending millions on this place if I buy it," he says. "They're the only ones who need to take a shower."

"Only you could say that and not sound arrogant," I comment.

"Because I see the influence of money as a fact," he states. "It's about knowing where your power comes from."

Knowing where your power comes from. Those words resonate with me, and in my mind, I believe my phone will ring now. Because I took the power I still had left, and used it when I left that message. I'm so lost in thought I don't immediately realize the woman is walking toward us, and not only is she elegant in black pants and blouse, she has spiky blond hair and her name is Jessica.

Instantly on the defensive, I try to pull my hand away from Shane and he catches it on the other side of his hip. "Shane, let go, damn it."

"She's already seen us, sweetheart, and I trust her. You can trust her too."

"Why didn't you at least warn me?"

"I didn't know she was going to be here until we walked in."

It's at that moment that we halt in front of Jessica, her attention settling on me. "Hello, Emily."

"Hi, Jessica," I say, giving an awkward wave. "Sorry I didn't tell you, but it just wasn't the right time."

"I'm using her to get information," Shane says. "Hiding in plain sight. Understood?"

"To protect her," Jessica concludes, her gaze flickering between the two of us. "Understood. You could have told me right out of the gate."

"We're telling you now," Shane says. "And Derek and my mother know."

"And your father?"

"Assume he does," Shane states, and obviously done with the topic, adds, "Let's get this viewing done and over with."

"All right then," she says. "But before I introduce you to Frank, our realtor today, you should know I'd describe him as 'difficult.'"

"My money isn't," Shane replies.

"Well then," she replies, "it seems that in your present mood, Frank doesn't stand a chance." She steps backward and leads us in his direction.

Frank, a fifty-something man with glasses and a pretentious attitude he doesn't need words to reinforce, greets us with handshakes, and quickly directs us to an elevator bank. Once inside, Shane stands behind me, one possessive hand on my shoulder. "This property will go fast," Frank states, standing near Shane. "How motivated are you to make a quick decision?"

"If I'm motivated," Shane says dryly, "you'll know."

Frank doesn't get the message to stand down, pressing onward. "I should tell you that I already have several interested parties."

"*If* I'm motivated," Shane repeats. "You'll know."

Frank shuts up at that point and the rest of the ride to the penthouse is silent. The car stops on our level, and Frank leads us to the one and only door on the floor, while Shane urges me inside the apartment for the first look. Upon entering, the wooden floor is dark, almost black, a striking difference to what Shane has now. Traveling a short hallway with stucco walls, I exit the other side to find myself in a half-moon-shaped room wrapped in windows. The view of downtown and the Rocky Mountains is so stunning, I barely glance at the black leather furnishings framing a fireplace running to the ceiling.

"What do you think?" Shane asks, stepping to my side.

I turn to face him. "So far, it's not that different from what you have now, though I haven't actually looked around it completely."

"You're right. It's got the same look and feel, down to the balcony off the living area." His hands settle on his hips. "The difference is that there I'm by the office."

"That has pros and cons," I say. "And your father sure won't be renting a room here."

"My father," he says, his look thoughtful, his fingers stroking the dark, sexy roughness of the stubble on his jaw, which he didn't shave this morning. "Won't be renting a room there either."

"I thought you said he was already?"

"I did."

Before I can ask what he means, Jessica appears between us, linking her arms with ours. "Let's look at the rest of the place," she urges. "Through the archway directly in front of us is a gorgeous gray stone kitchen and a sunken library." We start moving in that direction. "There's also an office and a bedroom, while the upstairs is expansive."

For the next ten minutes we do a walk-through of the re-

mainder of the apartment, including the rooms Jessica has indicated, along with a media room, and the second level, where we
find a ridiculous number of bathrooms and bedrooms. Through
it all, Shane is reserved, removed even, barely commenting on
anything. Finally, we reach the master bedroom, which is another half-moon-shaped room, with a massive four-poster bed
in the center, and another balcony to the right. Shane gives it
a thirty-second inspection, says nothing, and then crosses the
room to the balcony, which he opens, and steps outside.

Jessica lets out a frustrated sound and I turn to find her facing me. "I know you two started seeing each other before you
showed up at Brandon Enterprises," she says. "What I don't know
is how well you know him, so let me point out the obvious to me.
While other people throw things and curse when they're angry,
this is how Shane does pissed off. The quieter he is, the worse his
anger. So what happened and with who?"

Her observations resonate as correct, and since Shane trusts
her, I decide to answer. "Something Seth found out and shared
right before we got here. I don't know anything more."

"If Seth's involved, it's bad."

"Jessica," Frank shouts from the stairwell.

She grimaces. "I'll hold off Franky boy out there and give
you two some time."

I nod and she heads for the hallway, while I quickly join
Shane on the balcony, seeing nothing but his back, his shoulders
bunched under his T-shirt, and his gaze cast over the city.

"What can I say or do?" I ask, joining him, facing his direction, one of my hands closing around the steel railing.

He faces me, and his expression is all hard lines and shadows. "What can you do?"

"Yes. What can I do?"

He pulls me to him, his hands fanning out on my lower
back. "You can go home with me, get naked, and stay that way."

A few days ago his boldness would have flustered me, but not now, and this isn't about sex anyway. "Will that help?"

"Temporarily," he says. "Yes."

His voice is tight, controlled, but his heart thunders beneath my palm. "Then why are we still here?" I ask.

"I was just wondering the same thing." He cups the back of my head, an action he favors, and one I've come to like, and gives me a hard, fast kiss. "I'm going to deal with Frank." He sets me away from him and just that quickly, he's gone, and I'm leaning on the railing, watching him depart.

Jessica appears almost instantly, and I turn to face her. "I'm loyal to Shane but we are not, and never were, romantic," she says.

"I sensed that."

"He did something for my family in a time of need. A big something and I'm forever loyal. I cannot be turned by his family."

"Why are you telling me this?"

"Because it doesn't matter that he's pretending to use you to protect you. They will try to turn you. They will try to make you think he's betrayed you in some way, and I have to make sure I'm not a tool they use to do that."

"They who?" I ask, making sure I'm clear on the exact people she sees as enemies.

"His family and anyone working for them."

"*All* of them? Even his mother?"

"I don't trust any of them. They *will* make you doubt him."

"No, they won't."

"That wasn't a question, Emily. *They will make you doubt him.*"

"No, damn it, *they won't.*"

"They had better not," she says, her gaze sharpening, "because if you care about him at all, you cannot become the only weapon they have against him." She walks away and I hug myself, guilt clawing at me. Jessica's right. I can't be a weapon to tear him down. Every decision I make has to revolve around that absolute. And that's the moment my cell phone rings.

Digging my phone from my pocket, I move to the far side of the balcony, away from the open glass door, and hit the answer button. "Where have you been, Rick?" I demand softly.

"Do not call me and make threats like you did earlier," he growls.

"That wasn't a threat," I promise. "That was survival."

"I told you, the less we talk the safer we are."

"You also told me I'd be free of this in a month, two tops, and I'm headed toward that two."

"It's going to be a few more weeks."

"I can't do this for a few more weeks."

"You don't have a choice."

"I have a choice," I counter, "and yes. That's a threat."

"To yourself. You know the consequences."

"That you created and you said you had proof to make go away."

"Proof that has to be absolute, and it's not absolute yet. Stay your course. I'll be in touch. Get rid of the phone you're on and text me your new number."

"I need—"

He ends the call before I can say "money" and I stuff my phone back into my pocket, turning to face the railing, my hands settling on the steel. So much for using my power. I failed miserably and I lower my head, forcing myself to think. Suddenly Shane's hands are on my shoulders and I whirl around to face him, afraid he's heard my call.

"Hey," I say, his big body crowding mine, his eyes too attentive, searching my face. "What did you do about the apartment?"

"I bought it," he says, and the very fact that he's answered tells me no. He did not overhear my conversation.

"Already? How is that possible?"

"Money talks, but I'm not going to live here."

My brow furrows. "Then why buy it?"

"It's a damn good investment."

"So is Jessica lining up more places for you to look at?"

"Yes, and I might buy them too, but I'm staying at the Four Seasons."

"I'm confused, Shane. Does this mean you're leaving?"

"Leaving? No. I'm not going anywhere. It hit me when we were talking earlier: I decided to look for a place before I found out my father rented an apartment in my building for his mistress; if I leave now, he'll think he drove me out. I'm staying in the city, in the building, and I'm taking the apartment and the company." His hands come down on my arms, branding me, in that way his touch always brands me, and he closes the tiny space between us. "The way I'm going to take you when we get back to the Four Seasons."

"Yes. *Please.*"

"There's a word I like and haven't made you say near enough."

He kisses me, quick but perfect, and I'm getting used to the way he kisses me all the time. And when he grabs my hands and leads me toward the door, I let him. Because in the next few weeks, I'm either going to have to tell him the truth or leave, and the only way I can tell him the truth is if I fix my mess. Whatever the case, I'm going to savor every second I have with this man.

Nothing personal, it's just business.

—*Otto Berman*

CHAPTER SEVENTEEN

SHANE

I spend the rest of Sunday making good on my promise to keep Emily naked and saying "please," a remarkable feat, considering I now know I'm not just in bed with her. I'm in bed with the Martina cartel. They're running drugs through our trucking division, and getting them out will be no easy feat. They have the control, not my brother, who foolishly thinks he does. My desire to find Derek and beat the shit out of him is outside my normal calculated response.

Come Monday morning, I let Emily sleep while I shower, and adrenaline, not coffee, is fueling my thoughts. Brandon Enterprises *will not* become the Martina cartel's bitch and today I will come up with a plan to get them the hell out of our business. And while beating my brother's ass won't solve anything, when this is all over, I plan to give him the ass beating he deserves, purely for pleasure.

By the time I've texted my mother to find out what time my father starts his chemo, shaved, wrapped a towel around my hips, and entered the bedroom, Emily seems to be stirring. I cross to the closet and choose a dark gray suit. I'm dressed aside from my jacket and tie when Emily appears in the doorway wearing one of my T-shirts, her hair a wild, sexy mess.

"You didn't wake me."

"It's still early and you're dressing at home anyway." I pull open one of six built-in drawers, this one with a selection of ties. "Not to mention I kept you up late."

"Let me choose," she says, joining me at the drawer to inspect the options. "This one," she declares, reaching for a blue and gray striped Burberry tie. "One of my favorite brands," she adds, handing it to me.

"Expensive taste," I observe, fitting the tie under my collar and gently prodding her to fill me in on her past.

"Says the man with a fifty-thousand-dollar wardrobe," she says, reaching for my tie. "I'll do it."

I give her a quick nod and she starts working the knot like an expert. "You seem to have done this often," I comment, and I'm stunned to realize that I don't want her doing this for another man. *Ever.*

"My mother taught me," she says. "She used to do this for my father, and I wanted to help. One thing led to another and I took over doing it for him every morning."

When she was a kid. "You were close to him."

"Yes," she says, her voice softening ever so slightly. "Which was why him killing himself just didn't make sense to me. It didn't fit." She finishes off the knot and runs her hand down the tie. "All done. Actually," she says, reaching into the drawer again, removing a tiepin, and fitting it into place, "now you're done."

"Didn't make sense?" I ask, pulling my jacket off the hanger and shrugging into it.

"He loved life," she says. "There were no indicators he was suicidal. He didn't even drink."

"Do you think it was foul play?"

She hugs herself. "No." She hesitates. "I mean. Not anymore."

I arch a brow. "Not anymore?"

"I don't want to talk about this, Shane." The doorbell rings with the coffee order I placed, and I silently curse the timing. "I'm going to get dressed," she says, turning away.

I let her go for the moment, but she just told me that at some point she thought her father was murdered. I have a fleeting moment when I wonder if that has something to do with why she moved to Denver, but as I exit the closet and head downstairs, I deem that hypothesis unlikely, considering he'd died when she was a teen.

The doorbell rings again right as I reach the door and open it, accepting the Starbucks order from one of the hotel staff members. Hands full, I kick the door shut and turn to find Emily standing close, fully dressed in an all-black sweat suit, her purse over her shoulder. "I'm ready," she says, closing the distance between us, her skin pale perfection, and her hair not as wild as it was before. "Which one is mine?"

I offer her a cup and it hits me that she might be ashamed of something, and the minute she takes her drink, I flatten my hand on her lower back and pull her close. "You can tell me anything. Whatever you think I can't handle, believe me, sweetheart, I can." I don't wait for a reply or push her, releasing her and opening the door.

She stands there looking at me a moment, appearing a bit shell-shocked, but her eyes slowly soften. She reaches out, flattens her palm on my chest, holding it there a moment before she looks up at me. "Not yet," she says. "It's too soon." Her hand falls away as she steps into the hallway.

Pleased with an answer that wasn't "never" or "no," I join her in the hallway and we travel to the elevator. Stepping inside,

I punch the lobby level. "You know my father has chemo today, right?"

"Yes. I've never been around anyone going through this. Will he be in, do you think?"

"He's proven stubborn enough to work through it in the past, but I know nothing about how aggressive this flare-up is, or how intense the treatments are. I'm going to the hospital this morning to get a better picture of where he stands."

"I'm sorry, Shane." Her hand comes down on my arm, the touch cooling the burning emotion in my chest. "I know this sucks."

"Cancer is a monster." A jab of bitterness roughens my voice. "That it's found another monster is rather ironic."

"Shane—"

The door opens, giving me an escape from a moment when my emotions might get the best of me, and that would be unacceptable. Emily and I step into the lobby. "The car's waiting on us," I say, having ordered it brought around when I ordered the coffee. Her reply is to lace her arm with mine, the silent message of support exactly what I needed, even though I didn't know it.

We exit to the front of the hotel, and a doorman holds the door to the Bentley for Emily, while Tai waves to her and stops in front of me, lowering his voice. "Your father was here last night and when he left, he was coughing. One of my men said he saw blood on a napkin."

This news grinds through me and I reach into my pocket to offer him a tip. He holds up a hand. "No. Not this time."

I give him a nod, his actions offering me one more reason to respect him. I round the car and settle inside with Emily, shutting the door and resting my wrist on the steering wheel. "He was here last night with that woman."

"The night before chemo?" she asks, nailing exactly what is bothering me.

"Yes. The night before chemo." I place the car in drive.

"Oh my God. He's such a bastard."

"That's my old man." I cut the car onto the road, and I don't ask Emily's address and she doesn't offer, assuming I know it, and I do.

It's about three minutes later when I pull into the driveway of her apartment, an old warehouse converted to lofts, and park, turning to face her. "If you have any trouble today——"

"I'll call you," she supplies. "You've told me that many times. You take care of you and the business. I'll take care of me."

Take care of me. When was the last time anyone gave a shit about me? "Those things aren't mutually exclusive. I have meetings off site. I'm not sure when I'll be in, but call or text if you need me."

"I will."

"And I'll either meet you in the garage to pick you up or send a car for you."

"Okay." She hesitates as if she wants to say something, but seems to change her mind. "I should go, so you can get to the hospital."

I give a nod and she turns to the door but I grab her arm. She faces me and I don't have to pull her to me. Suddenly she's in my arms, and I'm not sure if it's me kissing her or her kissing me. My hands tangle in her hair, hers tunnel into mine, and the taste of desperation and fear in her kiss has me tearing my mouth from hers. Before I can speak, she says, "You call *me* if you need me." And then she turns and gets out of the car, shutting the door and leaving me alone.

I watch her walk to her door and disappear, and only then do I look away, her words replaying in my head. *You call me if you need me.* I haven't needed anyone, not for a long damn time, and yet . . . I put the Bentley in gear, and murmur, "What the hell are you doing to me, woman?"

Reaching the hospital, I'm unsurprised to find my father is in the private section that costs a hefty fee and ensures his room will be more of a luxury suite than the cold discomfort of a standard hospital room. I pass through security and head toward the corner of the west wing where I'm told he's registered. I'm almost to the door when my mother steps out of the room, dressed to kill in a tan pantsuit that screams fashion show, not cancer treatment. "I wondered if you were going to show up," she says, motioning behind me. "He wants coffee. Walk with me."

My brow furrows. "Coffee? They let him have coffee?"

"He's dying, Shane. We're prolonging it, not curing him, and do you really think they could stop him if he has his mind set on something?"

" 'Prolonging,' " I repeat. "You say that like you're reciting the weather."

"What am I supposed to do? Sit here and weep?"

"Yes. You are. He's your husband."

"And how do you think he'd react to me weeping? He'd crush me."

"Then why are you still with him?" I grind out, my voice low, taut.

She glances at the ceiling, as if she's grappling with emotions, which at least shows that she cares about something, though I question what that might be at this point. "Do you think I haven't asked myself that same question, over and over?" she hisses softly, fixing me with a bloodshot stare that suggests she's fighting tears.

"And how do you answer, Mom?"

"I can't leave him. Especially not now."

"Because you care?" I ask in disbelief. "Because he was with that woman at the Four Seasons this morning and you put him with her. That doesn't sound like caring to me."

"Do you really think me putting her with him means I want him to choose her?"

I arch a brow. "Doesn't it?"

She folds her arms in front of her. "Pretending he won't choose someone else doesn't make it true."

Frustration rolls through me and I step closer to her. "Do you know how crazy that sounds?"

"Don't you get on your high horse with me, Shane Brandon." She shoves a shaking hand through her long, dark hair. "You don't know what it's been like, and at least I know something about what is going on with him for you and for me. I'm surviving here the only way I can."

It's not the only way she can, but I force myself to remember that my father is a hard man who plays with people's heads. Years of getting the brunt of that had to have had an effect. "What's the prognosis, aside from terminal?"

"He had some extra testing today, and we won't have the results for a few days, but surprisingly good."

"He's coughing up blood. How can the words 'surprisingly good' even be in this conversation?"

"They gave me some long explanation about inflammation to describe why that's happening. The cancer's contained in his lungs and only stage one. His chemo will be aggressive but fairly moderate in intensity, which will limit side effects."

"What about the cancer in his brain?"

"Contained, but you know the story there. That could change any day."

I run my hand over my jaw. "I'm going in to talk to him."

She nods and starts to turn. "Mom," I say.

"Yes?" she asks, facing me.

"We'll get through this. I promise."

"I know," she says, and any remnants of tears or fears are gone, leaving me wondering if I'd imagined them.

She starts walking and I cross the small expanse to my father's room, pausing at the open door to hear him say, "Damn it to hell, Mike. I told you. I'm handling it."

I enter the room to find him wearing a hospital gown, and sitting in a fancy leather chair, in the corner by a window, a cell phone in his hand. My gaze flicks to the IV, and I swear, no matter how aware I am of his flaws, the scent of medicine and death is in the air, twisting my gut into knots. He glances up, seeming to sense my presence, and quickly tells Mike, "I need to call you back." There's a short silence and my father glowers. "*I said*, I'll call you back." He ends the call, and I pass the kitchen and bedroom area to join him in the mock living area, standing over him.

"Have what handled?" I ask, referencing what I'd overheard.

He scowls and snaps, "Nothing you need to worry about."

"If it's about the hedge fund you're hiding from me, you're wrong. I do."

"Hiding something infers I care what you think. I don't."

"You sure cared when I bailed you out of hot water."

His lips thin. "Until I make the damn thing come together, it might as well not exist. Why are you here?"

"I don't know," I say sarcastically. "I thought it was because my father's dying of cancer."

"Take care of business. I'll take care of me."

"In other words," I say, ignoring the brown leather couch and perching on the arm of a chair matching his. "Fuck you, Shane. Got it." I change the subject. "You're willing me the apartment. I'm drawing up the contract for you to sign."

"And because you draw them up, I should sign them why?"

"Because I'm your son and you love me. And because you

want me to sign off on that hedge fund that I couldn't give a shit about."

"It's worth fifty million."

"Like I said, I couldn't give a shit. I'll leave the contract with your new secretary. Unless you've already run her off."

"Emily doesn't intimidate easily," he says, his index finger thrumming on the arm of the chair. It's his "tell" he doesn't know he possesses, and I have one of the answers I came for. Derek or my mother told him about Emily, and considering he was coordinating the Nina Thompson payoff, it seems safe to assume he's well aware of the Martina cartel's involvement in the company. "It's rather refreshing," he adds.

"You'll have to step up your game then," I say dryly. "We wouldn't want people thinking you went soft. Speaking of the impression you're making. Unless you want me to know things like you were coughing up blood as you left the Four Seasons this morning, I'd change hotels. Though I do enjoy the flow of information." I stand. "I assume I won't see you at the office today since you don't like to appear weak, and you never know how the chemo cocktail they chose this time will affect you." I head for the door.

"That's it?" he calls out as I'm about to exit, and I know he's looking for a reaction to anything or everything, but that's not the way I win, thus it won't happen.

I pause at the door and look at him, and damn it to hell, my gut clenches at the sight of the IV running through his arm.

"What did you expect, Father?" I ask.

His gray eyes, hollowed though they seem, narrow on me for several beats before he snaps, "Not a fucking thing."

That's all the good-bye I need and I exit the room, striding toward the elevators to find Derek and my mother with their heads together. Derek's chin lifts, his gaze catching on me, hate he doesn't even try to hide anymore darkening his stare. He steps toward me, puffing up his chest in his expensive suit, while arrogance puffs up his head. "Is this where you tell me we should come together because he's dying?" he asks.

"I'm done pretending that's possible. I'm done with you." I step around him.

He calls out, "You'll never win."

I don't turn, and my lips curve with satisfaction at the words everyone I ever beat had said when they started to feel fear. I start walking and I don't look back. Not now and not ever again.

My next stop is at the bank to wrap up the purchase of the apartment Emily and I had looked at yesterday. I'm just finishing up the meeting when Seth calls to let me know he's arrived at Denver ground zero and is headed my way with company and the need for discretion. Seth arranges a showing at another downtown highrise apartment as a cover for the meeting. By the time I step off the elevator on the twenty-fifth floor it's nearly lunchtime.

Once I'm inside the unit that is filled with modern, artsy furnishings, I find myself at the head of a glass table. To my left is Seth and to my right is Nick Snyder, a man casually dressed in jeans and a T-shirt, his blondish hair starting to gray.

"As you know," Seth says, "Snyder X Security is the company I've contracted to work with us. Nick is the founder and the reason why I chose them."

"We met on an FBI-CIA combined task force," Nick offers. "And I was undercover in a biker gang for seven years. A gang that has some dealings with the Santos cartel, Martina's biggest rival."

"He took a bullet for me and saved my life," Seth adds.

I flick Nick a look. "Your credentials are good but I don't know you. I don't trust you. I trust Seth, and since he trusts you, I'll give you the benefit of the doubt."

"Good thing," Nick says, his glacier-green eyes glinting

hard. "Because you need me." He drops a small sealed baggie on the table. "That's what your trucking company is transporting for Martina."

"Coke," Seth says, confirming what I'd assumed, and sending a rush of anger through me that I quickly tap down.

"How long has this being going on?"

"Two weeks," Seth replies. "And we know this not from Riker, who won't talk to us, but from his right-hand man, who did. He's in this and wants out."

I have a small bit of relief with the news this is only two weeks old. "At least they don't have their teeth sunk in yet."

"But it won't take them long to," Nick warns. "They're testing the waters. If they like how this goes, this is just the beginning. They'll expand into all of your operations."

"How do we know they haven't already?" I ask.

"We don't," Seth says, "which is why we need to expedite your plan to control the rest of the stockholders."

"If we know your exposure is limited to the trucking division," Nick adds, "I have a friend at the Feds who can help."

"No Feds," I say. "The last thing I want is my family in jail and our company name all over the news."

"Understood," Nick says, "but my friend does side work for me. He can go in and nose around, flash his badge and then show up at Martina's restaurant and connect the dots. You've then successfully shut down your brother's attempt to go from dating to marriage with the cartel."

"Step one," Seth says, setting a folder in front of me. "That's the ammunition I have on the stockholders you wanted. Nick and I can split them up and have this done in the next few days."

I open the folder and the first thing I see is the only female stockholder's name, and next to it the word "miscarriage." My gaze shoots to Seth. "You have to be kidding me. You want to use a miscarriage against this woman?"

"Her husband is infertile," Seth says. "So yes. I do."

My temples begin to throb. "Let me get this straight. You're suggesting I become my family to fight my family."

"Better this than a cartel running drugs and killing people in your name," Nick states.

"Killing people in my name," I say. "That's the way to cut to the chase." I shut the folder and slide it to Seth. "Do what you have to do."

I stand and they follow, and I look at Seth. "I need an update by this time tomorrow." I don't wait for a reply, eager to get out of here and try to actually breathe again.

By the time I'm in the parking garage and sitting in my car, there is only one person on my mind. Emily. I remove my cell phone from my jacket to call her and it beeps with a text, from her of all people.

It appears that I'm going to lunch with your mother.

I like to be myself. Misery loves company.

CHAPTER EIGHTEEN

EMILY

It's no coincidence that lunch with Mrs. Brandon, or "Maggie," as I am now to call her, is at Jeffrey's Restaurant, the same place I'd gone with Shane the first night we met. It's her way of telling me she knows about Shane and me. Thankfully when we arrive, Susie isn't working or I'd be utterly cornered. Not that I think I'm going to escape some sort of full-frontal attack before this is over anyway, and of course, the elephant in the room is Mrs. Brandon's offer to pay me for information.

We settle at a table near the front of the restaurant, and Maggie doesn't bother to look at the menu. "The brown butter ravioli is to die for," she says. "I highly recommend it."

She might just love the ravioli, but I suspect she's baiting me, and I don't let her. "I've had it before," I say. "And I agree. It's fabulous."

"You've been here before. I had no idea. You didn't mention it when I made the suggestion."

Again with the baiting. "It was one of the first places recommended to me when I moved into town six weeks ago."

"That's right. You just moved here."

"I did, and not only do I love living close to my job, the food and shopping in this area are amazing."

She opens her mouth to ask a question I'm sure I won't want to answer, when our waitress, a pretty and young brunette, appears in front of us, and saves me, at least for the moment. "Welcome, Mrs. Brandon," she says, giving me a smile as well. "So nice to have you both in today."

My phone buzzes in my purse with yet another text I am certain is from Shane. I have yet to answer at least three others for fear of being obvious.

"Hello Lori," Maggie greets the waitress, then indicates me. "This is Emily." I wave and Maggie immediately says, "We're going to have the ravioli." She glances at me. "Wine?"

I hold up a hand. "Oh no. Thanks, but I'll fall asleep at my desk if I do that." I look at Lori. "Water, please." I grab my purse. "And on that note, I had better run to the ladies' room." I stand, running my hand down my simple navy blue dress, which is thankfully wrinkle free, since nothing else is right now.

Maggie's eyes hone in on me, amusement in their depths. "I guess you know where it is."

"I know where every bathroom in a place I've visited is, I promise you," I confirm, managing to sound amused despite my fear she's just made a masked reference to Shane and me kissing in the back hallway. "Everything I drink goes right through me."

"I'm the same way," she assures me. "Hurry back. My turn is coming."

More like hurry away, I think, rushing through the restaurant and down the hallway where Shane and I had first kissed, telling myself there is no way anyone, most especially Maggie, knows about that. We were alone. I enter the one-person bathroom and lock the door, opening my purse to grab my one remaining phone, having trashed the other one, as Rick demanded, on the walk to work this morning.

Leaning on the wall, I punch in Shane's number. "Why haven't you been answering me?" he demands after one ring, foregoing "hello."

"I'm with your mother and didn't want to seem rude. I came to the bathroom to call you."

"Where are you?" It's not a question but a demand. "I'm coming to you."

"What? No. You can't do that."

"I can and I am," he replies. "Where are you, Emily?"

"If you come to me, it will seem like you care about me and no one will believe you're using me."

"I *do* care about you and I'm not letting my mother fuck with you."

My heart softens. "I care about you too, Shane, which is why you have to trust me to handle this."

"It's not you I don't trust. It's my mother."

That statement makes me sad for him in too many ways. "I've got this, Shane. I promise. I have to get back to the table. I'll text you when I return to the office."

"She's going to try to mess with your head."

"I'm fully aware of your mother's intentions. And if you don't think I can manage her, and your father, why did we decide I'm staying?"

Silence stretches for several beats before I hear, "Do not let her turn you against me."

It hits me then that everyone close to him has turned against him. "She can't turn me against you. No one can. I promise." I just hope the same will be true in the reverse if he ever learns what I've been hiding.

"Text me when you're back," he orders.

"I will," I promise.

The line goes dead, and I stuff my phone back in my purse, and quickly step to the mirror, brushing my windblown hair back into place, and exit the bathroom. I dread my return to the table, but nevertheless hurry forward and rejoin Maggie. "My hair was a mess from all that wind on our walk over here," I say as I sit down.

"You look stunning as always." She settles her elbows on the table and rests her chin on her hand. "Tell me about yourself, Emily."

And just like that I am trapped, forced to tell her lies that will not match the truth I've told Shane, leaving me with no option but to dodge and weave. "I'm just a girl, learning her way around Denver."

"The food has arrived," Lori announces, saving me once again as she sets our plates in front of us. "Can I get either of you anything else?"

"Nothing for me," I reply, and thankfully Maggie and Lori chat for a moment, giving me time to plot my change of subject.

"Where were we?" Maggie asks, giving me her full attention again and reaching for a fork.

Nowhere I want to go again, I think, and quickly say, "I wanted to ask about Mr. Brandon. You mentioned he did well today when you first got to the office. Does that mean he'll be in tomorrow? There are a lot of people asking about him."

"I'm certain he will. Staying home today was a precaution to ensure he knew he'd tolerate treatment well."

"That's great news," I say, taking a bite, and despite this awkward meeting, the flavors explode in my mouth. "Oh man. I forgot how good this is."

She ignores my raves, her keen stare thoughtful, if not calculating. "You're close to my husband. You will see and hear things."

"If this is where you offer me money again, it won't work."

"This is how I get to know the person sitting outside his door."

"Do you do this with all his many assistants?"

"No. Because they didn't stand up to him and earn his respect. You have."

I'm not surprised I have his respect after our recent confrontations, but rather the fact that he's talked to her about me. "I've worked with men like him before. Retreating rarely works."

"You are correct, but even those who understand that premise tend to wilt under my husband's wrath."

"He's a hard man," I say. "But I assume that's part of why he's a success."

Something, bitterness perhaps, flits in her eyes and she stabs at a ravioli. "Tell me about yourself. You went to school in L.A., correct?"

"I guess you've been talking to human resources."

"I take that as a yes," she replies. "And your parents were attorneys?"

I reach for my water to help choke down the lies I clearly can't avoid. "Yes."

"Why didn't you go to law school?"

"Life happened," I say, quickly stuffing food into my mouth to shut myself up.

"Your parents died in a small plane crash."

My throat goes dry and I reach for my water. "Yes," I lie, though I've told the truth to Shane. I take a drink and set my glass down. "I guess I shouldn't have mentioned that to human resources if I didn't want it repeated."

"Nonsense," she says. "It's the little pieces of our past that bring us to the present."

"Indeed," I say, and she can't know just how profound those words are at this moment.

She pushes her plate aside. "Let's get to it, shall we?"

So much for the dodge and weave strategy. "All right," I say, scooting my plate away as well.

"You're in a unique position that will put you in the middle of a family war and you will become a casualty if you allow it."

"I'm sure I don't know what you mean."

"When I tried to buy you, it was with the intent of making it clear that you're loyal to me."

"If you did that, no one would have trusted me, to feed me the information you want."

She waves that off. "I get information on my own. I wanted them to believe you were no longer a target for their use."

"I don't understand."

"The Brandon men are motivated by power and money, and they will do whatever necessary to win those things. And at present, Shane and Derek are battling for control of the company, both in need of their father's vote with the board to claim the role of CEO. And, quite frankly, my husband enjoys watching them fight it out."

It's nothing Shane hasn't told me, but still incredulous to hear. "That's wrong on all kinds of levels."

"Honey, you can't know what it's like as a mother to watch the divide between my sons broaden, and at the hand of their father no less." Her voice cracks and suddenly, I think she might really be sincere about trying to help me. "All I can do is keep the playing field safe and even and protect those in the warpath, which includes you. In your role, both of my sons will most certainly see you as someone who can access critical information they might wish to possess."

Considering she knows about Shane and me, she's clearly inferring he's using me, and despite absolutely knowing better, there's a stupid hot spot in my chest. "The bottom line here," she says, continuing, "is that both of my sons will try to manipulate you and they will both have one agenda. Winning. You are inconsequential. Don't let them make you inconsequential."

Inconsequential. That word rips through me and hits raw

nerves I didn't realize were exposed, and have absolutely nothing to do with her, Shane, or my job. "You look stunned, honey," she says, giving me a sharp eye. "What are you thinking?"

"Thinking? Nothing really. I'm still just digesting it all."

She doesn't look pleased, as if she's expected some reaction I haven't given her, and thankfully her cell phone rings, giving me a few moments to compose my thoughts. I watch her grab her purse and remove her phone, and glance at a text. A nagging sense of her wanting me to lash out at Shane digs in and takes hold.

She gives an exaggerated sigh. "Alas, it seems I must end our lunch early. I've been ordered home. My husband's not feeling well after all, and needs me. And to think he was going to try to hide his new rounds of chemo from me." She tucks her phone back into her purse and hooks it over her shoulder. "Let's head back and finish talking on the way. They'll put the bill on my tab."

"Of course." Eager to end this encounter, I too grab my purse and we quickly make our way to the exit, stepping outside to gusting winds and droplets of rain that effectively save me by ending the conversation.

Once we've dashed back into the building, she faces me to softly say, "No one is to know about his cancer. Understood?"

"I would never tell something so private without permission."

"Excellent. You're a good girl, Emily. Let's keep you that way." She reaches up and drags my hair through her fingers, frowning as she does. "Emily, honey. You need to cover those blond roots. I'll text you my hairdresser's number. In the meantime, mascara on the roots. It works." She turns and walks away, oblivious of the bombshell she's just landed, leaving me stunned, my knees wobbling with the impact of yet another secret exposed.

My lies are everywhere, sucking me into a hole I fear I'll never escape, and my biggest fear is that they might be exposed and used not just against me, but against Shane. Mentally shaking myself, I hurry toward the public bathroom, dash to the back stall that has a sink and mirror inside, and inspect my hair, cringing at the blonde that seems to have appeared at my hairline overnight. Quickly taking Maggie's advice, I dig out my mascara, and manage with limited success to hide the lighter shade of my natural hair, resorting to a ton of hairspray to hide the rest.

Task complete, I exit the bathroom with my promise to call Shane weighing on my mind, and head to the coffee shop, where I hope to find privacy. With my phone already in my hand, I place an order, claim my drink, and sit down at a corner table, the sexy, funny memory of meeting Shane here playing in my mind. I'd been seduced from the moment I met him, and now . . . now I know I'm headed toward love with this man. I, of all people, know the death of love is lies.

My phone rings and sure enough, it's Shane. Drawing in a calming breath, I punch the answer button. "I was about to call you. Your father wasn't feeling well so she cut the lunch short, which suited me just fine."

"How did you even end up at lunch with her?" He doesn't wait for an answer. "Never mind. I know the answer. She bulldozed you."

"Much like her son, she doesn't take 'no' for an answer if she doesn't want 'no' for an answer."

"Unlike her son, she always has an agenda. What was she after?"

"She seemed to want me to stay away from you and Derek, and align myself with her."

"Me," he says flatly. "You're sure?"

"She never confronted me about seeing you, but she did say quite clearly that you and Derek would target me. Specifically, by seducing me or paying me for information that might help with the goal of taking over the company. And while it could be coincidence, she took me to lunch at Jeffrey's to deliver that warning."

"It wasn't a coincidence," he says tightly.

"That was what I thought too, I just didn't want to assume the worst of your mother." I hesitate. "She claims to be concerned about your divide with Derek, but she seemed to really want me to think the worst of you."

"And did it work?"

"Not for a minute."

"My light in the storm of betrayal," he says softly. "We'll talk more about my mother tonight, but I'm going to be off-site when you finish work. One of the partners from my old firm is in town and wants me to meet him for drinks, but I should be done by seven. I'll send a car to get you at six forty-five."

"I need to run a few errands after work," I say, thinking about dyeing my hair, and replacing the phone I threw away this morning. "Can the car pick me up at my apartment at eight?"

"I'll set it up," he confirms. "And I'm leaving an elevator card for you at the front desk and a key to the apartment just in case I run late."

A card and key feel like the trust that I so want to deserve. We say our good-byes and my mind lands on the moment at lunch when Maggie cornered me about my parents dying in a plane crash and I decide that lie is the one that is going to make *me* crash and burn. Shane's words replay in my head. *The light in my storm of betrayal.* The idea that the lies forced on me by another could make him believe I'm a part of that storm twists me in knots. I *have* to tell Shane that I lied to human resources and his mother before she says something and he finds out from her. If only I could safely tell him *everything.*

I leave work at five o'clock, a luxury I am certain I wouldn't have if Shane's father wasn't out today, and make my way to the pharmacy, where I buy a phone and hair color. As soon as I get home, I text Rick with my new number, but of course get no reply. By seven, I've colored my hair and I'm drying it, chasing my lies, and looking for solutions. By seven forty-five, I've dressed in my only pair of jeans, a slim-cut dark denim, and a light blue V-neck tee, wearing tennis shoes, because I have nothing else but heels. Come eight o'clock, I'm pacing my small apartment waiting on the car Shane's sending for me, and I've come to the conclusion I don't want to have. I want to tell Shane the truth, I do, but it's selfish and wrong. Once he knows, that's it, and that comes with a burden he doesn't deserve or need, not with all the hell he has going on. If he stays close to me, he will find out, and that leaves only one option. We can't see each other anymore.

There is a knock on the door and I glance out of the window to find a man in a suit and a black sedan idling nearby. A few minutes later, I'm at the Four Seasons, traveling the elevator up to Shane's suite, a small overnight bag on my shoulder. At Shane's door I knock but he doesn't answer, and the fact that he trusts me here alone only drives home why I have to be strong tonight. We *have* to stop seeing each other. I unlock the door and enter, setting my bag and purse on the coatrack by the door.

I pass the kitchen and glance up the stairs at the bedroom, wondering, *Can I really walk away if I make it up those stairs again?* But how do I miss one last night with Shane? Tormented, I walk through the living room and realize the patio door is open. Inhaling, I move forward to hear Shane's voice.

"What exactly are you suggesting, Eric?" Shane demands.

"I'm not suggesting anything," comes a male voice I assume to be Eric. "I'm telling you what my patient told my nurses. And not just any patient. The wife of a professional baseball player who says he's using performance-enhancing drugs he gets packaged as something else from your company."

I catch myself on the edge of the bar from the impact of

Shane being involved with more than just a family war. This is criminal, and it's everything I've tried to fight and escape in my life.

"Let me get this straight," Shane says. "The soon-to-be ex-wife says this drug my company is selling off-label can't be detected in blood tests?"

"That's what she claims," Eric says.

"This is the athlete that is paying for the plastic surgery you're doing on his soon-to-be ex-wife."

"Correct."

"This has dirty divorce settlement written all over it," Shane replies.

"Shane, man," Eric says. "I want that to be truth, but she swears that ballplayer who died last month of an unexplained heart attack was using it too."

"This isn't happening at Brandon Pharmaceuticals," Shane insists.

"I hope not, man," Eric says. "Look. We went to school together. We grew up together. I know you wouldn't do this, but your family is another story."

Shane brushes past that comment. "I need everything you can give me on this woman."

"You know I can't give you that."

"Of course you can't. I'll figure it out, but I need you to keep me in the loop."

"I will."

It's then I realize the conversation is ending and I'm standing here listening. I turn and rush for the door, messing with my bags as footsteps sound. "Emily."

Suddenly Shane is standing in the hallway in front of me, and a tall, good-looking man in a dark suit with wavy blond hair is with him. "Hi," I say with an awkward wave of my hand. "I knocked but you didn't answer."

"I was just leaving anyway," the other man says, giving me a nod and then eyeing Shane. "I'll be in touch." He steps around us and leaves.

The door shuts behind me, leaving Shane and me alone. Shane steps closer to me, his suit jacket gone, his tie loose, and he looks like sin and sex and torment. "We need to talk," he says, a lean away from touching me, but he doesn't. And I sense he doesn't want me to touch him either.

"I'm listening," I say, every nerve in my body on edge waiting for some bombshell beyond what I know already.

"There are things happening, Emily, that I can't, *I won't*, risk you becoming involved in. Tomorrow you make sure you get fired and I'll make sure you get the severance you need."

This is my out. I should take it and run, but instead I ask, "So that's it? I quit and go away?"

"For now. We talked about this."

"And yet you won't even touch me."

"If I touch you, I won't send you home, and I can't let that happen." He takes a step backward, as if solidifying those words. When his gray eyes meet mine, they are steel, his decision made. I wait to feel rejected by the coldness of the moment, but I do not. He really means to protect me. There is no other option to him and I am ashamed of how weak I was in protecting him.

I inhale a deep breath as I step to the coatrack, grabbing my purse and bag and turning for the door. I want him to stop me, but I know he won't. He believes this is the right decision. I'd believed that as well until I'd heard the trouble he's in. Sitting outside his father's door, I have a unique window into the family with whom Shane is at war. Leaving now is deserting a ship, and a battle post, in the middle of that war. I won't do that. I'm staying.

"Emily," he says. My hand is on the door, but the next thing I know, he's grabbed me, and his hand is on the back of my head. He's kissing me, deeply, passionately, and then he sets me away from him and opens the door. "If you don't make my father fire you, *I'll* fire you."

I leave without a word, the taste of his regret, and my own, on my lips, with no intention of anyone firing me. I'm more resourceful than he thinks, and I care too much about him to let his family win.

SHANE

Two hours after I gutted myself by forcing Emily out of my apartment and my life, at least for the time being, Seth and Nick join me at my apartment, Nick making a discreet entry separate from Seth. Convening at the island in the kitchen, both men look weary, Nick with a thick stubble on his jaw, and Seth with his tie loose and his jacket gone.

"I'm going to cut to the chase here," Nick says, opening the conversation, "and the news isn't good. I've talked to my buddy at the Feds and they are indeed investigating a performance-enhancing drug called 'Sub-Zero' on the streets."

"How do we know that connects the dots to my company?" I ask.

"It's being investigated as the cause of death of a professional athlete," he says, confirming what Eric's patient had claimed. "Toxicology, however, was negative but as you told Seth, that would be expected. And that's part of the buzz on the streets. Not only is it rumored to produce the same physical benefits of a steroid with an added boost of mental clarity, but it remains invisible."

"What about hair follicle testing?" I ask.

"Negative," Nick says. "There's a hypothesis the drug somehow mimics something naturally created in the body, but there's absolutely no supporting evidence. Aside from chatter on the streets, the FBI is flying blind on this one."

"And that chatter is going to lead them to me," I say, "like it did the doctor who came to me today."

"Does any of this chatter include the Martina cartel?" Seth asks.

"Negative again," Nick says. "At this point, they've been focusing on high-end sports clinics, college sports complexes, and doctors." His gaze cuts to me. "If you go to them—"

"Not no," I say, "but hell no."

"Think about this, Shane," Seth argues. "Protection. Immunity. And the chance to take down one of the largest, most dangerous cartels on the planet."

"That would infer I intend to get in bed with Martina, and I don't, nor will the Feds drag me, and people close to me, into said bed. It's a death wish in every possible sense of that saying. And don't tell me they'll offer protection that won't be needed if the two of you do your damn job, and get them the hell out of my business."

"At the risk of pissing off the man responsible for my generous payroll," Nick interjects, "I need to insert a warning here. If the Feds come to you before you go to them, they won't be your friends."

My jaw sets hard and I give him a steely look. "Are you working for me or them? Because you sound like you're pushing their agenda."

"Their agenda is to take down a cartel," he argues.

My lips thin with my growing agitation. "With acceptable losses along the way. Me, my company, and the people around me, *will not* be those losses. So I repeat. Who do you work for? Me or them?"

"You," he says, his voice low, tight.

"Then use that energy to get me out of this," I say. "Not six feet under." I glance between them. "At this point, I have nothing but an angry, soon-to-be ex-wife connecting BP to Sub-Zero. If it's in my building, I should have known before she did. How are we going to fix that?"

"You need an informant inside BP," Nick suggests.

I give a negative shake of my head. "I'm not risking the exposure that could represent unless I have no other options. If Sub-Zero is inside the BP facility, we need to hone in on who helped Derek get it there."

"William Nichols," Seth says, and I assume for Nick's benefit, he adds, "The head of research and development at BP. My gut says he's a problem and his behavior on the security film I watched has been suspicious, but far from conclusive."

"Does he have the control and resources to breach the facility with illegal drugs?" Nick asks.

"He does," I say, "and he's weak, which makes him a soft target for Derek, who is far too often shortsighted, considering that it also makes him a soft target for everyone else as well."

"Define 'soft target,'" Nick urges.

"Under the right pressure," I reply. "He'll buckle under the right pressure, be it from us, or someone else."

"We need to make sure it's to us," Seth concludes.

"Exactly," I say. "And the best way to shake down a soft target is to scare the shit out of said target, and see where they lead you. If we execute this correctly, we'll quickly know if we're looking in the right place with William."

"So we play Go Fish," Nick says. "What's our bait?"

We spend the next fifteen minutes debating exactly how Go Fish will play out, before Nick departs, while Seth lingers with me, on the other side of the island. "Emily," he says flatly, no lead-up, warning, or further explanation.

"I'm listening," I say cautiously, a muscle beginning to tick in my jaw.

"You're sleeping with her."

"That wasn't a question. Where are you going with this?"

He pushes off the counter and folds his arms in front of him. "How do you know she's not working for Derek?"

"I know," I say firmly. "And this conversation is irrelevant at this point. She's leaving the company and will be off everyone's radar. Watch her to protect her, but otherwise, leave her there."

His eyes narrow, harden with the set of his jaw. "Understood," he says, and without another word, he turns away to head for the door, but I know Seth, and Emily is no more off his radar than she is off mine. But better ours than Derek's or the Martina cartel's.

Look at me. I did this to you. Remember me.

—*Sonny LoSpecchio*

CHAPTER NINETEEN

SHANE

I wake the next morning to the sweet scent of Emily clinging to my sheets and the bitter memory of why I had to send her away. Drugs. Cartels. Enough lies to create a sinkhole that will swallow us all alive. This drives home why I did the right thing to push her away, but I regret sending her away, but it had to be that way. Had I touched her, *if* I touch her now, beyond that painful, searing last kiss, I'll forget how easily I could put her in harm's way. Knowing this, however, doesn't keep my mind off her as I shower. Nor does it stop me from pairing my navy suit with the same blue and gray striped Burberry tie she'd chosen for me yesterday. My way of telling her that she might be gone from my immediate life right now, but she is not forgotten.

Heading downstairs, I make coffee, and cup in hand, I head to my home office, where I settle behind the desk, my phone next to me, my gaze falling to the wall Emily and I worked our butts off to turn into a bulletin board. Among the data pinned there are true jewels of information I can use to grow the pharmaceutical division, none of it relevant if I don't shut down the threats to the company that the Martina family, and my own, represent.

Glancing down at my tie, my concern over Emily being too close to potential danger swells and I reach for my cell phone, punching in her number. The call goes straight to voice mail. Grimacing, I decide against a message to confirm today is her last day working for my father. It could be taken as cold, rather than concerned, which is what I intended. Whatever the case, her leaving the company today is not an option.

My cell phone rings and Seth is on the line. I turn my attention to the game of Go Fish, while Seth and I spend the next several hours setting our trap for William and hopefully Derek in the process. Namely, locking down surveillance on anyone either of them might contact after I've rattled a few cages today. By the time everyone we need to have eyes on is in view, it's nearly two o'clock, and I drive to a coffee shop practically in the parking lot of the pharmaceutical plant. Parking by the door, I dial William Nichols, our suspected traitor. "Mr. Brandon," he greets me amiably. "What can I do for you today?"

"I'm negotiating an acquisition that will directly impact your work and I need immediate feedback. I'm next door at Mountaintop Coffee. I need you to come over."

"Now?"

"Now."

"I'm right in the middle of—"

"Now," I repeat, adding a hard push to my voice.

"Yes sir."

I end the call and send a group text to Seth and Nick: *I'm here and he's on his way.* I exit the Bentley and head inside, claiming a booth that allows me to see the door and setting my phone on the table, only to have it buzz. Glancing at the caller ID, I answer and hear Freddy "Maverick" Woods, the head partner of the firm I left for all this joy I'm living, say, "Have you considered my offer from last night?"

"I don't remember saying I would."

"You'd be the youngest senior partner in our history."

Senior partner in New York, away from the Martina cartel, and with Emily by my side. I want it, but I can't have it. "We talked about this. My father's dying. I have a company to run."

"Let your brother run it."

"To the ground," I say. "No thank you." I push steel into my voice. "My answer is still no."

"Subject to change?"

"Balls to the wall," I say, repeating what he and I had said often in my days as his employee. "I'm here to stay."

"I'll ask again in a month." He ends the call and I set the phone down.

"Shane."

At the sound of a far too familiar female voice, I look up to find Lana Smith, an attractive brunette with her hair tied at the nape, standing at my table. She's also a brilliant scientist, Will's second-in-command, and a woman who'd been a much-regretted college fuck buddy I prefer not to acknowledge.

"Do you have a moment?" she asks.

"If that," I say. "I'm about to meet with your boss."

"I'll be fast," she says, wasting no time settling into the seat across from me, and in typical Lana style, she leans in to expose the ample cleavage of her gray dress, which I ignore, as she adds, "I seem to have bad timing with you, though you buying the company I work for seems like a twist of fate."

"Fate didn't bring us together. Business did."

"But what are the odds of you being the one behind the acquisition of a company I work for?"

"Big-money pharmaceuticals drawing the attention of a

major conglomerate like Brandon Enterprises is more likely than not."

"Right. Of course." She gives me a keen look. "You haven't forgiven me, have you?"

I don't pretend ignorance I don't appreciate in others. "It's ancient history, Lana, and better left there considering I'm one of your employers." My brow furrows as the past becomes a little too present to be ignored. "However, it is a bit ironic that you hid drugs in my car and almost cost me Harvard, considering you now work for a drug company."

Her eyes go wide with surprise. "It was weed and we were young. You can't seriously see that as an issue."

I look at her, trying to decide if this is a red flag or a bad coincidence.

She obviously reads the questions in my silence, straightening in her chair, her attempts to show her breasts forgotten. "I'm good at my job. I'm one of the best in my field, an expert in—"

"I know your credentials." My gaze flicks to the door, to the gray-haired, slender man in a white button-down and khakis. "Your boss is here," I say, leveling her with a stare. "Was there something you needed that I haven't addressed?"

"Nothing we can cover with an audience." She stands, and turns to greet William, who visibly jolts with her presence. "Hello, William."

He looks at me. "I didn't realize Lana was attending this meeting."

"I'm not," Lana says quickly. "If you remember, Mr. Brandon and I went to college together and I came for coffee and he was here and . . . I'm going back to work." She steps around him and walks toward the counter.

Already focused on William, I motion for him to sit. "Thanks for coming."

"It sounded urgent," he says, joining me.

"I'm not going to mince words. It is." He slips his hands under the table, a classic way to hide a tremble. "I didn't bring you here to talk about acquisitions," I continue. "I have a problem."

He swallows hard. "What kind of problem?"

"The board of directors is not pleased with our profit margins."

"That's crazy," he says, his hands finding their way to the table. "Our margins are exceptional."

"They aren't at the level you and I discussed."

"We set a one-year goal," he argues. "We're only halfway there and on pace to be right on target."

"That might be true, but I need something to excite the board, teasers that show we can be more and do more."

"I hope I'm not interrupting." I glance up at the sound of a male voice to find a man in a dark suit with graying hair standing by our table. "Actually," he adds, grabbing a chair at the end of our table and sitting down, "I really don't care if I'm interrupting."

"Who the fuck are you?" I demand.

"Richard Jones is the name." He reaches in his pocket, flashes a badge, and starts to put it in his pocket. "FBI."

As soon as he hears "FBI," William jerks his hands off the table, hiding them again, while turning fifty shades of green, proving my assessment of how soft he is to be true.

I tap the table. "I'll take a look at that badge."

The agent smirks but slides it across the table for my inspection. I give it a longer look than is necessary before sliding it back to him. "What can we do for you, Agent Jones?"

"I have questions," he says. "And what better time to ask them than when you're with your head of research and development?"

"You know who I am?" William asks, and then looks at me. "How does he know who I am?"

"It's my job to know, Mr. Nichols," Agent Jones answers.

"*What can I do for you*, Agent Jones?" I repeat.

His head snaps in my direction. "I'll be direct," he says. "I'm investigating a member of the FDA staff with some rather suspect drug approvals. In short, we believe he's been taking cash payouts to improperly approve sometimes quite dangerous drugs."

" 'Direct' means explaining what this has to do with us," I say. "Not throwing out the information in hope that we squirm."

"You recently had a drug approved by this FDA representative," Jones explains, his attention cutting sharply to William. "I assume in your role, you'd be the person deciding it was ready for submission?"

William pales. "I . . . I don't know what drug you're talking about. I submit many drugs for approval."

"An asthma drug," Agent Jones says. "The name escapes me, but then, I'm not a world-class scientist like you, William."

"Tenza," I supply the name of the drug connected to my brother's FDA bribe. "It's called Tenza." I glance at William. "Did we get the official approval?"

"Just yesterday," he replies. "I planned to document it in next week's reports."

"This approval must have been a shock," Agent Jones interjects. "I mean, from what I read in the reports, even to me, a complete nonacademic, especially when it comes to the complexity of drug manufacturing, it's not market ready. Surely a man with your experience, Mr. Nichols, knew that. Unless . . ." He looks at me. "Management told him to submit it, and you'd take care of the approval?"

"I don't think I like where you're going with this, Agent Jones," I say, my voice low, hard.

"The FBI is far less concerned with what you think, than what you're doing," Jones replies dryly. "And if this is going where

I *think* it is, it's a good thing you're an attorney. You might be needing those skills." He stands and sets the chair back at the table behind him before giving me a mock salute. "I'll be in touch." He walks away and I watch his every step until he disappears, only then turning my attention back to William, who has turned yet a deeper shade of green.

"Is there something you need to tell me?" I demand.

"What? No. Of course not."

"Agent Jones certainly seemed to think something is amiss."

"I admit I was shocked the drug was approved, but I did nothing but submit it."

Semantics, I think, leaning forward, and tightening my voice. "I plan to make Brandon Enterprises the greatest brand on the planet. *Do not* let me find out you're working against that."

"I'm not. I swear to you, I want the same thing."

I don't immediately reply, letting my gaze cut through him. "Go back to work."

"What about—"

"*Go back to work.*"

He nods and quickly stands, all but running across the coffee shop. My lips quirk and I dial Seth. "I'm pretty sure William's shitting his pants right now."

"I have eyes on him and the man stumbled twice on the way to his car."

"I'm headed to the office to show my outrage over what just happened and ensure the Brandon clan believes it was real," I say. "I fully intend to use this to back Derek the fuck off, and hope I keep him in the shadows long enough to take over the board, and get him out of it for good."

"Get him out for good," he repeats. "You've never said that before, and let me tell you, those words are music to my ears."

"Blood only goes so far," I say, wondering how I understood that with my clients but only now accept it with my family. "I'll give you an update after I talk to my father." I start to hang up, but pause to add, "By the way. Tell Nick I still have my reservations about contracting an active federal agent for this job, but his man Jones made that easier to swallow. He played William like a star quarterback. If he didn't break William today, he will."

Thanks to a hellish traffic jam, it's nearly an hour later when I arrive at the office and ride the elevator to our floor. Jessica lets me know that Derek is in the building, and that he shut his door about the time Seth observed William standing outside the pharmaceutical plant on a phone call. I also know Emily's still at her desk working. That's a problem I'll solve while chatting with my father about "Agent Jones."

Entering the lobby, I offer the receptionist a two-finger wave and head down the hallway toward my father's office, my blood pumping a little faster with the knowledge that I'm about to see Emily. Rounding the corner to her office, and my father's, I stop at the sight of her on the phone, her gaze averted, and damn if my heart doesn't race just looking at her. And my heart doesn't race in reaction to anything, not even a courtroom full of people during closing statements.

She ends her call and her attention lifts, her eyes going wide as they land on me. I stride toward her, stopping in front of her desk. "Hi," she says, her voice quavering ever so slightly; the high neckline of her black silk blouse reaches her collarbone, and is ten times sexier than Lana's deep V.

My gaze flicks to my father's office, and back to her. "Is he alone?"

"Yes."

I lean forward, resting my hands on the desk, my gaze meeting hers. "Why are you still here?"

"I don't want to leave." She lowers her voice. "Shane. I can help you."

"The way to help me is to give me the peace of mind to know whatever I do, won't put you at risk."

"Shane—"

"This isn't a debate, Emily. You *will not* stay here." I push off the desk and walk to my father's doors, opening them without knocking.

"Holy fuck, son," he grumbles as I step inside and shut the doors behind me. "Did I not bring you up with manners?"

"Mom brought me up with manners," I say, crossing to stand in front of his desk. "You just taught me to watch my back in case I have someone like you behind me."

"And now you're a killer in the courtroom," he says, leaning back in his chair, white lines around his mouth that I suspect indicate nausea.

"You better hope I am. I was having coffee with our head of research and development for BP this afternoon, when we had an interesting guest."

He arches a brow. "Was she pretty?"

I ignore the ridiculous comment. "She was a he and carrying an FBI badge."

He leans forward, snapping out, "What did he want?"

"He's investigating the FDA inspector Derek bribed, and now we're back on the Feds' radar."

"Get us out of this," he orders.

"I plan to, but you already know how fast things can escalate with the Feds. They won't just look at the BP division, especially with our track record. They will, and probably already are, looking at every one of our divisions. Put that leash back on Derek and don't tell me to do it. Not if you want me to be focused on fixing this."

His eyes glint, a hint of anger in their depths he doesn't try to hide. He might want my skills working for him, but he hates the power they give me. "I'll handle Derek," he says.

I give him a nod and begin to turn when he says, "One more thing, son."

I face him again with an arched brow. "Emily told me you fucked her."

Shocked at Emily's actions, I check my reaction. "Are we really talking about who I'm fucking right now?"

"She also told me she's *not* fucking you anymore," he continues, as if I haven't spoken. "She's afraid of being fired and since she's the only damn person who's sat at that desk in a year that I can actually tolerate, I need to be clear. She's staying."

A ball of anger forms in my chest. "And if I object?"

"I'll let you choose. Do you want me to control Derek or fire Emily?"

Ignoring the ridiculous question that dismisses the FBI threat we both know he isn't dismissing, I turn and walk to the door, with every intention of handling Emily on my own. Exiting the office, I shut the doors behind me and discover Emily is no longer at her desk. Jaw set hard, I stride through the office and down the hallway, pausing at the reception desk. "Where did Emily go?"

"She just got on the elevator with Jessica," Kelly replies.

The elevator it is. I start walking.

EMILY

Jessica and I step into the elevator and she punches the lobby level. "What's wrong?" she asks as the doors shut. "You sounded panicked when you called."

"I am," I say, pressing my hand to my forehead. "I mean, I did the right thing, but—"

"What did you do?"

The elevator stops only two floors down, and she rolls her

eyes. "Oh good gosh, not now," she says, as the doors open again, and four people crowd us into a corner.

"What did you do?" she whispers.

"Not yet," I say.

"Right. Not yet. This is killing me."

"Try being me," I murmur, enduring the rest of the ride by silently assuring myself I did the right thing, while worrying about Shane's reaction.

"Finally," Jessica says, as we hit ground level and follow the crowd out of the car.

"This way," she says, linking her arm with mine, and leading me toward the garage, where we exit into the parking lot. She releases me. "What did you do?"

"Shane ordered me to piss off his father and get fired so that no one thinks I left because Shane is protecting me."

She blanches. "What? Why? What happened to the whole 'using you' routine?"

"I don't know. Something must have happened, which is why me staying is more important than ever. I'm sitting at the window, open to his enemies."

She holds up her hands. "Okay. Okay. I have to tread cautiously here or Shane is going to hang me by my toes in some public place."

In other words, she agrees with me, but works for him. "I'm not leaving," I announce.

"Shane can just fire you himself."

I shake my head. "Not anymore."

"Once again. What did you do?"

"I told his father I slept with Shane, but that it's over. I told him Maggie warned me that I was being used, which she did, by the way."

"I told you that would happen."

"Yes and it sucked but it helped me today."

"This is holy batshit crazy."

"I'm not even done yet. I told Brandon Senior I was afraid Shane would fire me and he promised me job security."

"Oh my God, Emily. Major respect for you right now because that took courage, but Shane is going to be furious."

The garage door opens again and my gaze jerks in that direction, finding Shane standing there, his expression hard and his eyes steely gray. "Speak of the devil," Jessica murmurs softly.

Shane seems to hear her, flicking her a look. "Leave."

She grabs my arm and squeezes before walking to the door, but before she exits, she pauses next to Shane. "She's protecting you," she says. "Don't forget that." She doesn't wait for a reply— which I doubt she'd get—entering the building and leaving me alone with Shane.

He steps forward and I don't know how, but without ever touching me, the man backs me against the wall, his big body crowding mine. Everything about him is big and angry. "What the hell was that?" he demands, his voice a tight band, ready to snap.

Quite clear on what "that" is, considering he just met with his father, I state my case. "You *need* me to stay. I have access to information that can help you."

"What I need is for you to do what I tell you. No want. Need. *Demand.* Nothing has changed. Today is your last day. If you show up tomorrow, I will personally escort you out. Do you understand?"

I swallow hard against the hardness of his energy, and I want to argue, but I believe him. He will escort me out. I nod. "Say it," he demands.

"I understand."

He studies me for several heavy seconds, seeming to weigh my sincerity, before he steps back, giving me space I don't want, my gaze falling on his tie to discover it's the one I chose for him.

"Emily," he says, a soft command demanding I look at him, and when I do, that connection is like an electric charge going through me, touching me everywhere when he is touching me nowhere.

"I won't be the reason you get hurt," he says, a vehement rasp to his voice. He turns and leaves, the door shutting behind him.

I swallow against the sudden thickness in my throat, and while his coldness hurts, no matter what his intentions, I remember two things only. What I'd felt when I looked in his eyes, along with him wearing that tie, tells me no matter how hard he's pushing me away, it's not the choice he wants to make. And if he really feels this is the right move, I'll respect his wishes, but damn it, if today is my last day, I'm going to make it count. This good little soldier will leave here with every piece of data that can possibly help Shane win his war.

Don't mistake my kindness for weakness. I am kind to everyone, but when someone is unkind to me, weak is not what you are going to remember about me.

—*Al Capone*

CHAPTER TWENTY

SHANE

A full minute after leaving Emily in the garage, I can still smell the floral sweetness of her perfume, every muscle in my body tense with the effort it had taken to keep my hands off her. I reach the elevator, and step into a car, the steel doors sealing me inside, and I feel more caged animal than man right now. I need a release. A run. My fist in my brother's face. Emily *naked*. Seconds and floors tick by like hours, until finally I exit on the higher level, my gaze landing on the Brandon Enterprises logo, honing in on the lion. It's becoming clear that sharp leadership might not be enough to save this company. I might have to rip a few throats out to get the job done. And at this point, a few throats versus total annihilation of the brand, and my family, seems a fair trade-off.

Entering the reception area, I quickly make my way toward the end of the hallway that forks to my office and my brother's, noting his door is still shut before traveling to my own. Jessica stands on my approach.

"Not now," I say before she starts explaining herself. I'm

really not in the mood. I walk straight into my office and reso-
lutely shut the door.

I've barely sat down when she buzzes in on the intercom,
proving she is forever dogmatic about just about everything. "I'll
defend myself when you're a little less intense. But since 'intense'
only makes you a better negotiator, the bank is on the phone
about the Cherry Creek apartment and there's an attorney for a
class-action lawsuit on the phone."

"What class-action?"

"It's related to BP Pharmaceuticals."

I scrub my jaw. "Of course it is." And while this kind of thing
is common with drug companies, it hits one of about ten raw
nerves. "Put the attorney through."

From there, my work snowballs and it's nearly six when Seth
calls to report in. "Tell me something good," I say, leaning back
in my chair.

"If you define 'good' as me having no bad news, then I can.
My news amounts to not much. For now, all is quiet, and Nick's
team has widespread eyes on our watch targets."

"What I want is conclusive evidence that Sub-Zero is not in
my manufacturing facility."

"Nick's men entered BP on the pretense of a conveyor belt
repair, and managed to install a few added camera angles we
didn't have on the security feed. I'll be watching real-time surveillance tonight to see if we triggered any unusual activity when
we spooked William."

"Sounds like titillating viewing. Is it mobile?"

"On my laptop. Why?"

"I need out of this place almost as much as I need a drink.
If you meet me at my place and supply the movie entertainment,
I'll provide the expensive booze."

"Sold at expensive booze. I'll see you then."

Happily ending the call to get the hell out of here, I buzz Jessica. "I'm headed out," I say, already stuffing files in my brief-case. "You do the same."

Almost instantly, there's a knock on the door that's clearly more of a formality than a request, since Jessica immediately en-ters and shuts the door. "You can't leave without telling me what's going on."

I drape my briefcase strap over my shoulder, ignoring the question for what's really on my mind. "I hope like hell you didn't encourage Emily to pull that stunt."

"How can you even think that? She was just telling me what happened when you showed up in the garage. But she had to have been sideswiped by being pushed away and told to quit when you'd decided she could stay. What changed?"

"Nothing you need to know," I say, rounding the desk and crossing to stand in front of her. "Is she still here?"

"Your dad sent her on some errands and then I think she was headed home." Her lips tighten. "Shane——"

"Nothing you need to know," I repeat.

She inhales and lets it out. "This is one of those times I need to know my boundaries, right?"

"You always know your boundaries. You simply choose to ignore them and that would not be a good decision right now."

"Shit," she says. "You don't shut me out, so whatever hap-pened must be bad."

"It is," I confirm, "which is why I need you to color in the lines I give you, for once."

"Not my greatest skill, but I'll manage."

I give a quick nod and take a step toward the door.

"Wait," she says, surprising me by grabbing my arm. "Sorry," she says, releasing me, "but I just needed to say this. Emily really cares about you. And that isn't based on what she's said. It's in her eyes."

I feel that bittersweet observation like a punch in the gut, and my response is low, vehement. "And I'm doing my damnedest to make sure she doesn't regret that," I say, stepping around her to exit the office, and I don't stop until I'm at my car, about to climb inside, pausing at the sight of a note on my windshield. Brow furrowing, I snatch it, recognizing Emily's handwriting even before I read: *Confucius says—A tie can speak a million words.* I laugh, the tension in my spine sliding away, and once again, Emily has made me smile without even being present. I slide into the car and turn on the engine, more determined than ever to do *whatever it takes* to win this war. Or rather, *end this war.*

Three hours later, Seth and I are sitting in my living room, our ties and jackets gone, along with several pizzas, and a fair share of cognac. "I have to tell you, man," I say, indicating one of several laptops we have open on the coffee table, "the movie entertainment you provided just plain sucks."

"Welcome to my life," he says, lifting his glass and downing the contents. "I spend way too much time watching, and waiting, for assholes to become idiots." He refills his glass and mine. "And unfortunately the smart ones, like Adrian Martina, aren't easily spooked. They're smart and calculated, but that makes catching them all the sweeter."

A message pops up on the computer screen from Nick, as it has many times tonight, and we both lean in closer to read it: *Derek just arrived at Martina's restaurant.*

"Houston, we have contact," Seth murmurs, cutting me a look. "Looks like your brother decided he needs to consult the real boss. Let's hope this is a prelude to some sort of action at the pharmaceutical branch."

"Let's hope it's not, because that would mean Sub-Zero really is inside our facility." The house phone for the hotel rings from inside the kitchen and my brow furrows. "That's odd," I say, already moving in that direction. "You didn't order room service, did you?"

"Hell no," he calls out. "I just ate two pizzas."

I walk to the wall by the fridge and grab the handset. "Mr. Brandon," the front desk clerk says. "I have a Lana Smith here to see you."

"Here? As in, she's in the hotel?"

"Yes sir. She's standing right here." And then she must grab the line because I hear, "Shane. It's Lana. Or I guess he told you that."

"How the hell do you know where I live?"

"I know the receptionist at your office and she let it slip at a happy hour months ago."

And Lana is nothing if not an opportunist. "Why are you here?"

"There are some things going on at BP and I didn't think I should go to the office to tell you and alert anyone."

"That's why they make telephones."

"I didn't think that was smart either. Please, can I come upstairs?"

I generally believe most things Lana does are rooted in manipulation, but she works with William, and I need information. "Wait there," I order, ending the call and turning to find Seth has joined me.

"Problem?" he asks.

"That's one way to describe her. Lana Smith from BP is downstairs, insisting she has information we need to know. I told her we'd come and get her."

"On my way," he says, already on the move, while I round the bar to the kitchen and decide a pot of coffee, not a bottle of booze, is now in order. That, and about ten grains of salt, might get me through another encounter with Lana. The pot has just finished brewing when the door opens, and I forget the coffee, and claim a spot at the end of the island. Seth and Lana enter the kitchen, and as usual, Lana's dressed to seduce in skintight black jeans with a T-shirt that scoops low to expose her cleavage. She's a five-alarm fire, burning hot, and ironically, that very quality drew me to her in the past but does nothing but scream trouble to me now.

She approaches the island, but instead of stopping on the other side, she rounds the counter to stand by the sink a few steps from me. "Sorry about dropping in on you," she says, hugging herself and actually seeming a bit awkward.

"If there's a problem, I need to know," I say, offering her cautious encouragement. "What information do you have for us?"

"Us?" she asks, glancing up at Seth and back at me. "You. I'm not telling anyone but you."

"Anything you can say to me, you can say to Seth."

"I'm sorry," she replies. "But I don't know him and I need to talk to you alone."

I clench my teeth, but she has access to BP in a high-profile position, and if she knows something about illegal activity, I can't blame her for being guarded. I eye Seth, giving him a silent command. He nods and without a word, heads for the door.

"All right, Lana," I say as the door opens and shuts. "We're alone."

To my surprise, she wastes no time proving she's here for a real reason. "A man visits William every Monday and he always has a large envelope in his hand when he enters William's office, but not when he leaves."

"He could be a supplier."

"He could, yes," she agrees, "but I don't think he is."

"And you base this on what?"

"For one thing," she says, "he's very secretive and nervous, often going outside to make calls."

"That could be personal."

"No. Something isn't right with him, Shane. *Look.* I'm smart and observant and this man is my boss. I wouldn't make an accusation if I wasn't truly concerned."

"I need more than you being smart and observant to believe he's guilty of some unknown misstep."

"I know." She reaches into her purse where it hangs at her hip, and removes a piece of paper. "That's why I brought this." She steps closer and flattens it on the counter. "I made copies of two versions of the same inventory report, side by side."

"Two versions?"

"Right," she confirms. "The left is the one I found on his desk. The right is the one that got uploaded into our database. They don't match."

"Maybe the first wasn't final?" I ask, digging for an answer that doesn't end with the Martina cartel.

"He doesn't handle inventory," she says.

"That doesn't mean it didn't change from the time it was on his desk and the time it was entered," I argue.

She points to a particular line. "Right here. This indicates the sales for Ridel, an anti-inflammatory drug that's in low demand because of side effects and better patient options. I know this because I spent some time working on a new version and it got sidelined for more urgent projects. Column one indicates that low demand, but in the second version of the report, twenty times as many units have been sold."

"Has sales done a push on Ridel?"

"I can't say for sure. That's done through outside reps I have no exposure to, but considering the drug's history, I find that hard to believe." She hesitates and abandons the paper to focus on me. "That night—"

"Don't do this. Not now. Not when you've just dropped a bombshell on me. Fuck." I turn away and run my hand over my face, the magnitude of what she's just told me starting to hit. Could Sub-Zero be packaged and labeled as this anti-inflammatory drug?

I face her and all of a sudden, she's in front of me, one hand on my chest, scorching me through the material. I grab her wrist, and she steps into me, her legs pressed to mine. "I can help if you let me."

This was always her goal, I realize, and the truth is, she's exactly the kind of woman I should be fucking. Devious. Calculated. Incapable of being ruined by me and my screwed-up family. She belongs here. Emily does not.

EMILY

My plan to leave Brandon Enterprises with something, anything, to help Shane win this blood war gets easy when I return from running a million and one errands for his father and find the offices dark. Entering the lobby, I lock myself inside, drop my purse on my desk, and head straight for Brandon Senior's office. Opening the doors, I flip on the light, and while I really don't know what I'm looking for, one thing is certain. I promised Shane this would be my last day at Brandon Enterprises and that means this is my last chance to use my role in this company to help Shane in whatever way I can.

With that goal in mind, I cross the office and sit down behind the desk, and since Shane believes the hedge fund is being used to hide a secret that seems like a good place to start my investigation. Reaching for the drawer where I've seen him stick the file, I tug, but it doesn't move. I try another drawer with the same result. Not ready to give up, I search the desk for a tool of some sort, and grab a paper clip, inserting it into the lock with zero success.

Frowning, I scour my brain for a solution, and a crazy idea sends me to my desk, where I snag my own key, and return to Brandon Senior's desk and the locked drawer. Inhaling, I pray for luck, insert the key into the nemesis lock, and *bingo*, it turns. Pulling open the drawer, I snatch up the hedge-fund folder and one labeled MIKE ROGERS, who's both a board member and a key player in the hedge fund. I then spend a few minutes making varied selections of other folders. My prizes in hand, I hurry to the large file room behind the reception desk, flip on the light, and power up the copy machine to begin duplicating everything in the files.

I've just finished with the final documents, gathering all my paperwork, when I hear, "It's late to be working alone, isn't it?"

I jolt at the male voice, whirling around to find a dark-haired security guard I've never seen before, standing in the doorway. "What are you doing here?" I demand, his big body, and the empty office, hitting all of my many raw nerves.

"I saw the light on and thought something was amiss."

"Just catching up on my work."

"I see that," he says, eying the stack of files I've created, and with what strikes me as more interest than an outsider should have.

"Thanks for checking on me," I say, shutting the file I have open and scooping up the entire stack of files. "I'm fine. I'm going to leave soon."

"I know you think you are," he says, "but that's when people make mistakes."

My throat goes dry with what seems to be a hidden meaning. "Mistakes?"

"They let their guard down and forget to stay alert. Case in point, we've had a few strange reports in the building this week, which one wouldn't expect with our level of security. You said you're leaving soon. Why don't you let me walk you downstairs?"

"Oh no," I say, kicking myself for giving him that opening, and growing more uncomfortable by the moment. "Thank you, but 'soon' for me translates to the next hour or so."

He studies me for several more of those creepy moments in which I contemplate the heel of my shoe as a weapon, before he finally gives a quick nod and says, "Be careful on your way down." He disappears out of the door, and I have no idea what possesses me, considering he freaks me out, but I dart forward, catching him as he's about to exit the office.

"Excuse me," I call out.

He faces me, and I ask, "What strange happenings?"

"For tenant privacy reasons, I'm not at liberty to say."

"I understand. What's your name?"

"Randy," he says.

"Randy," I repeat. "Thank you, again."

He inclines his head and exits, and I quickly dart forward, locking the door that apparently won't keep "Randy" out anyway, his name nagging at my gut for some reason. Shaking off the feeling I can't place, I return to Brandon Senior's office, and start refiling the folders I'd taken, when I pause with realization. The guard who'd helped me with my lost phone my first night in the building had been Randy. Of course, they could share the name. Obviously, *they do* share the name, but something, no, *everything*, about this new "Randy" is bothering me.

Turning off the light and shutting Mr. Brandon's doors, and fighting a nagging sense of uneasiness, I sit down at my desk and retrieve a large interoffice envelope from a drawer. I'm about to insert all the documents I've copied inside it, when my gaze catches on a list of proposed investments for the hedge fund. "Brandon Transportation," I murmur, and then, "Rogers Athletics," a company famously owned by Mike Rogers. Those companies seem like curious choices, considering this particular hedge fund is brokered by Brandon Senior, but

I don't pretend to know if that is a problem or not. This is Shane's expertise, not mine.

I stuff all the documents in the folder and stand, one more task to complete before I say adios to this place. Trying not to think about Randy's potential return, I will away my nerves, and start walking, my path leading me down the dark hallway to Derek's door. Inhaling for courage, I reach for the knob, turn it, and find it locked. A sudden roaring sound from near the front of the offices has me whirling around toward the lobby, my heart thundering in my ears right along with the air conditioner that just kicked in. Okay. *That's it.* I'm done and I all but run to the front door, turn out the lights, and hesitate in the doorway. Wait. I never turned on the lights in this part of the offices. Did I? No. I did not and they weren't on when Randy left either.

Officially freaked out, adrenaline surges through me, and I flip the light switch off, lock the door, and cross to the elevator panel, where I punch the button over and over, until finally a car arrives. Stepping inside, I dig out my phone, holding it like the weapon I wish it was, and watch the hallway every second until the doors shut. Another thirty seconds that feel like thirty *years* later I exit into the downstairs corridor. I start walking for the front exit, glancing toward the security desk to discover the first Randy at the desk. More unease rolls through me, and as much as I want to confirm the other man really works here, I want out of this building more.

A few dozen fast steps, and I am outside, a chilly breeze lifting my hair, and without hesitation, I start walking toward the Four Seasons, punching in Shane's number as I do. It rings once and goes to voice mail, and in the short two-block walk, I try twice more, with no success. Arriving at the entrance of the hotel, I wave at Tai as he helps another visitor, and enter the lobby to make a beeline for the elevators.

Once inside, I key in the security code, and watch the floors tick by, certain this knot in my belly will disappear when I see Shane. So much so that I am out of the car the minute the doors open, and double-stepping for his door. Once I'm there, I resist the urge to just go in, forcing myself to punch the doorbell. Seconds tick by and he doesn't answer, and I finally dig out the key he'd given me. I'm reaching for the lock when the door opens and I come face-to-face with a stunning brunette.

"Oh," she says. "Hello." Her lips curve in a cat-that-ate-the-canary smile. "He's all yours." She steps around me and starts walking.

My stomach rolls, at the same moment Shane appears in the doorway, his Burberry tie I'd put so much meaning behind gone, along with his jacket. "Emily," he says, and before he can utter a lie I don't want to remember him by, I try to turn away.

He catches my arm, dragging me to him, and my hand flattens on his chest, but he doesn't say anything and he smells like perfume. No. He smells like *her.* "Let go of me," I say, my voice trembling with the pain I swore no man would cause me again.

Several beats pass and if I wanted some sort of denial from him, I don't get it. He releases me, and every warm spot this man ever created in me turns icy. I take a step backward, swallowing hard, and turning away. Somehow, my feet are moving, while the cold, hard truth is slowly, but precisely, seeping in and carving out a piece of my heart. This isn't even a betrayal. He'd cut ties with me last night and I'd simply chosen not to believe it to be true.

Reaching the end of the hall that leads to the elevator, I already know he's not following me, but some part of me needs that confirmation. Inhaling, I rotate to glance down the path I've just traveled to find Shane lingering in his doorway, now in profile, his hand on the jamb, his head tilted forward and low. Tormented, it seems, but I don't pretend to know what he's feeling. I don't pretend to know him at all. I leave then, turning the corner and moments later, stepping into the elevator, I have two thoughts. I'm still clutching the folder I never gave him against my chest, and I must have been falling in love with him to hurt this badly.

I step out of the Four Seasons and onto the street to start the six-block walk to my apartment, shoving aside the tears threatening to erupt. I will not cry. I will not be defined by the actions of one man. And the very idea that if Shane had declared that woman's presence in his home an innocent encounter, I'd have believed him—despite her scent clinging to his clothes—infuriates me. I will not become the fool my mother was with my stepfather, with Shane or any other man.

A half block later, I have found a cold, gray spot in my mind and taken residence there, not overthinking my relationship with Shane, when I so easily could. Instead, I occupy my mind by reading store names, never letting myself go to places that might test my emotions. By block four there is a prickling sensation on my neck, a sense of being watched I do not like. It quickens my pace, reminding me of more than Randy. It reminds me of why I'm in Denver, and it is with relief that I reach my apartment and lock myself inside.

Leaning on the door, I walk to the kitchen, and set the folder on the counter. I grab my purse and the new disposable phone inside, punching in Rick's number. He doesn't answer, of course. He never answers. "I think I'm in trouble," I say. "I need help. You have to call me back." I press end and then redial his number, with the same result. I try again and again, and I have this clawing feeling that Rick is gone for good. I set my phone on the counter, and stare at my apartment, absent of all furniture, and I have never felt so alone or without resources. That's not true. I do have a resource. *Shane and the Brandon family empire.*

Perfection is achieved, not when there is nothing more to add, but when there is nothing left to take away.

—*Carlo Gambino*

CHAPTER TWENTY-ONE

EMILY

What better place to hide than inside the Brandon family empire, outside the king's door? That is the idea I cling to as I fall asleep, and the same one I cling to come morning light. That one premise motivates me to get up and dress in what has become my go-to navy skirt and matching blouse and to apply bright pink lipstick to deflect from the dark circles under my eyes that concealer has failed to cover. Task complete, I end up in the kitchen, staring at the folder I'd left on the counter, not sure what to do with it. Ultimately, no matter how Shane and I ended, I do believe he's the better man, and I snatch it up and head for the door, deciding I'll leave it on his desk the first chance I can discreetly manage.

I exit my apartment, lock up, and find myself scanning for something, or someone, or I don't really know what. I just know that I still feel that creepy, being-watched sensation that has me taking longer strides on my path to work, and solidifies my decision to keep my job. I can't worry about a confrontation with Shane right now. No one can be as safely invisible as I am if I leave my job. Finally at the building, I head inside and waste no time making my way to the office and my desk outside Brandon Senior's still dark office, and stick the folder in my drawer.

It's then that the reality of Shane and me coming face-to-face hits me hard, but my phone buzzes, distracting me, and I spend the next hour juggling calls for Brandon Senior. A break comes and the need to go to the file room has me thinking of my visitor last night. I grab my Rolodex, and find the security desk number, punching it in.

"Security," a woman answers. "Can I help you?"

"Yes. Hi. This is Brandon Senior's assistant. Can you tell me the names of the guards who were on duty last night?"

"Was there a problem?"

"Oh no. The opposite. One of the men checked on me when I was working late and I want to tell his supervisor."

"Randy was the only guard working last night."

A bad feeling rolls through me, the memory of seeing the original Randy behind the desk crystal clear in my mind. "I thought there were two men named Randy on duty last night?"

"No. We only have one Randy working here."

My throat tightens. "Okay. I must be confused. Thank you." I hang up, a sick feeling expanding in my belly. Who was that man and how did he get into the office?

"Good morning."

I jolt at the sound of Jessica's voice, glancing up to find her standing in front of me. "Hi," I say cautiously, worried this is the start of a confrontation when I'm still reeling from the Randy revelation.

"Hi," she says, pressing her hands to the waist of her cream-colored dress. "Want to go downstairs and get coffee?"

"I'm not sure that's a good idea."

"Because of Shane?" she asks, and waves off the idea. "He's not here."

"Really? Okay then," I say, welcoming a friend right now,

and any hint about how Shane might react to my presence. "Coffee sounds really good." I stand and reach for my purse.

"It's on Shane," she says. "He has an account and he'll be happy to buy for us."

She can't begin to understand the many ways that feels wrong but I let it go, and we make our way to the elevator, where we end up sardines in a crowded car, a short reprieve from what I know will be her many questions. Sure enough, we step off the car and she gets right to the point of this coffee break. "Are you staying or leaving?"

"Staying," I say as we arrive at the coffee shop and take our place in line.

"Does Shane know?" she asks.

"Shane doesn't get to make this decision," I say, folding my arms in front of me and preparing for the attack that may follow. "Severance won't last forever and I have bills to pay."

"I did think of that," she surprises me by saying. "And you're getting paid well. But Emily, he's worried about you."

I don't even know how to reply to that and it turns out I don't have to, at least not now. The customer in front of us leaves and I step up to the register and place my order, quickly moving to the end of the counter to wait for my coffee. And damn it, I suddenly remember I'm wearing the same lipstick I'd been wearing the day I'd met Shane.

"Emily."

Shane's voice radiates through me, a wicked hot reminder of what might have been and will never be; facing him, I find him nearly on top of me. "What are you doing here?" he demands, the scent of him, spicy and male, somehow adding to the anger his question ignites in me.

"I need a jolt of caffeine," I say, cautiously containing my temper.

"Don't play innocent," he says, his gray eyes darkening to match the deep gray of his suit he wears too well to be such a jerk.

"I didn't sleep last night," I say. "I *needed* a jolt of caffeine."

He attacks again. "Why are you at work?"

"Because you aren't pushing me out. I need this job."

"I promised you severance pay," he reminds me, as if he's offered me a pot of gold at the end of the rainbow he's destroyed.

"Severance does not a career make," I say, grabbing my coffee as it's set on the counter. "I need to get back to work." I try to step around him.

He is quickly in front of me again. "You aren't staying, Emily."

"Yes," I reply firmly. "I am."

His eyes glint, and I see the obstinate determination in his stare even before he declares, "You have until the end of day and then I will ensure you're gone." He turns and leaves, and anger surges through me. He will *ensure* I'm gone? He is being so unfair and I can't believe I thought I could love that man.

"Wow," Jessica says, joining me. "You're trembling, honey." She reaches for my cup. "Let me hold that. What happened?"

"I'll let you know when it's over," I say, taking off after Shane, my steps fast, but not fast enough. I round the corner to the bank of elevators at the same moment he steps into a car. I will never make before it leaves.

Another elevator opens and I step inside, facing forward. Jessica joins me. "What are you about to do? And is it smart?" she demands, punching the button to our floor.

"Very and don't even think about taking his side right now."

"Easy, honey," she says, holding up her hands, and she obviously opted to leave our coffees behind. "I just think you should know that he was protecting you. There's something nasty going on in this company."

"You have no idea what has happened between us, so please don't try to make this about whatever is happening in the company."

"Oh shit. What did he do?"

The elevator opens and I don't even consider answering her, exiting in time to spot Shane in the lobby moments before I myself am there too. He cuts down his hallway and I pursue him, my heart in my throat, a cocktail of adrenaline and anger driving my every step. I round the corner and have a brief moment of hesitation when I spy Derek's door open, but it's so very brief, my focus on Shane and Shane alone, who is now entering his office. I'm there as his door shuts. Not even bothering to knock, I open the door and enter.

He turns at the sound of my entry, and I shut us inside to face off with him. "You don't get to fuck me and then do this to me. I need this job. I need the money. I need the security. I need it."

I blink and he's pressing me against the door, his big body framing mine, and I shove against him with all my force. "Get off me. You don't get to bully me, yet again." He doesn't budge, in fact, he ups his bully ranking by snagging my wrists. "Damn it. Let go, Shane."

"Calm down."

"Calm down?" I demand. "Do you know what saying 'calm down' does to a woman? It makes her *not* calm down. Back the fuck off, Shane."

"I'm trying to protect you."

"Yeah. I saw that last night, but it doesn't matter. I'm a grown adult. I don't need you to get rid of me because you fucked me."

"You think this is about fucking someone else?"

"I don't care, Shane. I just want to go back to my desk and do my job."

"I can't let you do that."

The absoluteness in his voice slams into me and desperateness, mixed with the tornado of emotions I'd battled all night, and thought I'd defeated, spurs me on. "Don't do this to me. This job is all I have right now."

"Emily," he breathes out, his expression and grip on my wrists softening. "Sweetheart."

The endearment punches me in the gut. "Please don't call me that."

He looks at the ceiling, seeming to battle within himself, before he levels me with a turbulent stare, his hands settling on my arms. "I didn't sleep with that woman."

The lie ignites my anger all over again. "You *smelled* like her," I hiss, tugging against his hold. "Stop bullying me."

"Lana's a user and manipulator. I didn't expect her last night. She just showed up unannounced."

"And you let her up."

"Seth was with me. She works at BP and had information I needed about a problem there."

"You *smelled like her*," I repeat, rejecting his tidy little explanation.

"She refused to share the information with me if Seth didn't leave, and yes, she pressed herself against me and yes, I knew her in college."

"*Fucked* her in college."

"Yes. I did and I won't lie to you. For a moment, the briefest of moments, I thought—she's what I deserve, and you were too good for me, and this screwed-up life I'm living. But even knowing that didn't matter. She wasn't you, and *you* are who I want. You, Emily." His hands settle on my waist, heating my skin through my clothes. "Just you."

"You really didn't . . ."

"No. I didn't and Lord help any man who tries to touch you."

I search his face, and he doesn't look away, or hide the truth in his eyes. I believe him but that doesn't erase the pain of last night. "Do you know what you did to me? Why wouldn't you just tell me last night?"

"Because what she shared with me was bad. Criminal, even. The kind of thing that gets people killed and I saw your anger as the way to ensure you stayed away until I fixed this."

"I already told you I'd quit."

"And then left that note on my window that made me need to see you, and touch you. I wasn't going to stay away from you."

My fingers curl on his chest where they've landed. "So you hurt me," I say, my throat thick with emotion.

"Yes. So I hurt you."

"That was really shitty, Shane."

"Why do you think I ran ten miles this morning after pacing my apartment all night? *I'm sorry.* More than you can possibly know." He cups my face. "Forgive me."

"I'm going to, but I'm still too angry to do it right this moment."

"Stay with me tonight."

"As long as you understand that I'm staying here too. I'm keeping my job."

"We'll talk about it tonight."

"No. We won't."

His hands drop from my face, and he leans in, pressing his cheek to mine, to murmur, "Do you know how badly I want to be inside you right now?" His hands settle over my ribs, his thumbs tracing the lower line of my breasts, tightening my nipples and sending shivers down my spine.

"Tonight," I say, catching his hands and leaning back to look at him. "But I'm still keeping my job."

The intercom buzzes and Jessica clears her throat and says, "Shane, sorry, but the realtor is here with the paperwork for the apartment."

He curses softly and pulls back, calling out, "Tell him I'll be right there." He refocuses on me. "Tonight."

"Yes. Tonight."

He leans in to kiss me, and I say, "Wait. I have on that lipstick that—"

His mouth comes down on mine, his tongue stroking deeply, and I forget the lipstick, and that Lana woman, and Rick, and everything else. I lean into him, kissing him back, this man who has become so much to me in such a short time. Every lick of his tongue is a promise of more, and I'm not sure it will ever be enough. Too soon it seems, our lips part, reality returning with his murmur of, "Tonight."

"Yes," I say. "Tonight."

He releases me then, reaching for the door and opening it, and I laugh at the sight of my pink lipstick on his mouth. "Pink really is your color," I say, before darting away, his low, sexy laughter following me to the edge of Jessica's desk.

Jessica grins at my smile and winks as I pass, but it's a short-lived, wonderful moment that ends as Derek steps to his doorway, his stare heavy as it falls on me. I have no choice but to move forward to the hallway that leads to the lobby, leaving me no escape from his attention, until suddenly his gaze lifts above my head. I cut left and pause, turning back to peek around the corner to find Shane and Derek staring each other down, hate etching the air and stealing my breath. They are enemies and it delivers a blade of reality I have yet to face. Blood doesn't mean loyalty, and that's what I've been counting on to save me.

SHANE

It's nearly eight when I finish an off-site meeting about a trademark dispute and send a car to pick up Emily at her apartment.

I arrive at the apartment before her, removing my jacket and tie before filling a glass with whiskey and stepping onto the balcony and finding the railing. I stare out at the city, the past twenty-four hours and all the revelations made heavy on my mind, with no movement on resolution. But nothing weighs as heavily on me as last night with Emily. Regret doesn't begin to describe what I'd felt when I'd seen the pain in Emily's eyes over what she thought was my betrayal. Nor does fear begin to describe what I feel when I think of her becoming a target for Derek or the Martina cartel either.

The door opens and I turn in anticipation of her presence, and when she steps into the open doorway, her long hair silky over her shoulders, that unnamed emotion she always makes me feel forms a name.

Love.

I'm falling in love with her and while that's damn good for me, I'm still not convinced it's good for her.

I motion her forward and meet her in the middle of the patio, directly under a light. I set my drink on the table next to us, my hands settling on her waist. "Hey," I say.

"Hey," she says, that sweet shyness she seduces me with clear and present.

"I have something for you." I look up, and her chin lifts, laughter bubbling from her lips as she spies the bra hanging there.

"Oh my God, Shane. Why is it still there and how did it get up there?"

"I have no clue how we managed that. Maybe I have a ghost."

"A ghost," she laughs. "Who puts bras on lights?"

"Maybe it has a sense of humor," I offer.

"Why didn't you take it down?"

"It's my prize," I say, my voice roughening with the rise of my desire. "Like you."

"Shane," she whispers, the air thickening around us.

I lean in to kiss her and the doorbell rings. "That can only be Seth. He's the only person with the code." I lean back and stroke her hair. "Sorry, sweetheart, but with some of the things going on, I have to let him in."

"Of course," she says. "I'll be out here."

I give her a nod and I head inside, crossing to the door and opening it, bringing Seth into view, the hard lines of his face telling me something is wrong. "Are you alone?" he asks.

"Emily's on the patio."

He lifts the folder in his hand and then sets it on the counter. "All the more reason you need to see this."

A bad feeling rolls through me and I step back, allowing him to enter, and we convene in the kitchen at the island. He sets the folder in front of me. I flip it open and stare down at a photo of Emily. "What is this?"

"I had her checked out and yes, her identity checks out, but it's a shell created by a hacker. The kind of shell that's created when someone is hiding who they really are. Witness protection, criminal, or undercover agents." He tosses an envelope on the counter. "I found that in her desk. It's a compilation of information ranging from bank accounts to investors."

"Holy fuck. You think she's setting us up."

"I don't have a clue, but you better find out and now. And because I'm thorough, I checked her fingerprints, too. There not on file."

The idea of Emily's betrayal slices through me, a wicked blade that is unforgiving. "Leave," I order.

He gives an incline of his head and disappears, and I press my hands to the counter, letting my head dip low, my mother's words coming back to me. *Once someone is in your bed, they're dangerously close to you. Watch your back with that woman.*

"Shane."

At the sound of Emily's voice, I inhale and push off the

counter, turning to find her standing in front of me. "It's time for some rules," I say.

"Rules?" she asks, her voice quavering. "What rules?"

I grab her and turn us both, pressing her against the counter, my hands caging her in. "Hard rules. And hard rule number one is, *no more lies.*"

Hello readers!

Remember that super sexy balcony scene where Emily is pressed to the glass enclosed railing, afraid she will fall, but Shane manages to make her forget everything but HIM?! Well, I'm excited to share what was going on in her mind while Shane was pushing her limits and claiming more than her pleasure. This was when he started to claim her heart.

I hope you enjoy!

XOXO,
Lisa

EMILY

Shane's eyes glint with satisfaction at my agreement but he doesn't release me. Instead, he spreads my arms until they align with the railing, his body draped over mine and my nipples rasping against the starched material of his shirt. He lingers there, pressed against me, his teeth scraping my shoulder. Tiny darts of pleasure shoot down my arm, intensified when he licks the offended area. I shut my eyes with the impact of a breeze rushing over me, and while it is chilly, it does nothing to cool all the places he's made hot.

His lips travel over the skin his teeth and tongue have already visited, to my neck, my jaw, and then settling a breath from my mouth, his breath a warm fan promising me a kiss he does not deliver. He lingers right there, teasing me, driving me crazy, his hands flexing over mine, as if in warning. A beat later, he releases them and me, putting a step between us, and leaving me free to let go of the railing, and I almost do but his withdrawal seems to be a message. He won't touch me if I let go of the railing. My grip tightens on the steel beneath my palm, holding on the way I want him to hold on to me.

"Close your eyes," he orders.

I blanch, already feeling exposed and vulnerable. "What?"

"Close your eyes, Emily."

This time it's a command and I have no idea why, but I not only willingly take the order, I'm wet and achy, and I want this man more than I have ever wanted anyone. My reward is the very thing I want most. Him touching me, anywhere, everywhere, and for now that means his hands cradling my neck. "Don't open them or—"

"You'll stop what you're doing," I supply.

His breath fans over my ear. "I'm glad you understand."

"You haven't done anything to stop yet so I feel—"

He kisses me, a lush slide of his tongue against mine gone too soon. "You feel what?"

"Like I want you to kiss me again."

"Not yet," he says, and like his mouth, his hands are once again gone, but I can feel him close. I can feel him everywhere and nowhere. I know he is a lean away, a reach of my hands that might as well be bound. But then, I wouldn't choose to give him control and I think . . . I think he is all about choices. I think I've given him more control than I've ever given anyone.

The air shifts abruptly and I know he is no longer as close as he was moments before. I listen for movement, and there are random, barely there sounds but nothing I can place. Is he undressing? I hope. Maybe? An array of sensations roll through me. Nerves. Eagerness. *Arousal.* I can barely take it. "Shane."

"Open your eyes."

I blink my eyes open and he's sitting in front of me on a chair. Another blink and he's moved it, and himself, closer. "*Don't* let go of the railing," he warns and I've barely processed that order before he's cupping my backside and dragging me to his lap to straddle him, the angle forcing me to lean into the glass wall behind me.

Fear rushes through me, my pulse all over the place. "Shane, damn it. What if the glass breaks?"

"Easy, sweetheart," he murmurs, his hand flattening on my belly. "It's reinforced and there's horizontal steel bands supporting it. I have you and I won't let you go. *Relax.*"

I inhale and try to calm my body. "You're sure it won't break?"

"One hundred percent." He leans over me and kisses the spot between my breasts, cupping one of them, and looks up at me, his eyes smoldering as he says, "Trust me."

Trust. The word guts me and throws me back into a reality I don't want to visit but he doesn't let me stay there long. He fingers my nipples, sending a rush of sensation through my body with the delicate, sensual caresses that become rougher and rougher. I am panting again, conflicting pain and pleasure wreaking havoc on my body.

And his assault on my senses doesn't stop there. His mouth is still between my breasts, tongue tracking toward my nipple. I arch into him, and on some level I know I'm increasing the pressure on the wall behind me, pressing harder, but I no longer seem to be capable of caring. His mouth closes around me and he suckles deeply, and at the same moment, his hand on my belly moves lower, his thumb stroking my clit. Every part of me is alive, aroused, and unaware of anything but what he is making me feel.

I am so on edge that I barely register the way he cups my backside and shifts our bodies. There is just the moment his mouth is in the most intimate part of me, closed around my nub, while his fingers slide inside me. And he is licking and teasing and I am . . . I am on the edge of that cliff where I want to be but don't want to leave. But he pumps his fingers into me, and suckles me deeper and I can't stop it. My body tightens and I can't move or breathe. Another second and my sex clenches around his fingers, my body spasming with such intensity I'm quaking inside and out. I slip into a sweet, pleasure-laden oblivion that seems to last forever and yet not long enough.

The present comes back to me with several blinks, and Shane seems to know, his fingers sliding from inside me, leaving me aware of the angle of my body that traps me against the glass at my back. "Shane," I whisper, a plea he answers by flattening his hand on my back and dragging me from the wall to sit fully on top of him.

He cups the back of my head, bringing my lips to his. "Now I taste like you," he proclaims, his lips slanting over mine, the taste of him, of his desire, raw and ripe, but there is more. There is a salty sweet taste that is me, and I don't expect it to turn me on, but it does, or he does. And the way my hands are on his shoulders, and his arms, and he isn't stopping me, only drives my need to a whole new level.

I moan, impossibly aroused all over again, brutally aware of the empty spot inside me yet to be filled. He deepens the kiss, and I sink into it, tunnel my hands in the thick, dark strands of his hair, but I can taste the restraint in him, the part of him he's containing, not yet setting free. And I want it free. "You have to get undressed," I pant into his mouth, and I have no idea what gets into me, but I reach up and grip his shirt, and yank, fully intending to repeat what he'd done to my blouse. I fail. Nothing happens aside from heat rushing to my cheeks. I look up at Shane, who is stone-faced as I admit, "In my mind that went much differently."

He stares at me, unreadable, intense, and then I don't know how it happens but we are both laughing. "Not as you planned, huh?"

"No. But I'm not exactly what anyone would call a seductress."

"I like you just the way you are."

"You don't even know me."

"But I'm about to." He seals that sexy promise by dragging my hands to his shoulders and announcing, "Hold on. We're going inside." He's standing by the time the warning is issued, cupping my backside.

He starts walking and I cling to his neck, my legs around his waist, my heels still somehow on my feet, thigh highs the only other thing I am wearing. But it's not being naked on the outside that has a hot spot in my chest. It's how oddly naked inside I feel with this man, like he really can see inside me and discover my secrets. It's guilt that makes me paranoid. I *hate* the guilt. I hate the bad decisions that have changed my life. No. *One* bad decision. One *stupid, stupid,* decision.

Shane stops in the living area, and sets me down on top of a giant tan ottoman, some sort of soft material framed by leather replacing his hands on my bare backside, and one of my shoes comes off. I kick the other one free of my foot and he settles on one knee in front of me, reaching for the buttons on his shirt, his lips curving. "I'll do it this time."

My worries fade, amazed that the same person who stirs darker emotions in me manages to make me smile so easily. "I could try again," I offer.

"Not necessary," he assures me, and already four buttons down, he reaches behind him, and pulls the shirt over his head, a sprinkle of dark hair over his chest, and delicious muscle ripping as he tosses it on the coffee table behind him.

My gaze immediately lands on the unexpected tattoo on his arm of a lion, with an eagle sitting on its head with its wings spread. I reach out and touch it. "Why a lion and an eagle?" I ask.

His expression tightens, unreadable but hard, and I do not miss the fact that he is not touching me.

"The eagle is knowledge, strength, and leadership. The lion is cunning and vicious. He'll rip your throat out if you give him the chance."

I blanch. "Are you the lion or the eagle? Or both?"

He reaches for me, dragging me to the floor in front of him and then turning me to face the ottoman, his big body framing mine, his hands cupping my breasts. "I'm the man who's wanted to fuck you for hours and it's time for me to be inside you."

An onslaught of sensations and emotions overwhelm me, and I decide I've hit a nerve with Shane, like he does too easily with me. "You're the one who won't get undressed," I accuse.

He nips my shoulder as if punishing me for seeing too much, and this time it's harder than when we were outside. "Shane," I object at the same instant his tongue licks away the sting, his mouth finding my ear.

"Don't move." He doesn't wait for my agreement, lifting off of me, and the truth is, I could turn around but I don't want to move. I've stirred some demon in him the way he has for me, and he is taking us back to the place we were meant to be. Sex. *Just* sex. He wants it. *I* want it.

There is movement behind me, the rip of a package that has to be a condom, and almost immediately Shane's wrapped around me again, his hand on my breast, the other sliding the thick ridge of his erection along my sex. And then he is inside me, burying himself to the hilt and I can't breathe for the sensations rolling through me.

His mouth finds my ear. "You feel as damn good as I knew you would." He pulls back then, and I am certain he will pull out, before he finally drives into me again, deep, hard, pleasure spiraling through me.

Now both hands are on my breasts, his body snugly molded to mine, and I swear I lose everything but this moment, and the next. My fingers curl into my palms, the ottoman too wide for me to hold the sides. I arch into the next thrust of his hips and he lifts me until we are both almost upright, me leaning into him. We stay like that a moment not moving, just breathing together, just feeling each other, and then he's moving again, his fingers sliding to my clit and caressing.

I can't move. Not at this angle, but I don't have to wither. He moves for us both, and oh so well. I give myself to it, to him, and just feel. A tight ball is forming in my sex, and somehow my hand is in his, and he's pressing it between my legs, using it to please me. And somehow he thrusts all the right ways and I'm gone. I'm lost and my head falls forward with the tightening of my body. I come with a fierce quake of my body, my sex spasming around him, and this deep, guttural sound rumbles from his chest, telling me that he's right there with me.

I have goose bumps all over my skin when I realize it's over, and we're just together, unmoving, still holding each other. Shane leans me forward, and I catch myself on my hands. He pulls out and I am instantly awash in emotion that has me spinning around only to find his hands on the cushion on either side of me, his strong arms caging me.

I turn around, and he sits there, staring at me. And he is stone, his expression is unreadable, his jaw set hard. I hold my breath, waiting for something I think he wants to say but has not. "There is nothing about you, or this night, that is uncomplicated or what I expected."

"I don't know what that means," I say, and it's true. Or maybe it's not, but this time it's not an intentional lie. "What are you saying?"

"Think about it. You'll figure it out. Stay here, I'll be right back." And just like that he's on his feet, pulling up his pants, which he never even took off. I've been naked on top of the damn city, and he *never even undressed.* He turns away and I watch as he crosses toward the fireplace and then disappears down a hallway.

ABOUT THE AUTHOR

New York Times and *USA Today* bestselling author LISA RENEE JONES is the author of the highly acclaimed Inside Out series, which is now in development for a cable television show to be produced by Suzanne Todd (*Alice in Wonderland*). In addition, her Tall, Dark, and Deadly series and The Secret Life of Amy Bensen series both spent several months on the *New York Times* and *USA Today* lists. Since beginning her publishing career in 2007, Lisa has published more than forty books translated around the world.